Dark Net

Kevin H. Hilton

To Mum, Dad, and Ceri

PROLOGUE

London.
As Gina Oakley ascended the boarding ramp to the Blohm & Voss cruise yacht, *Wave Forge*, her mind was buzzing. Moored at the docks off Thunderer Road, East of the Thames barrier, the vessel looked large enough to get lost aboard, reminding her of ones which she had seen in Monaco. Nevertheless, what was on Gina's mind was the distinct premonition that this was about to be a turning point in her career.

She had been picked up from the plastic surgery clinic in London's city centre by a chauffeur driven Daimler limousine. It had seemed a tad excessive for this initial meeting with Gerald Entwhistle, though she had known this sixty year old multi-billionaire to be something of a playboy. Nevertheless she had then expected to be driven across London for an office meeting, not to find that she was being ushered onto an enormous boat. As she made her way on board she saw the limousine take another ramp to her left into its garage in a side bay of the vessel, and glancing up to the right she could see there was a Dauphin Eurocopter on a pad at the stern. There was no shortage of resources here.

Even before she reached the end of the ramp her host was greeting her.

'Ah, Miss Oakley, welcome *aboard*.' The grey haired Entwhistle's voice oozed ego that had been with him even before he had made his billions in the chemical industry.

'Mister Entwhistle. Thank you for inviting me aboard this amazing boat.'

'Yacht,' he corrected.

'Yacht...?' She thought a yacht was a small boat with sails. 'I was only expecting to visit your office today.'

'Forgive me for my forwardness, but please think of this as my *mobile* office.'

'Okay.' Her voice gave away her uneasiness.

Entwhistle picked up on the tone of her response and wondered whether Oakley got seasick, but decided that now was not the time to ask. There were more pressing matters. As he shook her hand it struck him that she did not look as slim as he would have expected, particularly for someone in her profession of beauty enhancements. Nevertheless, she did match her ID photo, with that angelic face framed by hell's fire, her curly orange hair, which made her look something of an enigma to him. 'I'd like to take you below.'

'Sure.' As she followed Entwhistle below it was like she was entering a dream world, or a Bond movie set, it felt rather unreal. Uniformed men and women strode purposefully by in the corridor all of them acknowledging Entwhistle as they passed. Everything seemed so new, it even had that *new yacht* smell, she guessed. 'She been with you long?'

'Who?' Entwhistle sounded almost suspicious as he turned to look at her through narrowed eyes.

'The b...Yacht.'

'Oh…About three weeks actually.' He continued on with Gina in tow. 'The last one was a bit on the big side. It rather limited which ports I could moor at,' he explained, opening a door and walking through.

'Oh...*OH*!' she repeated in surprise as she followed him through what looked like a pre-op room into an operating theatre at the stern. 'I...I thought we were just going to discuss the contract for the surgery for your *girlfriend*.'

'There's not much to discuss Miss Oakley. A number of my girls will be requiring breast implants.'

'A *number*?...Well we did wonder why you didn't just book your girlfriend in for surgery at the clinic.'

'I didn't want to be on a waiting list to use your facilities, especially when, as you see, I have my own.'

'I'm surprised you don't have your own surgeon to go with it.'

'We *did* have, but sadly he had to leave us at short notice…So depending on how well things go today, maybe I will have a *replacement*.'

'Oh I see. So this meeting is *actually* a job interview is it?'

'Let's say I'm very particular who I have on staff, I've read your résumé and I'm impressed, but I want to see how you handle things under pressure.'

'*Pressure*?'

Entwhistle gave a nod to a male nurse to one side who then went into the adjoining room to return with additional staff and a patient on a gurney with a drip, who appeared to be already anaesthetised.

'What's this?' Gina's tone gave away her uneasiness again, only more so this time.

'Well you know what women are like, I'm sure. When they want something they want it *now.*'

'Well I'm sorry Mister Entwhistle but I don't work like this. There is due process. I need to discuss the client's needs.'

'*I'm* your client.'

'My *patient* then,' she said taking a closer look at the young olive-skinned woman on the gurney. She looked Middle Eastern, or possibly even Pakistani. 'I need to check everything is in order.'

'It *is.*' Entwhistle urged. Then with a smile he softened his voice. 'You have everything you need here.'

Gina stood her ethical high ground. 'I require *her* consent,' she insisted, tapping the patient's forehead, as if *she* was the missing paperwork. Gina was actually checking the woman was indeed unconscious and that this was not some sort of hoax, but the woman did not even flinch.

With a click of his fingers Entwhistle was handed a wad of paperwork by the medical administrator, which he then brandished in front of Gina. 'Here we go. One step ahead of you and all signed, so we're ready for the op.'

'It doesn't work like this. I need to go through her medical records, so that I'm fully apprised of the patient's medical history.'

Again his fingers clicked and she was handed a folder of notes. Realising she had to slow things down Gina went over to a desk and pulled its chair out to sit down. Entwhistle followed, and stood over her impatiently.

Nevertheless she took her time reading through the documentation, wondering how she was going to talk her way out from under Entwhistle's insistence. And as if this wasn't pressure enough she noticed something else. The hum of the vessel had changed, and she thought she detected movement.

'Are we moving?' she asked looking into Entwhistle's pale green eyes.

'Yes I'm sorry but I have to be on my way. But don't worry I can have you flown back by helicopter after the op. I understand the procedure only takes an hour or so these days.'

'Well yes if everything goes smoothly.'

Gina didn't like this at all. The devil sitting on her left shoulder was telling her with a smirk that she was officially heading into some deep water now. Meanwhile the angel plugged into her right ear, which was supposed to be providing back-up was apparently dead even after a couple of firm taps. She just had to hope she could still be heard.

'So where are you off to, anywhere nice?'

'Just down to the Med,' he answered in a clipped tone which suggested he was not interested in getting side-tracked.

'Oh I love the Med...Majorca...Greece...' she tried to stall. 'I remember one time I went…'

'So are you finished with the notes? Can we get on?'

'Oh sorry, I'll just run through the last of them.' She felt more like running up on deck and diving over the side, but that would be getting ahead of herself. She needed the evidence she had been sent in for first. But this all too fragile cover story wasn't going to last much longer in this revised scenario, as it would become patently obvious that she was in fact not a surgeon at all, and abandoning ship would mean abandoning this patient to goodness knows what fate, in addition to which it sounded like there may be others aboard too. She knew that MI5 had the Special Boat Service primed to come aboard if necessary, but even the London contingent would take fifteen minutes once scrambled. It looked increasingly likely she was going to have to take things into her own hands *before* any intervention arrived.

This was just meant to be a simple fact finding mission, to get some damning evidence on Entwhistle and his suspected terrorist plans. Publically he had been heard to speak out against terrorism, particularly al Qaeda and the unidentified man now calling himself *Allah's Fist* who was helping fund jihadist activities through services provided on the fast developing Dark Net. That could have been a smokescreen of course, and he might actually *be* Allah's Fist. But so far he was only *rumoured* to be *associated* with terrorism and human trafficking. The big question facing Gina right now, as she tried to use her powers of intuition to connect the dots, was what on Earth had all that got to do with boob jobs?

Entwhistle clearly had the money to grant girls wishes, he just didn't have the surgeon. Gina was sure that she had seen enough Nip/Tuck, Grey's Anatomy, and surgical documentaries to play her cover out a little further. However, there was no way she wanted to be putting anyone under the knife today, *if* she could avoid it. It did occur to Gina however, that the array of surgical instruments still waiting behind her might have been better used to get some answers from Entwhistle. Put her alone in a cell with him and she was pretty sure she could induce enough fear with the scalpels to get all the information *Five* needed.

'Okay then,' she said slowly as if she was only half sure. 'I need to see the implant certificates now.'

'The *implant certificates*?' Entwhistle growled impatiently.

'Yes. I need to know they are of an approved standard.'

'*Approved standard*? What do you take me for?'

A member of staff, not waiting for Entwhistle to click his fingers, handed him more paperwork, which he in turn passed to Gina, with an irritated shake of the sheets.

She turned to examine them. They seemed in order, to her untrained eye, which only meant that they could in fact be forgeries. But why would Entwhistle need to forge breast implant certificates? She needed to find something incriminating. She knew the SBS wouldn't be allowed to sneak aboard, certainly not burst into the operating theatre, until she had confirmed that she had found what *Five* were looking for. Otherwise it could lead to an embarrassing headline: *Special Forces rescue incompetent operative*. All she could do was keep going, but how? If that meant opening this woman up she would remain in that condition when it became clear that Gina was in fact no surgeon. Then what would happen to the two of them?

She got up, took off the jacket of her business suit, to reveal her short sleeved tailored blouse. She placed the jacket over the back of the chair and moved over to the sink and began slowly scrubbing up. As she dried off, a nurse came and helped her don her surgical gown, cap, mask and gloves. Oakley continued to take her time.

Next she went to examine the patient again who had now been placed on the operating table. The woman was young enough to be Entwhistle's daughter. She failed to see the attraction of old men herself, even if they were filthy rich, but clearly there were plenty of young women who *were* attracted to such prospects.

The staff watched on as she lifted each eyelid in turn and then checked for unconsciousness.

'She's fine,' assured the anaesthetist.

'Okay. Where are the implants?' She was shown to the trolley with two containers. Removing both lids and looking inside she took a translucent sack from the containers in each hand. They felt far more fluid than she expected. She had always imagined that they would have a firmer gel consistency. Suddenly she squeezed them both with all her might, hoping one might burst so the op would be postponed.

'What the hell are you doing, woman?!!' Entwhistle squealed stumbling away from her, his previous confidence instantly replaced by shock horror.

The medical staff, similarly anxious, gasped in chorus.

'Sorry, it's standard operating procedure. We have to test for leaks. We don't want silicone getting into the girl's body,' she explained as she examined the implants for signs of moisture.

'There're no *bloody* leaks...They've already been checked!'

Entwhistle's fearful frustration seemed to Gina to be giving something away, and at that moment she had one of her *camera zoom out* insight moments.

It occurred to her that she could be holding both components of a binary explosive compound, safe separate, but mix them together and ka-boom.

It was pure evil, the idea that women could be turned into walking bombs. Would they even know? Did they self-initiate with a double puncture or slash, or did a second person open them up? Oakley's mind raced.

Was it more complicated? Was this to target aircraft? Everyone knew you were not allowed to take liquids aboard planes. Did this means of bypassing security searches require these women to go to the toilet in mid-flight and milk themselves, to mix the two solutions for twenty minutes or so to produce the unstable crystalline explosive? Or was this a whole new compound?

Scarily she knew this would all too easily get through present security checks. It didn't bear thinking about. But maybe she had been reading too many thrillers and was just letting her imagination run away with her again and this really was just a straight forward boob job.

With neither implant having provided opportunity for postponement she realised that what she should be turning her imagination to was other ways of getting out of this mess, alive. As was often her way, Gina submitted to her intuitive nature and training. Replacing the implants momentarily, and taking a scalpel from the tray to her right, she lifted the young woman's left breast and demanded 'Swab.'

The nurse directly across from her lent forward with a swab in forceps to sterilise and mark the expected incision line with the brown antiseptic fluid. Gina didn't waste a second. Before the swab was even half way across the section of skin, the scalpel went in deep and fast, slashing the nurse's left wrist.

As the shocked nurse screamed out, Oakley used the opportunity to open up the jugular of the anaesthetist to her left, and as the male nurse to her right stepped back raising his hands in defence she followed through by opening up both of his wrists for good measure.

'OH MY GOD!!' Entwhistle squealed.

Blood fountained over the patient, none of it her own. She was the only person in the room able to remain calm. Gina's plan was working. The medical crew were each self-absorbed, attempting to staunch the bleeding, as Gina turned to look to Entwhistle. She just caught the back of him as he vanished into the adjoining room to escape the *crazy woman*. She threw her scalpel at the closing gap, but too late. It hit the panelling and flew aside.

Quickly she grabbed both implants again. This time holding them both cradled in her left arm, protected close to her chest. Then she took three scalpels in her right fist, one between each finger looking rather like Wolverine from the X-Men and went after Entwhistle. He was some way ahead of her now going for help no doubt, but she was faster on her feet after years of parkour and running marathons, not to mention her regular armed and unarmed combat training that kept her sharp.

Though *she* had Entwhistle on the run, on *his* yacht, she was hopelessly outnumbered by his crew. She saw him look back over his shoulder to confirm his fears before flying down a staircase to the next level. The sixty year old almost dived as he grabbed the metal banisters on either side and swung his feet ahead of him to jump clear of the last step, creating more ground again. This was something Gina could not attempt, with her hands full. She took the stairs two steps at a time.

Just as she reached the next deck she saw Entwhistle pass one of his men. She fully expected the crewman to be ordered to attack her, however, the order Entwhistle was heard to scream was 'RUN!!'

Now she was after two men and it occurred to her that surely there couldn't be much further to run astern as she closed in on them. But then they split, Entwhistle heading down another flight of stairs as the crewman carried straight on jumping through a bulkhead to seal the door after him.

Arriving at the top of the next stairs time seemed to slow for Gina as she took in what was waiting on the next deck down, and intuitively she stopped dead in her tracks. The next deck had jet-skis and no doubt a way out across the water. Entwhistle was about to make his escape, but not if she could help it.

She punctured one of the implants with a scalpel. Dropping that blade and a second as she placed the third between her teeth, she passed the pierced implant to her right hand and threw it at Entwhistle's back. As it travelled through the air in a blur of motion, Gina took the scalpel from her teeth and punctured the second implant, discarded that blade too and threw the remaining sack of fluid. The first one had missed its target, bursting on the floor ahead of Entwhistle to his left, but it caused him to slip in its greasiness and he went down hard on the steel deck, winding himself. He turned to look back, seeing the second implant on its way to him, and he raised a hand as if to swat it aside.

'NO!!' he screamed at the madness of it all.

The already slowed time seemed to freeze for the two of them. If these implants were legitimate Gina Oakley's career could be over. Gerald Entwhistle would be reporting a plastic surgeon who had gone mentally unstable on his yacht, cutting up his medical staff and chasing after him with a couple of silicone breast implants. None of which would not look good on her MI5 dossier.

However, if her intuition proved correct then the prime suspect could end up with third degree burns, or worse dead. A key lead lost. Something of a lose-lose situation. But should she have simply dived overboard with the implants as possible evidence and taken the risk of letting him get away with more? How bad could these two fluids react anyway? Oakley thought back to her chemistry lessons where an acid reacted with an alkali in an exothermic reaction. She suspected it would be more advanced than that but it wasn't going to be anything like say a plutonium core being inserted into its female component to achieve 'atom-splitting' critical mass, was it?

Gina's commanding officer, Penelope Ryder, had also become uneasy as it became clear that her agent's cover was about to be compromised now that surgery was required. If only Gina had considered faking a fit, Penelope thought, but the sounds she was hearing from Gina's mike suggested she hadn't. Penelope saw nothing else for it and ordered her *extraction*. Penelope was concerned that Gina could be heading for one of her *incidents*.

Minutes later, as the *Wave Forge* had reached the Queen Elizabeth II Bridge, the SBS Augusta Westland helicopter overtook the river police who had already been on site with their launches if required to board.

At that very moment the SBS commander saw what reminded him of HMS Antelope going up in the Falklands. Just ahead, the stern of the yacht suddenly lifted its bulk out of the water, engulfed in a massive fireball that shook the bridge above as it momentarily plunged the bow under the river. The blast lifted Entwhistle's helicopter like a firework, narrowly missing the bridge, but its crumpled body plunged into the Thames just short of the bank.

This turn of events changed the mission brief somewhat. Now the SBS had to board a sinking

17

vessel to extract any evidence of terrorist activity before it was destroyed. The search rather than rescue might have seemed a bit cold hearted when there would be people aboard burning and drowning, but the police would be at hand to fish out any swimming survivors, and floaters.

By rights Gina ought to have evaporated along with Entwhistle when the second implant split against his swatting fingers, but the force of the second throw had caused Gina to lose her balance.

She was falling back towards the deck when the shockwave came. It hurled her along the corridor which she had only moments before sprinted along, just ahead of the angriest fireball she had ever seen first-hand. She narrowly missed the set of stairs that she had previous descended, but landed very heavily with what felt like a rib or two round the back cracking. Then the fire caught up with her. She attempted to roll under the stairs for whatever shelter that afforded.

The surgical clothing gave a little extra protection, but it could not save her eyelashes and eyebrows being singed off.

First there was no air because the flame had taken it all then there was no air because there were thousands of gallons of water rushing in. The cold of the Thames revived Gina enough to keep her conscious but as it swamped her smouldering face mask it felt like she was being water-boarded. So she yanked it from her stinging face, and her cap with it. She had to get up the stairs, but the chaotic force of the water was almost too great. She grabbed the banister and pulled herself round. It was then that she became aware of just how badly the vessel was listing to starboard and stern. She had to get to the unconscious woman above, and get her out. There would be others trapped somewhere, but she had no idea where.

Escaping the foaming clutches of the water and finding her way back to the operating theatre she saw the blood drenched woman was now on the floor on the lower side of the room.

She was tangled in intravenous tubing and wires, but still unconscious. Gina removed the IV kit and pulled her loose of the wires.

Attempting a fireman's lift Gina made her way across the tilted theatre to the door, but just then water rushed into the room. The force of the water prevented escape the way she had come in, it was too strong even to close the door against it. Gina turned and made for the other door. Making it into the corridor beyond was still a distance from freedom, and as the vessel made horrible metallic death groans, Gina got the sensation of an underground train coming. She turned to see a wall of white-water rushing up the corridor to meet the two of them.

While the police were pulling back from the turbulent water around the sinking vessel in case their launches got drawn down with it, the SBS were actually jumping aboard and going inside. They would have boarded sooner, but the blast from the implants had almost caused their Augusta to ditch as it had descended for the *Wave Forge's* double H helipad.

Watched by onlookers from the bridge, the police fished out the last of the survivors as the vessel vanished from sight, ferrying them to shore where other police vehicles and ambulances waited.

As the minutes dragged on it didn't look too good for anyone else, unless there were people locked inside airtight compartments which the SBS could reach with their re-breathers.

Finally the SBS captain turned to see Penelope Ryder's enquiring look and shook his head. She took it on the chin that Gina Oakley had not made it this time. She hadn't known an agent like her for finding trouble. Whilst it was true that she got results, they were *always* the sort of results that were followed by mounds of paperwork and having to devise credible explanations for what *actually* happened.

Penelope took one last look out onto the Thames just as a beacon of orange hair suddenly surfaced with a head of dark hair bobbing up next to it, supported under an arm. Penelope sighed with a mixture of relief and exasperation over the incident, 'Agent Orange.'

1

Five years later.
Peter Trent drummed his fingers on the arm of his chair, barely listening to the employee in front of his desk. He had heard it all before. The new ones always thought they knew better. *If* they survived in this profession it was because they accepted the rules of *good business* in computer software design, the main one being the financial necessity of *change for change's sake*.

If a new release was not put out on a regular basis the company shares dropped, so revisions *had* to be hyped-up and delivered. If there was sufficient inspirational user feedback or a technological innovation to work with then an upgrade *was* possible. However, as the programmer in front of Peter had realised and was pointing out, if you already had the software working just right, then any change was likely to be experienced as a *downgrade*.

Downgrades, still referred to as upgrades, were a sad fact of good business, it gave companies the excuse to keep charging for software support in order to correct the mess. The trick was to keep the annual maintenance charges preferable to the client's only other option of buying into a competitors system.

The employee went on to suggest that they were behaving little better than those security software houses that pay people to develop viruses and Trojans to keep their market buoyant. Peter decided he had given the lad enough of his precious time, and dismissed him with a promise to *look into it*. He had no intention of sacking him, after all his employment just added to the overheads he could charge against. Nevertheless, he couldn't stop the guy quitting, as some did.

With the idea of heading home to the Docklands now foremost in his mind, Peter checked his watch. He was finishing work late again that Friday night. Putting the day's irritations behind him he went home via Lidl's where he picked up a frozen meal for one, and a bottle of wine.

The girl at the checkout recognised him. She looked fit but he wasn't about to ask her out. He'd been down that road enough times with girls to know it did not work out well, though it wasn't that there were no girls into geeks out there. At thirty-two he knew that though the long hours and lack of free time in the job certainly didn't help maintain a working relationship, the real problem was a clash of interests.

With the red wine being given time to breathe as he nuked his pasta bake he went through to his lounge. It was pretty bare. He didn't have a sofa just a single recliner chair, positioned in front of a widescreen smart HDTV.

He never had people round to his new flat. Most of his friends were *virtual* anyway. It was a sad fact that his home life was just as much in front of a screen as his working life, but that was the way of things as he saw it, so he wasn't about to be offering his right arm for anything better.

Taking the remote in hand Peter flicked through the TV guide list to see what was on his selection of adult channels. He had a ten terabyte solid state drive over half full of stuff he had downloaded over the last few years, but he was always on the lookout for new material.

It had all started on the slippery slope of *porn-am*, much of which was free, but like millions of others this taste for porn on stream developed a need for something harder, and then came the move to subscriber channels. But the development of his needs did not stop there, and like with all too many others it awakened a preference for *abuse-porn* and then *torture-porn*.

There was a time that this sort of material would have scared him, but he had now become desensitized to ordinary porn and discovered he was left only feeling aroused by degrading scenes of violence.

From there it was an easy slip to becoming an avid user of what was now commonly called the Dark Net. This was an underground use of the Internet. Only certain types of people were invited in, or found their way in.

The Dark Net provided apparently anonymous access to far more illegal and immoral materials, using *Onion Ring* routers, through systems like *Tor*. Peter also relied on his heavy duty firewall and encryption systems for further security. Nevertheless, even if someone was able to penetrate all of those security barriers, all they would appear to find on his drives nowadays would be a large collection of relatively harmless image and video files.

These images and videos were accessed from legitimate poster and video suppliers on the Internet. These suppliers were in some cases unaware of the misery they were helping pedal, because they were not yet sufficiently aware of the Dark Net and how it worked to question the source of the submissions to their online libraries.

The first clue to Dark Net content was overly large file sizes. Opening the files in standard software revealed the harmless *cover* image or video, but with the Dark Net software and access codes the files revealed hidden contents including images and video embedded in the content code; Image and video material hidden for good reason.

Much of these visual materials on the Dark Net were generated under duress, with no respect for human rights. It was often associated with human trafficking activities.

The long arm of the law continued to be powerless to deal with this increasing misuse of the Internet. While there were people like Peter out there, excited enough by the range of content to pay for darker experiences, then it was a market with a promising future.

The microwave beeped and Peter went to the kitchen to pick up his supper. Returning with a bowl and fork in one hand and a bottle and glass in the other, he placed the bowl on his lap and poured himself a glass of wine. Placing the bottle beside the chair he used the remote to select and play one of his favourite torture-porn films.

Later, when the bottle of wine was empty and the film almost over, an email notification came through from one of the Dark Net product suppliers. Knowing well how the film he was watching ended and now more excited by the prospect of something new Peter put the video on pause and opened his mail. The email read Trailer. And when he opened it up there was the access code and price for the complete video access code.

Quickly he downloaded the attachment then opened it with his special video software. He input the access code and then watched the trailer. He liked what he saw. Though it did not give much away, it was enough. Peter agreed the transaction through his account with the supplier, a legitimate purchase to all but the deepest of investigations, and returned to the torture-porn while he waited for delivery.

It only took a few minutes to arrive in his inbox. Though the porn film he had returned to watching was still not quite over he quit it. With the access code for the new purchase Peter soon had it up on screen.

There was rarely anything close to a storyline to this darker material, not like the thinly scripted softer porn movies. This was clearly real people and real reactions to intense distress. No acting necessary.

It made Peter's palms sweat and his heart rate increase with the thrill. He wouldn't pass for a psychopath however he was pretty sure he had some sort of mental health issue. It was just too much fun to want to do anything about it.

He shifted about on his chair, unable to contain himself as ten minutes in he realised what he had bought into, and in a hushed groan of amazement at his good fortune he blurted 'Oh yeah...they are *actually* going to kill him.'

He always took great pleasure in identifying with the victims suffering their brutal treatment; he often indulged in fantasies of these situations happening to him, but was secure in the knowledge that he was safe.

At that very moment a black van pulled up unheard outside Peter's London Docklands address. Its driver didn't need to shout to be heard by those waiting in the back. The throat mike conveyed the 'Go, go, go,' signal to their ear pieces.

The rear doors swung open and four black clad figures bounded out, carrying their suppressed HK MP7 submachine guns. Closing the well-oiled doors behind them before racing up the stairs of the five-storey flats, two went straight to the roof while the other two headed along Peter's fifth-floor corridor.

He was just disposing of a paper hanky in a waste basket by the chair when he noticed a red laser dot on his outstretched hand.

Spinning around, puzzled, as he got out of his chair, he saw what looked like two masked and armed SAS troopers standing on his balcony. They were aiming their weapon sites at his chest and forehead through his curtainless windows.

It was like something out of a nightmare. He stood there dazed for what felt like an eternity of confusion. This couldn't be happening. What did they want with him? Then it became all so obvious, Dark Net.

He ran. He didn't have a thought where to go, just out and away. He expected to hear the smashing of glass as the troopers gave chase, but there was only the sound of his panicked breathing. He whipped open the door to his flat where he then met the other two troopers.

There was no getting past them. He turned and ran back turning off to the left and into his bedroom, cursing. He slammed the door and locked it then backed over to the emotional security of his single bed. There were a tense few moments when nothing happened.

He racked his brain for a plan but before one was forthcoming the door was kicked in with a single blow of such force he thought they had used C4.

The four troopers surrounded him where he shook uncontrollably on his duvet, and watched as one of them unfolded a body-bag. He begged them not to hurt him, and tried to explain that he hadn't done anything wrong, that he didn't understand what this was all about.

Nevertheless, it didn't stop the syringe going in as he was pinned down by three gloved hands and the muzzles of two submachine guns. Then his theatrical display of injustice became a fade to black and all his tension just slipped away, for a while.

The extraction team quietly and efficiently bagged up all the evidence in the flat, and slipped Peter into his own bag before taking their latest bust to the waiting van and out of London.

Meanwhile, up in Birmingham, fourteen year old Ethan Best slept fitfully as he dreamed once again about the biological parents he had never known.

A woman who Ethan took to be his mother, who this time was in her thirties stood on a stage being applauded, while a man he took to be his father, now in his eighties, sat in the front row of the audience barely able to remain upright never mind clap his hands. The mother was being awarded for her contribution to science.

Her highly coveted research practice involved identifying appropriate names for new species of plants and insects, and this award related to the nomination for her greatly admired naming of *Wet-Nurse's Phlegm*.

'Thank you all so much for voting for me…This,' she held up her golden statuette of what looked like two beetles copulating next to an otter spraint, 'has come as a result of years of hard but highly rewarding work. My dedication to my work has been so much more rewarding than it would have been to bring up the son I abandoned at birth.'

The audience fell silent and Ethan woke, fists clenched, to the sound of his animal-like growl. Not all adopted children felt the same way, but Ethan hated his biological parents so much, especially his mother. This struck Ethan as irrational which irritated him all the more. He liked to be in control.

It was still dark so he knew he had to get back to sleep, but he could hear his hamster scratching around in its cage.

'Don't push me Percy.'

Percy stopped for a moment on hearing Ethan's voice but then started gnawing its bars.

2

Dave Fendor, based in London, had been regularly teased by his close colleagues at MI5 since 2009, when Woody Harrelson played a wannabe superhero character, Defendor. However, Dave never let their humour deter him from a job at hand.

He saw himself as a doer who was unlikely to rise further in the ranks, and also as someone with a propensity to try and do *the right thing* when needed, even if that meant doing it in his own time. He stood watching Gina admiringly from the rear of her firing booth. He missed working with her.

They had once dated and he found himself wondering *this* Saturday night what might have been. They had gone their separate ways since the unfortunate incidents that had led to her losing her job with the security services five years ago.

It had been a case of *three strikes and you're out*. He was not alone in considering her a good agent, but things did just seem to go wrong around her. So much so that after the second strike, involving a failed interception and a multiple pile-up on the M25, the department started referring to her as Agent Orange, on account of her flaming curly hair and the name for the defoliant toxin 2,4,5-T used in the Viet Nam war of the 60's.

There was no denying her final mission had all gone tits up, he thought, and smiled at his unintended pun. Nevertheless as he recalled it the Special Boat Service had retrieved enough data off the *Wave Forge* to explain what had been happening on board, and what would have happened had Gina not taken things in hand.

A large number of Eastern and Middle Eastern women had been given free boob-jobs, not knowing they were walking bombs.

Entwhistle had intended that they all be set of in shopping malls and on airliners over Islamic dominated countries. In his mind this was his own jihad to give them a taste of their own medicine.

There were a number of problems with Entwhistle's idea, not least being the large number of innocent people who would have been injured and killed. The main problem as MI5 saw it was the fact that Islamic terrorists seem *all too happy* to skip the day to day grind and go straight to the afterlife and the bizarre promise of virgins on tap. But then maybe Entwhistle had never watched The Four Lions movie.

Luckily, once Gina had reported what she had discovered, which helped make sense of what the SBS managed to retrieve, those implanted women who were not aboard the cruiser were traced very quickly, and neutralised.

That is, they were all operated on, to remove the unexploded breasts. It should have been a happy ending to a terrible story, maybe not a promotion for Gina but *not* dismissal. Nevertheless it was argued from higher up that she had caused millions of pounds of damage, what with the blocked shipping lane in the Thames, and the closure of the Queen Elizabeth II Bridge for checks and repairs, so someone had to take the fallout. After all, it took weeks for the remainder of the explosives to be located and removed safely, and the wreck salvaged from the mud.

Gina slid a fresh magazine home and aimed the Sig P266 at the card figure fifty metres down the track. In quick succession she fired six times, then removed her ear defenders and pressed the 'target forward' button.

'I thought you were away up Birmingham these days?' Dave announced his presence.

After a year of looking for work in private security and finding that no-one wanted to touch her, Gina had decided it was time to put her belongings into storage and travel the world.

When she returned from her year out she found that the Thames incident was water under the bridge and actually started getting some contract work. More recently however, she had been offered, and accepted, a permanent position working for DNA, Devereux-Norton Associates detective agency, in Birmingham.

She turned and smiled at Dave. 'Yeah, I just thought I'd pop in for a practice, while I'm down to pick up the rest of my stuff.'

'So how's the new job?'

'Oh you know, still settling in to the mundane and trivial.'

She turned to inspect the target. To a novice it might have appeared that she had missed, but target figures did not come with eye-holes.

'Always a perfect shot *Agent Orange*…But considering you no longer have a license to carry a firearm on the street, even as a PI, isn't all this just a waste of rounds?'

'You never know *Defendor*, there're an increasing number of people out there who don't deserve to be, and sometimes situations can change as quickly as the weather.'

That evening as Ethan Best reached into his school bag, which he took around with him even on weekends, he felt a great calm come over him. He drew out one of his humane traps he'd retrieved from the waste ground on his way home from the park in King's Heath. He walked over to the plastic cage by his bedroom window and looked in.

'Look Percy, one of your mates has come to *save* you.'

A sad looking hamster peered out from its little nest, which needed cleaning out. It was beginning to smell. Unless that was the leftovers of Ethan's Frey Bentos pie he'd scraped into the cage a few days ago which seemed to have gone untouched.

Ethan considered that this might be a hunger strike and he tutted. It wasn't a good idea to be any source of trouble to Ethan. The wheel had already been removed, some months ago, because the first hamster had made too much noise and had kept him awake. However, it was a no-win situation, as even inaction could spell doom.

He well knew his desire to be in control of the *helpless* and of their suffering and eventual demise was not a commonly shared personality trait. Otherwise he would have bumped into like-minded individuals at the pet shops and areas of waste ground that he frequented.

He considered himself an intelligent person. After all, he always did well in his school tests. Nevertheless he couldn't decide whether his behaviour, which he expected others to find unacceptable, was something he could not change, or simply *would* not.

He got such a sense of calm release from his internal turmoil over his being adopted when he watched others suffer. He was convinced that the reason for this lay in the lack of parental love he may have craved in his infancy.

The apparent abandonment by his parents, for unknown reasons, and his inadequate adoption by folk who simply serviced his basic needs like a pet, combined as a shortfall in stability and social role modelling.

As much as Ethan despised his adoptive parents, they didn't tend to ask too many questions, and often got him whatever he asked for. This was possibly in the hope of getting him to open up more to them.

He was not a very talkative child at four when they took him away from the care home, or now at fourteen. Not with *them* anyway. He hadn't shown an interest in sports, and wasn't particularly fussed with TV. He did read novels and manuals however, and like many other kids he enjoyed spending a lot of time on the computer, involved in gaming and other Internet activities.

His adoptive parents decided not to push, just to *be there* for him. So they had said nothing when his South American bird eating Goliath Tarantula had spontaneously combust. Even though that was within a day of the Zebra Finch dying of starvation in the tarantulas tank rather than being consumed.

More recently, on cleaning parts of Ethan's room Mrs Best had begun to notice that the hamster they had bought him actually seemed to have the capacity to change colour, but again no mention was made.

With a low laugh that was almost a hum Ethan turned his back on Percy and moved from the cage to the fish tank, where he opened the lid to empty in the occupant of the trap, with an inappropriately playful *plop*.

He watched eagerly as the shrew, vole, mouse, whatever it was this time, paddled frantically against the glass, before the water below its little feet erupted with three pairs of hungry razor sharp teeth that tore it to ribbons in seconds.

He moved back to the cage. 'Did you see that Percy? Aren't Piranhas jawsome?' Ethan laughed, but Percy seemed to sneeze as if in contempt. 'I *so* want to see you in there, but I *mustn't*…But soon maybe, soon.'

When not in heels, or propping up a bar, Gina stood five foot eleven inches. Although she liked her drink she was blessed with a metabolism that kept her beer-belly free. In fact she'd heard it said that she was a *fit lass for a size 16*. She had of course had worse things said about her in the past, from Ginger Gina the nickname at school, to Orangina as a WPC, which had stuck with her even as she made DI.

Her move to Scotland Yard's SCD9 had not lasted. Although her suspension from duty couldn't exactly state that she was jinxed, that is what its author had wanted to record.

Her shooting of Sir Alistair Bernard and subsequent successful release of a large number of Chinese children from a dockland container yard, would have worked in her favour, had her handling of the operation not resulted in a block of flats burning to the ground.

She had attempted to give chase to Bernard's right-hand man in the only available vehicle, a petrol tanker. Not having a HGV license she didn't have a clue how to detach the rig, but at least found the cab unlocked and the keys in the ignition, only because the driver had nipped out to ask for directions from a security guard office. She crashed the tanker only half a mile further on.

The suspension from duty had not stopped her applying to join MI5's ranks, or for that matter being welcomed aboard, impressed by her quick wittedness and determination as they were.

Gina really enjoyed the work with MI5 and it began to be the only thing in her life. That was until Five ditched her. Now she was back working in Birmingham, where she had worked the beat as a WPC. There she reacquired her nickname of Orangina, reinforcing the sense of a step backwards, thanks to the local grapevine. Her knack for decimation continued too, with one in ten cases ending badly.

Behind where Gina now sat on a bar stool was what sounded like some conspiracy theorist, who was babbling away to his drinking buddy or unfortunate acquaintance. He was suggesting that the Internet and social networks were getting so pervasive that it could naturally enable psychopaths and supervillains to be drawn to one another, to create dark synergies.

He sounded like an academic, or a fiction writer, either way not connected with the real world. He had gone on to argue that 'This is why you are getting these bizarre cases of satanic human sacrifices now, because these sorts of people would *never* have met up by chance in the past. Social networking now allows people to connect anonymously under false identities but truly dark needs.'

Gina was tiring of his bullshit fast, and wanted to get on with what she had to do and get out. In front of her, better late than never, Dick Tennyson, an observed regular, took his usual stool.

He was a mortgage advisor from a local building society, whose wife had paid for evidence that Dick was cheating. She had paid for a month but in that time Gina had turned up nothing. Nevertheless, Gina was convinced Mrs Tennyson was right and talked her into a month's extension to her contract. At the end of this time there was still nothing, and though Mrs Tennyson was now satisfied, Gina was not. Her intuition told her that *Dick* was exactly what it said of the man.

Sliding her left index finger between her wet-look orange lips and fingering her tongue she watched Dick's face. Slowly drawing the finger out and leaning forward to give a better view of her low-cut top she ran her finger-tip round the rim of his pint glass to make it sing.

However, the pint of bitter was still over half-full and didn't want to play any tune; Dick having only arrived five minutes ago.

In that time he had barely said a word to this redhead who was now even more overtly coming on to him.

'You look like someone who's more used to wine glasses,' he said with a smile.

'Well then, maybe you should come over mine,' she said pushing her chest further forward, her breasts almost popping out of her emerald green sequin mini-dress, 'if you've got the bottle.'

Not waiting for a reply she slipped off the stool and took a few steps towards the door, with an air of the confident drunk, turning to check that he was indeed following, before investigating the contents of her clutch-bag.

Dick turned to the barman, 'As I always say, never look a gift-whore in the mouth.' He gulped down a further two mouthfuls of his pint and moved after her. It was then that the two pound coin rolled across the floor, heading between his feet.

Before he could move, Gina charged after it and planted the crown of her head right in his crotch. As he doubled over in pain she brought her head up hard and fast to feel the bridge of his nose shatter against the back of her thick skull.

'Gotcha!' Gina announced holding up the coin with a smile.

'Fuuuuck!' Blood was pouring from Dick's now exploded nose, and the barman started complaining about the mess.

'Are you okay? What happened?' Gina played the innocent.

'You've fucking broke my nose you dumb slag!'

'Shit...Some people!' Gina put her coin back in the bag and swayed her way out of the pub.

Once outside her gait changed and she strolled round to the car park to her old copper Tigra. She felt closer to satisfied that the wait in the bar had been worth it. However, she expected that if Dick happened to describe her to his wife, she'd probably work out what had happened, but then say nothing.

The following Monday morning, on his way to school, Ethan replaced the trap he had removed from the waste ground, not forgetting to put in a piece of cheese from his sandwich, before balancing it in position in its sheltered spot.

A number of these traps failed because of the wind shifting them, as they were really designed for indoor use. What he wanted to do was get a larger trap and maybe catch a rat. He thought that would be good to watch.

In the playground he waited for Bertie Brookes. Bertie was one of the first years' who had *easy target* written all over him, lacking confidence *and* friends, due in no small part to his eczema. Ethan had been trying to tap him for money but getting nowhere. Then Bertie's father had died in a freak accident on the

London underground, falling onto the rails as the train was coming.

It had sounded like suicide, but Ethan told Bertie that *he* had pushed his father because Bertie hadn't paid when he'd asked nicely. It was a warning, plain and simple.

Bertie had threatened to go to the police, but Ethan had laughed and warned that he had enough people under his control to provide him with an alibi.

Anyway, he explained, he was still too young for the police to prosecute him. He had then told Bertie that if he did not bring him five quid a week, or if he found he had tried telling anyone about any of this, Bertie's mum would be the next bit of paste coming out of the tube.

Eventually Bertie came through the gates and noticed Ethan almost immediately, then looked as if he was going to pretend he hadn't seen him so that he could walk on by, but Ethan shook his head and then flicked it backwards to beckon him over. Bertie reluctantly approached.

'It's that time of the week Bertie.'

'What?'

'Time…to…pay…up,' he prompted him in a way that he considered fit for a slow learner.

'But…'

'Protection costs money. And you wouldn't like your mummy to take a fall would you? Knowing that it was all your fault, *again.*'

Bertie reached into his pocket and took out his wallet.

'Thanks.'

'Hey!' Bertie tried to grab it back but Ethan was holding it way out of his reach and laughing. It never occurred to poor Bertie to punch Ethan in the testicles and smashing his knee into his face, which Gina would certainly have done without a second's thought at his age.

Ethan found fifteen pounds and took it, emptying the wallet.

'That's my dinner money Ethan.'

'Well let's just say that now it is an advance on next week.'

'But I'll starve.'

'Starve? Fuck off! You don't know the meaning of the word. You get breakfast and tea don't you?'

'Yeah,' Bertie wasn't sure what his tormentor was trying to argue.

'Well there're kids in Africa that don't even get that. Have a thought for others you tactless twat.'

'Sorry Ethan. But my stomach will rumble and hurt.'

'Well you just need something to numb it.' Without warning he thumped Bertie so hard in the stomach it lifted the first years' feet off the ground and he fell, scuffing his knees.

'There now...Don't say I never give you anything Bertie.' He held the wallet out for him, but he was too winded to take it, blinking back the flashing lights and tears. Ethan just tossed the wallet onto the playground at his feet. 'If you do get hungry lunchtime, come and see me and I'll see if I can do you right, again,' he chuckled.

Ethan's actions had gone unseen by the other children, and more importantly the staff member who was standing by the school entrance dreading another day of chaos.

However, Ethan's actions had not gone totally unnoticed. A temporary resident of a block of flats, which overlooked the school, lowered a pair of high-powered binoculars and a directional microphone.

3

In her office in the Chiltern Hills Kate Handy looked up from her tablet, quitting the file she was reviewing as Peter Trent was brought in. He looked confused and was certainly full of questions having spent a whole weekend in a cell, albeit nicely furnished.

'Where am I?' he demanded, still struggling irritably with his cuffs.

'The Clinic,' said Kate pointing to the logo on the gown he had been provided in place of the clothes he had arrived in.

'Yes I know it's some sort of a *clinic*,' Peter said irritably, 'I've already been told that, but where *is* this place?'

'You don't need to trouble yourself with such details while you're with us.'

'Am I under arrest?' he was clearly angling to be released.

'No Peter, you are not under arrest, you are under *treatment*.'

'What for?'

'Oh I think we both know what for, *don't we*,' she smiled, 'after all we do have plenty of evidence to further inform our approach.'

'What approach?'

'It is my intention to rid you, and others like you, of your, shall we say, anti-social inclinations and behaviours. You will find that we work to a four phase treatment plan here, and like most who get brought to us you are presently in Phase Two.'

'*Two*? What happened to *One*?'

'The first phase is a period of self-healing. This is only possible if an individual acknowledges they have a problem, identifies a way to overcome it *and* successfully achieves their goal. You *had* that chance Peter. The phases cannot be allowed to go on indefinitely, so now you find yourself in Phase Two.'

'What does that involve then?'

'Science has shown that for certain low-boredom threshold individuals it is possible to almost rewire their desires.'

'You mean brainwash them?'

'Only in the gentlest sense, because here you manage the process yourself. It makes use of reflective practice and what is called brain plasticity. Do you think you have a low-boredom threshold Peter?'

'I'm guessing not. I'm a computer gamer and programmer after all.'

'Oh dear,' Kate pursed her lips. 'Well we *will* give phase two a try, but if you turn out to be correct then we *will* have to move into Phase Three.'

'And what's that involve?'

'We will deal with that *if* we need to. But there *will* be a cost attached to Phases Three *and* Four if you *have* to be progressed that far of course. Phase Two is a free service though, so use it wisely.'

'And it sounds like I don't have a choice,' he shook his cuffs to emphasis his point.

'Not really, no. So for now you will try Phase Two. This will involve the monitoring of EEG and ECG readouts while you watch a selection of images and video clips. The approach we take for Phase Two is writing therapy.'

'*Writing therapy*?' he scoffed. 'It sounds like a crock to me.'

'Let's hope not, for your sake. You will not be permitted to return to the community Peter *unless* we can bring an end to the darkness in you.'

'What will I have to write, *I will not kill*, a million times? And pray every day?' he was clearly still not taking this seriously.

'No, you will have to describe in the greatest detail all of your darkest fantasies. Then you will edit them adding more detail and thinking about what excites you the most. When you have exhausted all of these fantasies you will be required to develop new works, building on what you learned from the earlier works. If need be you will be given creative writing lessons by one of our therapists.'

'Ha. Are you for *real*? That would just make a person worse! Why not go straight to Phase Three and get down to the real business.'

Kate nodded. 'At first the arousal levels are heightened yes, but for the low-boredom threshold individuals the brain begins to rebalance and rewrite the problem pathways neutralising those desires. The arousal is no longer experienced on viewing the previous or similar imagery.'

'And you believe this will *fix* me?' his tone was still derisory, doubting her so called research.

'Fixing is not the term I would use, no. We do not retrain you to behave a particular way, beyond removing your desire for harm to self and others.'

'Self?' He wondered if they already knew what he fantasised about.

'Yes. Forms of self-harm can be treated in this way. We deal with a number of mental health issues at this unit Peter.'

'But I'm not mental!'

'Well your behaviour has not been deemed healthy has it, or you wouldn't be here.'

'What right...!'

Kate raised a hand, 'I think you will find we don't concern ourselves with the grey world of rights here Peter. It is about power and control involving treatment and monitoring without interference, so no visiting rights, no phone calls, and no complaints protocols.

'All through Phase Two you will receive EEG and ECG checks on your responses to the selected materials. If you make good progress you will be tested for responses to a fresh set of material. If the results are deemed acceptable to those then you will be returned to your home.'

'And if not, I will be progressed to Phase Three,' he used a bored tone in showing that he had been listening.

'I'm glad I'm boring you Peter. That shows more promise than you previously gave yourself credit for. However, Phase Two is hard work, and your clock *is* ticking.'

That Monday evening, in Somerset, Rupert Marchant lowered the book he was holding and listened. It had sounded like his wife had screamed something. Thinking he better go check he put the book down on the table, walked out of the study and into the hall.

'Dorothy?!' he called up the stairs.

Straining his ears he thought he could hear movement in her studio and then what sounded like a smothered cry, but no obvious reply to his call.

It was then that he felt the draft at the back of his neck and turned to see that the front door was wide open. This raised further concern, and not stopping to close the door he took the stairs two at a time, but only till he was half-way and then took them just one at a time.

He had argued with his wife that they should downsize to a bungalow, but she had said he was talking nonsense. Even at his age stairs were good exercise, and he shouldn't believe all that modern medical poppy-cock about heart strain.

Nevertheless, by the time he had reached the studio he was out of breath with a heart which could almost knock on the door in front of him.

The door was ajar but as he swung it open his jaw dropped. There in front of him were four black clad troopers piling computer equipment into bags, and with no sign of Dorothy he was left to assume she had already been packed in the body bag by the door.

'I say chaps, what on *earth* do you think you are doing?!' he lent down to unzip the body bag.

He only got the zip down far enough to confirm that the bag did indeed contain his wife when a trooper strode across, weapon in hand, and struck his head with the butt.

Later, when Rupert came round they had gone, and suddenly his life, like his wife's studio, felt very empty. Picking himself up, he went to their bedroom and rifled through his bedside table draw. His memory was not as dependable as it used to be, but he soon found his old note book and turned to the Hereford number he was looking for.

'This is Brigadier Marchant.'

'Who?' came the suspicious reply from the duty-sergeant.

'Brigadier Rupert Marchant. Is Edwards there?'

'Who?' the sergeant repeated, starting to sound to Rupert's mind a little like one of the WI women off Little Britain.

'Captain Edwards man!'

'I think you have the wrong number sir.'

'No!' he snapped, looking at the number in his book. 'I've just had four of your chaps storm into my home and take my wife away. What do you think this is Nazi Germany?!'

'Sir, you need to calm down. I don't know how you got this number, but…'

'I served in The Regiment you bloody fool.' He liked to think of himself as the original Rupert. 'Now just tell your lads to bring my good wife back, or she'll have their guts for garters!'

'Hold on…' the duty-sergeant put the phone down for a couple of minutes while he checked the roster. 'Sorry sir, but we don't have any active ops this evening.'

The very next morning, at DNA, Gina was getting it in the ear.

'It had to be *you* didn't it,' exclaimed her boss, Tom Norton.

'Sorry Tom.'

'What *were* you thinking?'

'Well actually, I was thinking the fucker shouldn't get away with it.'

'Mrs Tennyson was relatively happy with the lack of evidence, but now she's complaining you made her pay more than she could afford and then assaulted her innocent husband.'

'He must have known he was under surveillance…But he wasn't innocent, just careful.'

'Then *you* should have been *more careful*.'

'No. I think she must have made him suspicious.'

'Whatever…I've refunded her money.'

Gina sighed, 'I thought she'd appreciate what I'd done.'

'Yet again you thought wrong.'

'What's the matter with women these days?'

'Good question *Orangina*.'

Ethan, as per his routine, walked back to his house in King's Heath after school via the waste ground, but this time there was nothing in any of the traps. Maybe there would be something there tomorrow, he thought, or maybe he needed to find a new hunting ground, like the local park. In the meantime it meant doubling back into town, to Pet Barn.

He didn't rush his purchase at the store. He knew exactly what he was there for, but liked looking at the other animals and letting his imagination run wild. Wondering how long a kitten or a puppy might last in the tank. He also liked watching the monkeys. They were like little humans with tails. The way they looked back at you. It amused him, their intelligence, imagining those eyes searching for his soul, asking why he was doing what he did. But he'd need a bigger tank. Some people might call him wicked, but he liked to think of himself as creative with his cruelties.

'I'd like to buy a hamster,' he said to the lad at the counter.

'Are you looking to breed them?'

'What?'

'Breed them.'

'Why would you think that?'

'Well, you bought one here a few weeks back. So I assumed you might be thinking of breeding them.'

'Oh…no,' Ethan tried to recover quickly from his surprise of being recognised, whilst also now considering the idea of breading animals for his tank. 'The other one escaped.'

'Well they *are* good at that.'

'Yeah, he must have forced the gate spring open.'

'If you had a plastic tank they have no bars to climb to escape.'

'Ur, no thanks. I'll just…Peg the gate,' he lied. He already had a plastic tank, for that very reason.

'They can chew right through pegs.'

'Well I'll use wire then.'

'They can unwind wire.'

'Can they?!' Ethan was suddenly impressed.

'No, just kidding.'

'Oh,' Ethan was disappointed and found himself contemplating possible payback for the jest.

'Okay...If the other one turns up though, I can't take this one back.'

'Fine...No worries.'

'Junk,' Gina mumbled shaking her head as she sat at her desk deleting yet another string of emails, without opening them. Her mind was on going home at that point. She wasn't going to do another late one for DNA, or even to fulfil her own sense of justice. She was intending to take it easy.

'Well that's me done.' None of the others said a word. She got up, took her lime green jacket from the coat hanger behind her, and just carried it out. 'See you tomorrow.' She noted a couple of heads lift, which suggested she wasn't completely invisible. In fact she noticed the new guy even smiled.

In the car park she climbed into her Tigra, and joined the heavy Birmingham traffic. Edging forward through one set of lights after another, she wondered if Henry Ford ever imagined a time when cars would be unable to move faster than one of his production lines.

She had the feeling that she was being sucked down into a rut. That wasn't to say her work was like some dead end factory job, but these matrimonial dispute cases were rather lacklustre, and actually had a rather negative effect on her attitude towards relationships, not just marriage. Things had certainly not worked out between her and Sigh, a detective who she was partnered with back when she was on the force in Birmingham. Nevertheless the memory of it still lurked in the shadows of her mind like a case of mental thrush.

'This traffic's no good for your health!' she moaned, and on impulse pulled the car over in the hope that the traffic might be somewhat easier later, and went for a kebab.

At home Ethan went straight upstairs with his school bag then returned to the kitchen where his mother was preparing tea.

'Had a good day Ethan?'

'Of course not, it was school…Remember? *Suffer all ye children*,' he quoted his favourite line from bible class, as hurtfully as possible.

'What are you looking for?' she asked, ignoring his response as she looked down at him there on his knees, wondering if providing some help might make him happier.

Ethan was searching under the sink. 'I'm cleaning Percy's cage out. Here it is,' he had located the pine disinfectant.

'You are a good lad. There's no messing with you. Other children would leave that to their parents you know, but you really take care of your pets.'

'I certainly do,' he smiled at her unintended double meaning, as he placed the bottle in the bucket he took from behind the back door, then grabbed a cloth and some old newspaper before heading upstairs again.

Closing his bedroom door he went straight to the cage, putting the bucket to one side. Taking the lid off the cage he removed the sleepy hamster from its nest. It seemed to waken quickly and become inquisitive. It could smell the scent of the other hamster on his hands. Ethan began to stroke it as he turned towards the tank.

'Tonight's your big night Percy. You are *so* in for a treat. *Lucky you*. Now I hope you can swim. I'll be watching. Just squeak out if you've had enough.' He opened the lid of the tank and dropped Percy in. The hamster made a bigger splash than the smaller rodent had the evening before and made more of a commotion as it tried to keep its head above water, but this time the fish just watched.

'What's up lads?' They just floated around near the bottom. 'Oh you can't be full. Maybe you're bored of rodent. Maybe you'd like a bit of duckling next time.'

Ethan looked down beside the tank and picked up the little net there. Then lowered it to the surface of the water, offering it to Percy, 'Come on then lad.'

The hamster's forepaws grabbed onto the square of wire, only to find it was being plunged under. 'Oops. What *am* I thinking?'

Still the Piranhas held back for some reason, keeping to the far panel of the tank. 'Oh come on,' Ethan was growing disappointed.

After Percy had let go and tried to swim for the surface only to be pushed back down by the back of the neck, Ethan seemed to relent and pulled Percy out, dropping him into the bucket with a squeak. Maybe he smelled different. Maybe he was too clean.

Removing the bottle of disinfectant and the newspaper from the bucket Ethan then lifted out Percy and the cloth and began to dry the sodden rodent off. 'I'm sorry. Will you forgive me? Best laid plans of hamsters and men.'

Ethan reached into his school bag and pulled out the carton from the Pet Barn, opening the top to reveal its contents.

'Look Percy. This is your replacement. Isn't he nice? Now because you've been such a good sport with your swimming, and diving, I've got something for you in my pencil case.' He placed Percy on the carpet and took out a pencil and a sharpener, and as he sharpened the pencil Percy sniffed at the shavings that fell to the floor.

'No they are not for you...This is.' Ethan plunged the sharpened lead into the side of the hamster which squealed in agony. Ethan experienced no remorse, not even any excitement, though he was aware of how he wanted to feel *something* as he took Percy with two fingers by the scruff of the neck and dropped him back into the tank. This time the blood in the water was an irresistible signal and the surface of the water soon churned red.

'Just look at daddy Percy. It's going to be *alright* Percy. Just look at daddy's big smile.' Percy lasted longer than the previous meal. In fact Ethan thought he might even have been the longest lasting Percy so far.

As the bones and last strips of flesh and fur came to rest on the gravel at the bottom Ethan wondered what his parents would think if they saw this, would there be any reaction at all?

As soon as he had cleaned out the cage onto the newspaper he fished out the remains of the bones from the tank and put them with the sawdust and straw on the newspaper, then after a wipe of the cage he put clean sawdust in. Only then did he introduce his new victim to death row. Ethan's last task was getting rid of the evidence, taking the bundle downstairs to shove in the bin, before cleaning and replacing his mother's utensils.

'Tea's almost ready now Ethan.'

'What are we having?'

'Your favourite…Veal.'

'Great.'

All things considered, it was little wonder that the headmaster at Ethan's school had no grounds to disagree when staff complained about him. As a case in point, following a class discussion on whether or not animals had souls, Ethan's R.E. teacher wanted it noted that it was only the lack of a cane that had prevented the return of corporal punishment for the remarks and behaviour of this *evil cunt*.

4

Abaduna, Nigeria.
On the Monday afternoon, in the dry heat of Nigeria the rickety old Bedford truck, sounding none too healthy, had bounced its way down the rough dirt road to arrive at a bush village, carrying four black women in chains and a number of crates. The two armed white men in the cab had passed a number of checkpoints on their way, and paid the expected bribes for what they were trafficking. As they had neared the village they had been told to drive to, they had seen the villagers ahead becoming anxious and starting to run from hut to hut, hiding children.

The village of Abaduna was now composed of only women and children. Their men, young and old, had been taken away to fight *other people's* wars, and then with them gone, the traffickers had started to come and take some of their young women. The women of the village had no guns, and were not particularly able to defend themselves with sticks. Their men had never taught them how to fight. That was man's work. So they turned to the only defence they had, and wailed.

The truck arrived to the welcome of an ululating din, which the men ignored. Jumping down from their cab, brandishing their AK47s, they moved aggressively from hut to hut, pulling women aside as easy as their door screens, searching for something, or someone. Their eyes were very keen, reading body language and watching for any unwanted surprises, or traps, knowing not to underestimate the female of the species. These men considered themselves professionals, and knew they had to keep control of any given situation. Even though the women were unarmed, they outnumbered these men fifteen to one.

Finding the elder of the village the two men dragged her out into the middle of the cluster of huts where a number of hunting and farming tools had previously been burned by someone, leaving only bits of metal among the ashes. The elder knew better than to resist such visitors. She realised these men were about to make an example of her. It would be some imagined or trumped up action against the new order of things. An evil had come to their land of recent times that resistance only seemed to fuel.

The din died as the villagers gathered around the men, as seemed expected of them. Then in the villager's own language, so there would be no excuse for any misunderstanding, one of the men explained what was going to happen.

The men had chosen one hut, and as the silent man pointed it out the other explained that they would be emptying this. Whoever lived there would need to share a hut with someone else.

The hut would be used to store what was on the truck. If anyone resisted they would be shot and taken away to feed the animals. They were told that the truck contained drugs and slaves, and that they would return in a day or so, with a better truck, and would pick them back up.

If, on their return, they found their goods had been tampered with, the hut entered, there would be trouble. If the women had been spoken to or even offered food or water, the villagers would also be taken as slaves, never to return.

The men would know if there had been any rule-breaking because their slaves feared them and would tell them what happened in their absence.

The man went on to explain that *if* villagers heard a loud pop and a hiss it would mean that one of the slaves had attempted to escape and would have set off the *cloud of evil*. If this happened they should keep away from the cloud that would bring death to those who breathed it.

However, the slaves knew not to bring out the cloud. The cloud device would be connected to a spike after it was hammered into the ground to secure their chains to. Finally the villagers were asked if they understood.

It seemed a lot to take in, but the message was clear. The elder spoke for her people declaring that the men's demands were understood. She was thankful that they had not beaten her. She still had bruising from other visitors.

Satisfied, the men moved over to the chosen hut, which sat to one side of the village with a view of the central ground where the villagers had just gathered. There were very few belongings in the chosen hut, and as the silent man went inside and threw things out onto the ground, the other stood guard, watching its owners scrabble to pick up their belongings.

The man also noticed that the owners of the neighbouring two huts seemed to be removing some of their things, possibly fearful of the *cloud of death*. This could only be a good thing.

Next the truck was backed up to the hut and the crates offloaded. The slaves could be heard moaning with the uncertainty of what was to happen to them next.

They were removed from the truck by their chains, aware that the villagers were watching from a distance with trauma numbed expressions, powerless to help.

One of the slaves cried out either from pain or fear, before vanishing from sight into the hut. As the villagers heard the hammering in of the spike they watched as the windows were covered on the inside and then an additional screen put up to cover the doorway. It was going to be stifling for the slaves in that hut with only the hole in the apex of the grass-roof to provide ventilation.

The sun was beginning to get low as the men returned to their truck and pulled away. The villagers watched them for only a few moments, the tension easing, before returning to the last of their day's tasks.

Early the next morning, as a couple of the villagers were already tending to their goats, the rumble of engines was heard and they looked up to see three trucks approaching. The signal was given, rousing everyone to hide the children out in the bush again.

As the trucks pulled up on the edge of the village and their occupants got out it was obvious that the previous two white men were not among them. These were the other men who had been before and taken some of their daughters. As their leader strode into the village the elder came out to greet him and attempt to plead for their lives.

It did not bode well for any of the villagers as armed men from each truck spread out in preparation for what was to follow. Without a word the leader drew his weapon beaming a smile and placed the muzzle on the pleading elder's forehead.

There came a sound like the buzz of a bee and the leader dropped his weapon; a hole in his wrist, as three of his men simultaneously collapsed with holes in their heads.

The villagers scattered, and as the leader clutched his injured wrist he cried out a warning to the rest of his men. Another four of his men fell dead, their weapons only half raised, as their leader dropped to a crouch and ran for cover, pulling his neckerchief loose to stem the alarming flow of blood from his right wrist.

Out of the slaves hut burst four figures each armed with a suppressed HK416. Splitting up in pairs, covering each other's backs, their first objective was to mop up the three remaining traffickers they had counted, to be immediately followed by checking out the vehicles for more hostiles.

They had expected at least one of the trucks to be loaded with back-up. It was almost disappointing to find them empty; ready to harvest all of the villagers. Shortly, with the village secured, two troopers caught up with the leader as he attempted to make a run for it into the bush. A hard blow from a weapon sent him reeling into the dust. Trying to pick himself up it was his turn to try pleading.

'Mercenaries…listen. My boss can pay you double, triple, what *you* are getting,' he offered, though he had no idea who was paying them, but knew it couldn't be the villagers.

One of his captors pulled down the cloth covering her nose and mouth. 'Not mercenaries.'

'Women?' he almost laughed at the surprise. How could women have done this? They would pay dearly. He began to smile again.

'Get up!'

He was marched towards the middle of the village, aware that the eyes on him now saw him in a different light, and his smile faltered. He was expecting to be shot as an example of a hoped change in the winds of power, but they were wrong, his death would change nothing.

'Keep going.'

Confused, he was marched towards one of his trucks, where he met another of his men caught by the other troopers, and guessed the rest of his men were now dead, but he frowned. They couldn't just be letting them go, surely.

The leader and his surviving man were made to get into the back of one of the trucks, where they were cuffed to the metalwork by three troopers who then stayed to guard them.

Satisfied, the fourth trooper climbed into the cab, and without a word to the villagers they were off, but the truck had only travelled half a mile when it stopped. The villagers watched, but could see little.

The leader, his right wrist further agonised by the cuff, was distracted from his pain by the unexpected stop. He heard the sound of something being broken in the cab. It was the radio being smashed. Then the trooper came round to join the other three. The leader was removed from the metalwork and forced to lie down on the wooden boards of the truck.

His colleague could only look on as the troopers drew knives they had removed from the other men and in a synchronised motion pinned the leader's arms and legs firmly to the deck of the truck. His trousers were pulled down and without a pause another blade was used to castrate him. His severed genitals were shoved into his screaming mouth, choking him.

Then the second man was taken down, screaming with fear and fury, expecting the same treatment, but was pulled off the back of the truck and led around to the cab.

'Go back to your camp with this message. Tell your boss's boss that if a return is made to this village the Devil's Angels will wipe his men out again and then pay *his* village a visit.'

The man said nothing as he climbed up into the cab with his chance of escape. He smiled inwardly. He was going to get away from these stupid bitches. They were so full of themselves, for killing these men, one of whom was his brother. However, when he reported back to camp what they had done to his boss the camp leader would go ballistic. He would rain all hell down on the village. There would be nothing left but scorched earth.

As the villagers watched the truck start up again and drive away, they saw the four troopers returning on foot. When they got back to the camp the troopers all pulled down their dust scarves to show their friendly faces. Only then did their team leader turn to the village elder and apologised for their tactics.

'We are sorry we had to deceive you. It was the only way to ensure you would not give things away by your behaviour, if you had known that you had help.'

'But I am not sure you *have* helped us.'

'No?'

'You have stirred up an ants nest. There are only four of you, and there are many many more of *them*. They *will* come.'

'Have faith.'

'How can we have faith? We don't even know who sent you.'

Before an answer was given another warning was raised and a young woman came rushing to the elder. 'It is the two white men.'

The elder looked at the team leader for reassurance.

'It's fine. They will be nicer this time, I promise.'

When the truck arrived it was bigger. The two men got out, this time with a wave of hands not weapons, and went straight round to the back. The truck carried food and medical supplies, and new tools.

The elder was invited to come and see the gift to the village as the troopers moved to lend a hand unloading.

As the delivery was shared out, things set up and repairs made the night closed in and the troopers were offered back some of the food.

'I only wish,' the team leader said to the elder 'that we could find and return your loved ones.'

'That would be a miracle, but at the moment the miracle we need is to survive the wrath that soon faces us all. You do not seem to be prepared.'

'Don't we?' The team leader broke into a knowing grin. 'Have you ever heard the old saying, *a red sky at night is a shepherd's delight*?'

From her office Kate Handy had been following her team's progress with their Nigerian mission via the satellite feeds on her tablet, which she had tapped into through the control centre down stairs. She listened intently to their Sit-Reps, keen not to miss a thing that might spoil her plan. She could have played back the recordings from the satellites to track where the three trucks had originated from, but it was so much more fun to watch the GPS tracker, which her girls had fitted, trundle onwards to its target.

The truck pulled up at a very large camp which Kate had already had her suspicions about and the camp burst into activity. A person, possibly the big boss of the traffickers, came to see the dead man pinned to the back of the truck. Orders were assumed to have been issued because a little later more vehicles arrived, recalled, to make a return to the women's village with their own message. Now Kate was satisfied, and gave the order, 'Execute Shepherd's Delight.'

She appreciated that there would be some collateral damage, but that's why governments felt powerless to deal with these anti-social elements.

In Abuja, the capital of Nigeria, the city's defence headquarters, at Ship House, suddenly went into something of a flap as one of their computer guided missiles managed to self-initiate and then launch from a nearby barracks.

The level of concern only grew when it was identified what payload the missile was carrying. Even if it was aborted there would be collateral damage wherever it came down. They pressed the abort button, but found it was refusing to acknowledge.

The arms dealer who had supplied the weapon system would have some explaining to do. Their air force was scrambled far too late. Luckily for them the missile was not about to initiate war with their neighbour Cameroon, as it was coming down somewhere in their own back yard, where a certain GPS tracker was signalling for it.

Hearing Kate's confirmation in her earpiece the team leader checked her G-Shock watch and then her compass then called for the village elder and whoever else was within earshot. As they gathered round, the team leader checked her watch one more time and pointed to the East. 'Behold what a bit of faith can do.'

The sky lit up as if the sun were trying to rise early, but then came a great crown of smoke that the sun never wore, sending a simple but deadly message to all involved that a new game *was* in fact on.

5

Birmingham.
Gina slid the DVD caddy in and slumped onto the sofa with her bottle of Peroni to watch *Enter the Dragon* again. She knew it was now considered a very dated film, and compared to modern camera work and stunts it was easy to spot the missed contacts, but it was a classic and one of her favourites. The whole idea of infiltrating a villain's base and physically kicking the shit out of them all struck a chord with her. She certainly felt like drumming some sense into a few heads with her own nunchaku tonight.

The movie only got as far as the scene where Bruce Lee's art of *fighting without fighting* managed to trick the jerk on the junk into getting in the dinghy for a fight when Oakley's mobile began the *Enter the Dragon* theme music. She didn't notice it immediately. It wasn't the first time this had happened either, and her caller was close to being directed to voicemail before she answered it. It was Simon Dunn.

'Orangina.'

'Sigh.'

'What you up to?'

'Oh you know, watching Bruce.'

'Well I wondered if you'd be interested in looking at something for me.'

'What is it?'

He gave a big sigh, as was his thing. 'I'd rather not say. Come see for yourself.'

'Where are you?'

Gina shortly stood waiting by the cordon tape at the scene of crime, as DI Dunn came out of the warehouse, and beckoned her across. He was six foot two, with broad shoulders and greying brown hair.

Gina stepped over the tape and joined him. 'So what is it then Sigh?'

'Take a look in here. You're into Friends of the Earth and all that shit aren't you?'

'Well I don't know about the *shit*, but I certainly support *not fucking up the planet any more than we already have, Dunn.*'

'Okay then. Do you have any idea who might be responsible for this?' He led her inside where she saw a man hanging by his neck from a girder.

The first thing that struck her beyond the fact that the man was dead, was the corrugated cardboard on a piece of string round his neck. In green marker it read 'Stop killing the fish!'

'Who is he?' Gina asked.

'Birdseye driver,' he pointed at the truck parked beside them.

'But what do we know about him?'

'Nothing much yet,' he said splashing a foot on the wet floor. 'He's just an unlucky truck driver, I guess. I just thought before we get into the routine of the investigation you might be able to solve it with your *super insight.*'

'You've been watching too many re-runs of Heroes, Sigh.'

'I know, it's just you *do* have an uncanny knack of seeing the world differently.'

'Yeah, and so far Sigh it's just got me into trouble.'

'Well if you don't want to help us to get the responsible party before they get away, then I guess I can't detain you,' he said in a sulky tone that suggested he'd prefer she hung around.

'The responsible party is not going anywhere.'

'What do you mean?'

'He's hanging around in here now.'

'He is? Who?' DI Dunn looked around suspiciously at his colleagues.

'The dead guy.'

'What?'

'It's suicide.'

'But there're no steps. Someone had to have put him up there and took them away.'

Gina shook her head and led him to the back of the truck and opened it up. Apart from a little bit of ice on the bed of the refrigerated container it was empty. DI Dunn frowned at her, still confused. She pointed at the warehouse floor, the big puddle they had been standing in. He continued to frown. 'It's a classic lateral thinking puzzle scenario.'

'Durr,' DI Dunn made the sound that he thought *she* should be giving *him*. 'But I don't get it.'

'Check the writing on the cardboard with his. Check his pockets for a bye-bye note. I think you'll find he drove in here with the truck loaded with ice, dumped it in a pile below the girder. Climbed up, threw the rope over the girder made a noose, put his head in and waited for the ice to melt.'

After a pause while DI Dunn thought this through, he asked 'Why?'

'Oh that's a whole other question…Are we done?'

'I…'

'See you around then,' Gina turned and left, shaking her head.

DI Dunn watched her go and wondered whether he would have stood a better chance with Orangina if she wasn't such a bright spark, then he sighed again.

Dorothy had come round in her room. It didn't look like a police cell, or military interrogation room for that matter. However, her wrists were cuffed in front of her.

It almost looked like a hotel room, if you ignored the padded walls. There was no inside handle on the door, so she decided to go and thump on it for attention. But it was like clubbing a leather chair; no one came.

It was outrageous that she had been taken from her own home. Had they taken Rupert too? There were going to be heads rolling when she got out. She found herself imagining what she would like to do to the persons responsible for this, and that brought a smile to her face.

Ethan growled in his sleep. He was dreaming about his biological parents again. This time however, he saw himself *with* them; just a baby.

His father was pushing an antique wicker basket pram, full of bits of bread, while the infant Ethan was being carried by his mother in a plastic carrier bag, the bottom of which occasionally scuffed the paving as it stretched under his weight.

'Where did you say we were going again dear?' the father asked.

'The park,' she snapped.

'Oh good, I do enjoy the park, especially the swings.'

'You are *not* going to go on those swings again.'

'Why not?' Childishly disappointed.

'You always swing high and then jump off. The last time you did that you twisted your ankle and then I had to do *all* the chores with the boy.'

'So why *are* we going then?'

'To feed bread to the ducks.'

'But I thought we were not supposed to feed bread to ducks, because it makes them sink.'

'Sink?! Nonsense!'

'Well that's what I heard.'

'Well consider this an experiment then.'

They shortly arrived at the duck pond and Ethan's mother ordered the father to throw all the bread out onto the water. Even doing this with both hands it took an age to empty the pram. However, when he was done he revealed that there was a screw driver and spanner at the bottom.

Ethan had been left in the carrier bag at the side of the pond. He didn't like the feeling of the now loose plastic touching his face and attempted to crawl out with that sort of *two shuffles forward and three shuffles back* that infants are keen on perfecting. His mother paid his struggles no attention whatsoever; she was watching the quacking ducks go crazy over the bread-polluted pond water.

'What are these for?' The father asked, holding up the tools.

'Detaching the basket from the chassis of course,' she snapped again as if it was obvious to all, pointing at the pram and them waving her finger at it in the hope her husband would understand better that way.

'Why?'

'Another experiment…Come along, get on with it!'

The father set to with the tools and shortly had the basket off. 'Now what?'

'Place the boy in the basket and push it out into the reeds over there,' she said pointing irritably again.

'Why ever would we want to do that?'

'Don't question me! I'm a forensic historian, and this is to test out the story of Moses.'

'But surely this will just leak like a sieve? I believe Moses's basket would have been lined with tar, wouldn't it?'

'Well we don't *have* any tar *do we*!'

The father picked up Ethan just as he had escaped from the bag and dropped him into the basket. At the edge of the reeds he leaned out from the bank to lower Ethan in.

'Not there you idiot!' She waved him to wade to the far edge of the reeds. 'Further out!'

'But…'

'Man up!' She glared at him till he complied.

At the edge of the reeds he let go of the basket. It hit the water with a splash and immediately started going down. He looked back across to the mother. 'I warned you about the sinking dear.'

She looked to see him pointing at a group of three ducks apparently drowning.

Ethan could feel the pond water and woke up. He had wet himself, again.

6

Ethan hadn't long been at the waste ground the next morning when a car pulled up. This was *not good* he decided, even before the two women got out. Cars never came onto this bit of land. They could have been fly-tipping he considered for a moment. Nevertheless, that came to look less likely as they split up and walked empty handed in the beginnings of a pincer movement. They both removed wallets from their jackets which were still too distant for him to make out any detail.

'Police!' one of them yelled. 'We'd like to ask you a few questions.'

'About what?'

'We need you to come to the station with us, Ethan.'

He became more concerned when he heard his name and started edging away, had that idiot Bertie gone to the cops after all that he'd said?

'If you run it won't go well for you Ethan. It will be taken as a sign of guilt.'

He stopped 'For what?'

'That's what we need to confirm. How much of the story is true.' One said as they closed in.

'What story?'

'Come on Ethan. Don't make this worse for your parents.'

'Fuck off! You don't know what you are talking about.' He grabbed a stone and threw it with great force and accuracy. It hit one of the officers on the side of the head. She went down like a sack of potatoes and the other rushed to her aid.

Ethan took his chance and fled.

'Clare? Can you hear me? It's Jane.' But Clare was out cold. 'Bollocks!'

Clare *had* said this wasn't a good idea. Ethan was a big lad for his age and unpredictable.

Jane was new to this and had just wanted it sorted. She was getting tired of surveillance. She wanted to see some *action* but now all she had was a *situation*. Clare was down, and *she* couldn't drive. She called it in.

Even when out of sight of the women Ethan kept running. His whole day was thrown. He couldn't go to school now that he'd just assaulted a police officer. Then it dawned on him, he couldn't even go home, *and* he'd forgotten his phone. What was he going to do? He needed to find somewhere to think. He headed for the park.

Dorothy glared across the desk at Kate who was trying to give her the induction spiel but kept being interrupted.

'I don't know what crack-pot department this is, but you have made a grave mistake young lady. I have a close friend in MI5, and once he hears about this he will have me out of here, and your department closed down quicker than you can say *Jim'll Fix It*.'

'Ironic turn of phrase don't you think Dorothy, considering your own use of the Tor system.'

'I don't know what you are talking about.'

'So who is this person in MI5?'

'That's for me to know and you to worry about.'

'Well while I get on with this *worrying,* you need to make progress with your *treatment,* as explained.'

Gina sat at her desk, in no good mood, when Tom walked up and dumped two files in front of her cup of mint tea. 'Here are your next two cases Orangina. You can choose what order you start them, just get them done *properly.*'

'Yeah, well I…' She wasn't sure what the remainder of that sentence was going to be, but then he hadn't stayed around to listen.

She took one glance at the thinner of the two files, and seeing it was another matrimonial dispute snorted derisively. She flicked it to the far corner of her table, except that it overshot and spread across the floor. She didn't rush to pick it up, instead she turned over the cover of the thicker file and peered at the top sheet. However, before she got far into the summary she heard the first few bars of *Enter the Dragon* and reached into her fleece jacket. She checked the caller ID.

'Sigh.'

'You'll never guess.'

'You've had a promotion for solving the suicide.'

'What? No…I found it on the Internet.'

'What?'

'You know you said it was a lateral thinking puzzle.'

'Yeah?'

'Well I looked it up on the Internet and there it was.'

'Whoop dee doo.'

'Eh?'

'Sigh man, I'm sure there're loads of lateral thinking puzzles on the Internet. Have you let some of your IQ spill out on the way into work?'

'What? No...' He sighed. 'Listen. When I looked up the puzzle I found *video footage* of Mister Birdseye hanging his self.'

'Right,' she sounded surprised rather than sarcastic now.

'Yeah,' he sounded smug.

'And?' she wanted more now.

'Well, it couldn't be suicide then, because there was no video equipment at the scene, so someone else must have killed him.'

'Or it was a chance voyeur.'

'What?...Is that likely?'

'I don't know. This world is filling up with sick bastards. We've not got enough mental institutes or prisons to keep them all in. We could be reaching a tipping point.' It occurred to Gina that she was starting to sound like the conspiracy theorist she had heard at the bar the other night.

'A tipping point?'

'How the fuck should *I know*,' she retorted crossly. 'I'm just trying to get through another day of shit, hoping something good will come my way...So why did you really phone?'

'Oh, well I was just about to ask IT to run checks on the video to see if we can tell who downloaded it, but thought I'd, you know... Ring and let you know...'

'What? That I was *wrong*?'

'Well…'
'To give me a bit of a *lift*?'
'Eh, no.'
'Fuck off Sigh.'

Hours later, two cars returned to The Clinic driving straight down into the underground garage in the ops wing, bringing Jane and the still unconscious Clare back.

'Take Clare straight down to sick-bay,' ordered Kate who met them in the garage with Eleanor, her right hand woman. 'Let me know her condition as soon as you know.'

'Yes Kate,' said Eleanor.

In the sick-bay, Clare was placed on a padded table, her pupils checked and her pulse, then her wound cleaned and examined, but without facilities for an MRI scan or even x-ray they had to guess the rest. After conferring over Jane's account of what happened, the medical staff concluded that Clare should regain consciousness sometime soon, and they reported this to Eleanor.

The basics of a plan were coming together now for Ethan as he headed West to reach a canal towpath. What he needed to do first was rid himself of his school uniform, and appear more like a sixteen or seventeen year old. He knew gardens backed onto the path further South along where the canal ran round the edge of a housing estate.

There was no-one on the path that morning, all the better for him, as he soon slowed his pace and began looking through and over people's fences. Ideally he wanted to see clothes drying on lines, but there were few obliging households.

The first was possibly an all-female household, and desperate as he was, like most lads, he would rather get caught in school uniform than be seen disguised as a girl.

Finally, peering through a knot hole in a high wooden fence, he spotted washing on a rotary line, which seemed to include a grey and green track suit, and some T-shirts, among other items.

Conveniently, this garden had a back gate. Inconveniently there was someone in the kitchen. Ethan reasoned that they wouldn't stay in the kitchen all the time. At the very least they'd need to go to the toilet at some point, and he had to be prepared.

He tested the latch on the gate. It wasn't locked. It opened with a squeak. He pulled it closed, and listened for any sound of a dog as he peered through the knot hole again.

Eventually he observed the occupant leave their kitchen for another room and he made his move. It only took seconds but if felt like minutes. He decided to take the pegs too, thinking what Bear Grylls might have done in his place.

He wondered if there was anything else he might find useful that he could lift while he was there, but thought it best not to hang around.

Closing the gate behind him he shoved the damp clothing into his school bag and headed off down the towpath beyond the estate. He passed under a bridge beyond which the canal began to run through fields.

He kept going until he found a dense group of bushes. Quickly he changed out of his uniform. The damp stolen clothes were uncomfortable but his body heat would soon sort that if he kept moving. The track suit was a little on the large side but not noticeably so. He tucked the trouser legs into his socks. He put his uniform in his bag, not wanting to leave evidence, and also because the extra clothes could help him keep warm later.

Next he decided he would need food and water, and if possible a better bag. After that he knew he was going to have to decide in what direction his future lay.

David Johnson sat on an embankment over a hundred miles away from Ethan, considering his own future. He had heard that the public were beginning to catch on, and already some were referring to his line of work for the Highways Maintenance department as *Gratuitous Coning,* but he didn't give a damn about that, it was easy money.

The fact was in the 1990's the government had entered into a contract that it was legally unable to back out of. This contract was for an annual supply of traffic cones, at five pounds a shot. In the first year and a half the cone situation improved as the national shortfall was met, so no questions seemed to need asking.

That was until year four when it was pointed out that the supply of orange cones had exceeded the needs. Nevertheless the annual supply continued.

Highways Maintenance tried to cancel the contract but it was tied up too tight because of job security guarantees, plus the government's commitment to plastic recycling quotas.

They tried to sell the surplus abroad to countries which didn't use cones yet. They even tried different colours like green and blue to make them more interesting. A few hundred were successfully sold overseas, just for the look of them, but by far the majority remained in the UK.

It never occurred to anyone to suggest that the tax payer's money could continue to employ the cone moulders but for some other more useful product production. Instead, resourceful minds had been turned to consider other *solutions*.

As a result the likes of David Johnson found themselves placing and moving cones on the road, day in day out. Much to the irritation of motorists as the gratuitous coning only added to congestion.

Some motorists passed coned-off sections never to see them again, while others passed them a number of times and never thought to question them. However, a growing number *did* begin to notice that, for all the delays the coned sections created, no actual work seemed to be getting done in return.

David could vouch for this. He and his colleagues simply laid the cones out along a designated stretch of road, which to his mind seemed to be put on his briefing sheet purely at random, and once the job was done they left.

Later, his or another team would be sent back to remove them or just move them, plus any accompanying traffic lights. They never saw any work being done, either. The road never got dug up, the verges remained untidy, the hedges unclipped. That wasn't to say that maintenance didn't go on somewhere, just not anywhere he was sent.

The truth of the matter was that the increasing number of cones had reached a point where the councils could no longer afford the storage space to hold the surplus. They tried to return them to source, but the trucks returned and played havoc in the council car parks, until somebody had what the Highways Maintenance department thought was an *inspired idea*.

The roads and motorways became the storage area. Employing people to keep putting them out and moving them about addressed another political hot potato too, the reduction of unemployment.

There was some resistance to this from those who drove to work rather than used the failing public transport system, on the grounds of needless congestion. However, this was dealt with by getting a sponsored university to prove that congestion by gratuitous coning improved traffic flow and was therefore *green*.

So the farce of gratuitous coning continued to plague British roads, and as the years rolled by one Highways Maintenance cone truck became two, and then three, and then the gratuitous coners, like David, had to lay them more closely together on the roads to fit them all in, sometimes even doubling them up.

What David liked best about his mindless job was that it gave him loads of time to plan how he was going to become famous, or rather *infamous*.

He had been using the Dark Net for many months now, not just for entertainment, but to inspire ideas of how to capture a young woman and keep her alive through a protracted period of torture in the soundproofed basement he had now built.

In preparation for this, what he liked to do was practice speed-walking in other people's neighbourhoods to try and identify what type of person would make a good abductee and how he might pluck them off the street.

It was on one of these evening speed-walks that he passed a black van. He remembered being aware of someone up front watching him approach in the mirror. Then there was the sound of well-oiled rear doors opening as he passed, just before *he* was grabbed from behind and plucked off the street.

Later, in the ops wing of The Clinic the body bag containing David was placed on a gurney and wheeled away by two nurses, leaving cyber-forensics to unload and investigate the evidence removed from his home following his extraction.

The extraction team, made up of four troopers and their driver were shortly changing in front of their lockers and storing their kit away. Gloves came off first to make the rest of the task easier. Then the masks came off and for a moment the all women team shared a smile and hi-fived each other for another *client* bagged.

7

'Hey, Tango,' said the new guy at DNA, trying to give a funny first impression as he noticed how the woman in front of him wore pearlescent orange nail varnish and lipstick that pretty much matched her flaming orange hair. He had been there a week now and had spoken to everyone but her, and thought it about time he bit the bullet.

'The nickname's *Orangina*,' she corrected, looking up from her tablet where she was busy checking case details.

'What's the difference?'

'Mmm, you've got me there, though either is preferable to Agent Orange.'

'Who's that, someone from Captain Scarlet?'

'No, someone from MI5.'

'Oh, *you're* the *Belgrano in the Thames woman*, gotcha, sorry, my bad.'

She wasn't sure whether his continued tactlessness was all part of the wind-up or whether he really was this dim witted. 'My name's actually Gina, Gina Oakley, but most people here now know me as Orangina…Agent Orange was my MI5 tag, as well as being a chemical spray delivered by planes to defoliate canopy cover in Viet Nam, to reveal the Viet Cong. Though I understand it just forced them to dig tunnels and live in them…Since I've been accused of having a similarly devastating effect on cases I got called Agent Orange.'

'Why not just *Dumbass*?'

'I guess my MI5 colleagues were just better *educated* than you,' she said playing with a lock of her hair. 'So what do *you* want?'

'Oh…I was told you would need magazines for your stakeout.' He removed them from the carrier bag and dropped them next to her tablet.

'OK and Hello?…*Seriously*?'

'What?'

'You actually went and bought these?…Or are they on loan from your *personal collection*?'

'What? I wouldn't read that stuff...'

'Oh, and *I* would?'

'Well I thought you'd like to look at the clothes.'

'Fair assumption, but why not Vogue then, or Marie Claire even, instead of Celebrity Face-Lift and Royal's Spoils?'

'I guess they were right?'

'What?'

'I was told not to be fooled by the good looks…You can get your own stakeout reading material in future.'

'Sound advice…What was your name again?'

'Will…Will Norton.'

'Norton. Like…'

'…Old Uncle Tom, yeah.'

Jane entered Kate's office, having requested a meeting with her.

'How's Clare?' Kate enquired.

'Still unconscious,' Jane replied. 'I've been mulling over what happened this morning and…the lad is clearly dangerous, as we already noted during surveillance, so why can't we just sanction a normal extraction?'

'*Because* he's just a *kid*. When we go in and remove an adult, if things go wrong it may require something of a cover-up, but at least it would most likely be manageable.

'A failed or especially a witnessed extraction of a child would however go straight to front page news. Vicious school bully and potential animal abuser or not, people would be in uproar, looking for who was responsible.

'We need the soft approach that I briefed you both for, to encourage him to come to us. As it stands now, we have lost him. It won't be long before he is reported missing by his parents and then it gets a whole lot more challenging.'

'Do we *really* need to extract him right now?'

'Yes. Don't question my judgment. Find him.'

Gina sat in the Astra doing face exercises which were meant to keep signs of aging at bay by keeping the skin supple. Presently and more importantly however, they served as her penultimate resort before admitting she was hellishly bored.

She had been sat in the car for hours, just a few doors down and on the opposite side of the road from the target's King's Heath address, waiting for any sign of activity. It was now 6:35 and as a distraction, from her now rumbling tummy, she picked up OK from the passenger seat rested it on the steering wheel and began to flick through.

'Why on Earth wear something like that?' she mumbled her derision, then tried to imagine. *Oh*

I'm wearing Chelsea Flower Show today, to attract a keen gardener, as I have a bush that needs some attention,' she snickered, before flipping through some more pages.

'Oh look at me. I'm an executive at Drab & Drabber Associates…Who designs those suits? Have they got no sense of what clothing is supposed to do for a person? Oh God, and that, that just says *Look away. I'm not interested in a relationship*.'

Then, as if answering for the wearer, in a drone she continued '*But I like being lonely. I dress down to prove men don't find me attractive*.'

To which she then added 'That one ought to come with a free boob-tube which reads *My other dress is a potato sack*.'

She stopped talking to herself as she caught movement across the street. Not at the target's address but directly opposite the car. A woman had come out of her front door, walked to the gate and looked up the street, then turned and looked the other way. She glanced at her watch and went back inside not seeming to notice Gina.

After 11:00 with no sign of her quarry, and now reclined somewhat in her seat with the collar of her leather jacket up round her neck, Gina noticed a WPC call at the house opposite.

When the knock on the door came, Mrs Best hoped it was Ethan but just knew it wouldn't be as he had keys. Unless he'd lost them or been mugged, she reasoned as she went to answer it, mumbling 'Oh poor lad.'

'Hello…Mrs Best?'

'Yes.'

'I'm WPC Dixon.'

'Dixon you say? Like the policeman?'

'Ur…I guess…I'm here about the call you made…around 6.43.'

'Yes, yes. My son is missing.'

'He's still not come home then?'

'That's what I said.'

'Do you mind if I come in to ask a few question.'

'I told the officer on the phone all I knew, but if you must. The house is a tip. Come through to the lounge.' She left WPC Dixon to close the door as she led her through. 'Don't mind him,' she said, pointing to her husband now fast asleep in his chair.

WPC Dixon sat on the sofa next to the knitting, and noticed the ball of wool had rolled over near the TV, which Mrs Best was now switching off.

'Such rubbish on these days I don't know why we bother paying our licence.'

'So we don't arrest you I guess.'

'What?!'

'Sorry. Just a joke…to, you know…lighten the mood a bit.'

'Oh…I see,' she stepped closer. 'Would you like a cup of tea PC Dock?'

'WPC Dixon…and no thanks.'

'I have Earl Grey, Camomile, Nettle, and Tai Chi.'

'Tai Chi?'

'Yes…Do you want some?'

'No. No thanks.'

'Suit yourself PC…WPC…ur Green…I'm going to have one.'

'WPC Dixon.'

'Dixon, Dixon,' Mrs Best repeated as she left the room.

Looking round the room WPC Dixon noticed that other than the widescreen HDTV the room looked like a set from an 80's sitcom.

Then she noticed that Mr Best was not snoring, and wondered whether he might actually be faking sleep.

She took her smart phone out and held the screen close to his mouth then looked at it. It had steamed up so she had no need to worry about him being dead.

As an afterthought she took a flash photo of him with his glasses askew and mouth agape. 'You want to watch out Mr Best. *That's* invasion of privacy.'

He didn't stir, even when Mrs Best returned with a mug of what smelled like lemon disinfectant.

'Fire away then.'

'Sorry Mrs Best I left my gun at the station.'

'What?'

'So I wouldn't shoot anyone.'

'What?!' She almost spilled her hot drink, sitting down on a knitting needle.

'Sorry. I really must stop with the jokes. My desk sergeant says it will get me in trouble one day. But if I can just bring a smile to at least one person's face each day, then I think that should make up for those I upset. And show a more caring side to policing…So do you have any reason to think your son is in trouble, overdosed on drugs maybe, lying unconscious anywhere in particular?'

'Good heavens. What made you ask that?'

'Well we checked the hospitals before I came, and he's not come in, under his own name, at least…And well….You did tell us he's *fourteen*.'

'Yes but…'

'And boys do like to experiment with a lot of things at that age.'

'Do they? But Ethan…Is such a good boy.'

'Right…' she seemed to stifle a laugh, making it sound like maybe Ethan was well known down the local station, for one thing or another. On the other hand maybe the WPC was just joking again. 'So when did you see him last?'

'Ur…Just after 8:00 this morning. I tried ringing him, but he seems to have left his phone in his room.'

'Seems to have? Or has?'

'Well has.'

'Okay then, you can never be too careful with details as a police officer. So, where was he going? A friend's house?'

'No, to school.'

'Right…Well where does he go to school?'

'Mortonfield Comprehensive.'

'Oh dear. So…Why did he leave so early?'

'I…I don't know…He always leaves around that time.'

'So who *are* his friends?...Did you call *them* before ringing *us*?'

'Ethan…Doesn't have any friends.'

'Doesn't have any friends…that you *know about*.'

'He's a very quiet lad; Keeps to himself. Stays in his room most the time.'

'Ha…Oh…You have *checked* in his room Mrs Best?...Only there have been cases of a full scale search for children, and they turn out to be fast asleep down the side of the bed.'

'Ethan sleeps in a hammock.'

'A hammock? Does he?'

'Yes. He said he liked to imagine he's in a jungle, once he'd wet the bed a few times.'

'Right…' WPC Dixon frowned. 'So what time does he normally come home?'

'Around 5:00, for his tea.'

'Does he never go to the pictures?'

'No, he seems to watch whatever he wants on his computer these days. He used to love his Disney films, Silence of the Lambs, and the Red Dragon. I think he also mentioned a box set of Hannibal once. I think that's the one with the elephant.'

'No you're thinking of Dumbo…And I think you'll find those titles are all Lecter videos.'

'Well yes, he does enjoy his more academic documentaries.'

'Do you have a recent photograph of Ethan?'

'We don't have many, but there is this one of him holding one of his sheriffs badges.' She retrieved the photo from a shelf. 'He quite likes making them at school.'

'Mmm…Looks more like a shuriken to me Mrs Best.'

'I wouldn't know about that.'

'No. I'm sure you wouldn't.' The WPC took out her mobile again and took a shot of the photograph. 'This will save taking it away.'

'Wonderful.'

'I think that's all for now. We'll let you know as soon as we spot him…Sorry, did that make him sound like a lost dog? I mean when we find his…Him.'

8

By Ethan's G-Shock watch it was just after eight in the morning. He had spent the night huddled under a bush, but it had taken him a while to get to sleep. Bugs had insisted on landing on the warm skin of his face, until he took his school jumper and wrapped it round his head.

He slept fitfully as the real nightmares came out to play.

His father looked younger this time, but more confused as he listened to Ethan's mother explaining how her experience with fluid dynamics was helping her company sell more toilets.

'The effectiveness of the flush is influenced by a number of factors: quantity of water, height of delivery, and flow management. That's where I come in, dear.

'I devised a connector between the cistern and the bowl that induces a spin into the flow, creating a vortex which looks, to anyone watching, like it should clear the bowl. Whereas in fact it stops all but the most runny matter from going round the U-bend by putting most of the faecal matter into a tumble.'

'Sorry luv I don't follow?'

'Faecal matter is just jargon for turds.'

'Oh,' he continued to frown.

'So in combination with the reduced capacity of the cistern, *to save water*, it encourages the user to flush, and flush again.'

'Right…'

'Oh do keep up. Thereby it wears the components out sooner, or sometimes even frustrates the user enough to want to buy another bathroom suite entirely.'

'I see.'

'No you don't. It's a good thing we abandoned our son, I don't know how I would have coped with bringing up someone with your moronic genes.'

Waking with a moan, blinking his eyes, Ethan shook off the dream and tried to focus on the day ahead. He decided that while moving outside of town gave him a low profile it did take him away from more accessible food options, like bins.

On the outskirts desperation had led him to use one of the shuriken throwing-stars he had made in metalwork to try and kill a rabbit. Taking one from the bottom of his school bag he approached the animal quietly and slowly enough to get up close and he hit it too. It stuck in its side good and proper, but then it did an unexpected back flip followed by a front roll and sped off up the track. Ethan tried to follow but he lost both the rabbit and his shuriken to the undergrowth. He cursed it for not having the decency to die on impact, but made do with imagining its slow death as payback.

Peter was getting into this writing malarkey he was finding it quite arousing. He didn't want to mention this because that might not be in his favour, but then he thought the monitoring would surely pick it up anyway. He wished he'd thought of writing this stuff down before now.

He realised it was more fun than he would have imagined.

Dorothy, a few doors down, in her own sound proofed room didn't seem to have the heart for this approach. She just stared at the tablet, hands in her lap, thinking she would rather do things the traditional way, lying on a couch and talking to someone.

David, across the corridor, was shaking. He had written a few words but now whenever his fingers came close to the screen keys he felt the need to scream at someone. He didn't want to get any of his thoughts out into the open. He had heard a saying that you should only ever put into writing what you don't mind the whole world knowing, because there was no such thing as secrecy, especially in these days of computer aided hacking. His dark thoughts were private property. This therapy process was making him feel violated and he resented that.

He went to the door and tried banging on it, but the padding just made a dull thump. 'I can't do this!'

There was no response.

'Do you hear?' He wondered whether he was being observed through cameras and microphones. He had searched before but if there were any there they must be away from reach and in the stitching of the padding.

'I've had enough of this!'

When the nurse came to take David for monitoring she found him on his bed arms folded, or as close as he could manage with the cuffs on.

'Looking for inspiration?' the nurse asked.

'Looking to get out,' he retorted and noticed her hand move closer to the Taser on her belt.

'Well you can have a break. It's time for your tests,' the nurse led him out of his room, 'and maybe you can get a visit from your creative writing tutor after lunch to feed your imagination.'

'I really don't think that will help.'

'That's not the attitude for the road to recovery.'

'Fuck recovery,' David said angrily. 'I have more imagination than I can cope with. I just don't want to share what is mine!'

'Well no one is interested in what you write. This is *your* process of behaviour modification. We are only here to facilitate you.'

They arrived at the monitoring facility and a second nurse came across to help connect up the EEG and ECG devices.

'What does Phase Three involve?' David asked, hoping the nurses might be more forthcoming than Kate had been at induction.

'Can we just deal with this first?' asked the nurse who had collected him.

David sighed and let them get on with it, besides which he found the material they showed him of people's terror and bloodshed quite calming. In fact, to his mind, it was over all too soon. Then the first nurse removed his 3D video goggles and the monitor leads whilst the second checked for any change in his responses and reported that they had remained stable.

David didn't care. Maybe this was good reason to move to Phase Three. He knew there was a cost involved but he was sure he could string them along about settling up. He just wanted out.

'Do I still have to wear these in Phase Three?' he asked lifting his cuffed wrists.

'Well that depends on how you behave, but a number of people in the Phase Three wing don't wear them no.'

'But they are all staff, right?' he suspected a catch.

'No. I'm referring to clients.'

'Well I can't cope with any more of Phase Two. I want to go to Three.'

'Are you sure?'

'I'm sure I can't do Two any longer.'

'Okay.' The nurse lifted her radio from her breast pocket. 'Eleanor its Michelle, I've got Mr Johnson down here at Monitoring, says he wants to move onto Phase Three.'

Eleanor's reply could just be heard by David. 'He is requesting that, or you've recommended he goes?'

'No *he's* asking. Says he's had his fill of writing therapy, and he doesn't want to have to wear cuffs anymore.'

'That can be arranged. I will get Kate's approval and get back to you. Stay in Monitoring.'

'Will do,' the nurse said turning to David, 'Could be your lucky break.'

David felt relieved even though confirmation was not yet through, but there was something odd about these nurses. He couldn't decide whether their smiles were because they were happy for him, or for themselves. He wasn't even sure why that should matter.

Another nurse arrived, this one from the Phase Three wing, as noted on her badge. She was pushing a gurney. 'David Johnson for Phase Three assessment.'

David stepped forward. 'Assessment?'

'Yes to ensure you are prepared.'

'Prepared? For what? If I can't do Phase Two what other option is there?'

'Just come and lie down on here please sir.' She pointed at the gurney.

'Can't I just walk with you?'

She shook her head, 'It's procedure.'

David sighed stepped closer and got up onto the gurney. Lying down he felt his arm being pulled to the side and his wrist being strapped down. 'Oh *come on*! Don't you think these cuffs are enough?!'

'It's standard procedure. I'm removing your cuffs.' She unlocked them and took them off.

'Oh.'

Then his other wrist was strapped down. Next the nurse's attention turned to his ankles, strapping them in place. This should have been an end to it, to David's mind. However, she then proceeded to buckle down a chest strap followed by one across his thighs.

'This is ridiculous!'

'Just be patient sir.' With a nod to the Phase Two and Monitoring nurses the Phase Three nurse wheeled him away.

There were security ID checks between Monitoring and Phase Three wing and then he was rolling again.

David was placed to one side of a corridor by some double doors and told to wait there.

'Can't do fuck all else now can I,' he muttered.

After what felt like an hour the nurse returned.

'Where have you been? I want my lunch.'

'They are ready for you now.'

David was wheeled through the double doors into what looked like a theatre. He tried to crane his head one way then another to get a better look. To his surprise the nurse span the gurney to help him see all around before arriving where a group of what looked like surgeons stood waiting.

'What's going on?' he asked nervously as he noticed people taking seats in the 360 degree gallery above. 'Is this some sort of med school?'

'Just relax Mr Johnson,' said a new nurse. 'My name is Sandra, and I'm going to explain some of Phase Three to you.'

'Right,' he lowered his head and settled to listen.

'Phase Three assessment is an invasive procedure. Do you understand what *invasive* means Mr Johnson?'

'I…'

'It means penetrating the body.' Sandra gave a nod and two colleagues placed IV lines into his arms.

'Are they the drip and anaesthetic?' David enquired.

'No, somewhat the opposite. One supplies adrenalin, and the other delivers a form of amphetamine.'

'What?!'

'We have to keep you conscious for this assessment Mr Johnson.'

'*Conscious*?!' David started to pull at his restraints.

'Calm down. Have you watched brain surgery on TV before? It has to be undertaken with the patient conscious for reasons of watching responses.'

'Please no! Not my brain! I DON'T GIVE MY CONSENT! Don't operate on my brain!'

'Mr Johnson!' Sandra chided, 'We don't *need* any further consent, and we are *not* going to operate on your brain, today.'

'Thank fuck for that!'

'However,' she explained as she released the thigh straps, with support from other nurses, 'we are going to remove your genitals.'

9

Ethan's forearm swung over his eyes in his sleep as if to block out the dream of his father sneezing till his nose bled.

'That'll be the man-flu I guess,' Ethan's mother commented with little sympathy.

'Very funny,' he replied, spraying blood that was running over his lips.

'No I'm serious. It's what I've been working on at the government department of bioweapons at Pilton Down.'

'What?!' he sprayed more blood.

'Yes, the government needs to know how various bacteria and viruses spread, so what I do is design a new strain to have specific symptoms so that we can trace it in the community, which of course already has other contagion present. So to make it quite obvious I decided to design it to be gender specific, and now we have real man-flu.'

'Thanks a bunch luv. I feel like I'm dying.'

'Oh man up.'

'No seriously.'

'Well there *will* be a small percentage of fatalities to be expected. With any luck that unwanted child of ours will come down with it and pop his clogs, wherever he is.'

Ethan groaned himself awake and found he was shivering with cold and his nose running. He had to get moving and warm up so he gathered up his kit.

Gemma Dearly had been sent early Saturday morning on a potential recruitment mission to the Peak District. She now stood outside an old farmhouse on the edge of moorland.

It seemed quiet except for the occasional call from a curlew. This was where Abby Carlton, posing as a Forestry Commission Ranger lived alone.

Gem had considered parking down the lane where she had seen what looked like a small lay-by. However, she wasn't sure she should because it might have been a passing space. These lanes were rather narrow in places. So she had gone for the *park right there on the driveway* option.

No sooner had she got out of the Prius than Abby came out of the front door. 'Are you lost?' she smiled.

'Urr no actually, I don't think so.'

'Oh.' Abby had not expected that response.

'No. I came to see *you*…Abby Carlton…Isn't it?'

'Yes,' she said warily.

'My Names Gem…Gemma Dearly. But you can call me Gem.'

'Thanks…But whatever you're selling out here, I don't need it.'

'I'm not sure that's true, but then I'm not really here to sell…I'm here to *tell*.'

'Tell?'

'Yes. I believe we share a common interest.'

'The great outdoors?' she ventured.

'Urr, no…I'm talking about a more unusual interest in…shall we say in creating *challenging experiences*.'

Abby frowned, wondering who this person really was. 'I don't know what you mean.'

'Don't worry. I'm not police. Can I come in and talk.'

There was a pause as Abby thought this through. 'It's not really convenient for me right now. I have to be getting on with my job.'

'Surely *ranging* can wait for half an hour?' Gem pretended she accepted Abby's cover.

After further consideration Abby suggested 'Why don't you come with me up on the moor, and get some fresh air while you explain then.'

'I don't have any walking boots.' She declined, shaking her head. 'Why don't we go inside and you can put the kettle on.'

Abby looked over her shoulder. It was clear from her body language she wasn't comfortable with anyone going inside. 'What size feet are you?' she enquired.

'Seven.'

'Right, I have some wellingtons you can use.'

'Oh…Okay.'

As Abby went inside for the boots, Gem went to the car for her jacket then sat with the passenger door open unfastening her shoes.

'Here,' Abby returned, her tone still rather cold, and dropped the boots in front of the uninvited visitor.

'Thanks.'

'What did you say your name was again?'

'Gem.'

'So where are you from Gem?'

'Oh down south.'

'Well that covers a lot of ground.' She changed tack. 'Who do you work for?'

'I work for a group of *Specialists*.'

'*Specialists*?' Abby scoffed at Gem's second vague response.

'They run a clinic.' The borrowed boots now on, Gem stood up and locked the car.

'A *clinic*?' Abby began to walk, prompting Gem to follow, towards a stile over a dry-stone wall just down the lane from her property.

'Yes a clinic where we offer a very specific treatment.'

'Which involves what exactly?'

'To any outsider, not that we allow visits, it would appear that we are curing people of anti-social behavioural problems, which we *may* actually manage in some cases.'

Having crossed the stile they headed up the fell.

'Why would I be interested in a clinic?' Abby didn't see where Gem was going with this.

'What The Clinic is actually doing is serving a select group of women who need to watch and carry out torture.'

'What?!' She couldn't believe what she was hearing. 'Who are you really working for, the government?'

'Not exactly, but let's say we have access to government experience and information.'

Abby had difficulty believing this. Why would a stranger come and tell her such things? Could it be an attempt to catch her out? 'Sounds like you are making quite a commitment being this open with me. Either you are very sure I will want to join you, or this is all bullshit. Maybe this is a form of entrapment.'

'No we have no need for entrapment. We already have the evidence on you. We just want to offer you a place with us.'

'I'm not particularly a *people person.*'

'I wouldn't say that any of us are, by definition, nevertheless we have learned there are benefits from working together.'

'The idea sounds all very strange.'

'By bringing such *atypical* people as us together into a secure environment where interests can be shared, we can better control our quality of life, living out some of our fantasies, just as some more *typical* people do theirs.'

'Mmm…' Abby was still unconvinced.

'At The Clinic we have some advanced hacking and monitoring technologies, including spyware that enables us to track users of Tor and other Onion Ring router systems. This enables us to search out like minded individuals and recruit them before they get into trouble.'

'This is starting to sound like X-Men.'

'Well I don't know about that. As I said we are an all women group, though we do use men from time to time.

'Mainly we track typical Internet search patterns used by those showing an interest in methods and practices of abduction, torture and killing. We also use Trojans in downloadable content from the Dark Net.'

This worried Abby as she had understood the Dark Net to be fully secure. 'I'm just a Forestry Commission ranger. I really don't know *what* you think you know about me.'

'Yes you do Abby, or you would not have listened to me for this long. I'm being up front with you. We know you've not only been accessing videos of people in distress, but also now make a living out of producing and selling your own video material on the Dark Net.'

Abby stopped walking and Gem almost bumped into her.

'Come on, it's a natural progression for people like us,' Gem continued. 'We have been putting material onto Dark Net ourselves for some time now, containing our embedded spyware for tracking people. So with us you wouldn't have to hide your work away. You'd be amazed the rush you get sharing experiences and ideas, as a group.'

Abby seemed to slip into a trance looking aside. 'I'm finding this all a bit much to take in…Gem,' her denial was becoming less convincing, she needed a bit more of a push.

'You know the amputation video you watched last night?'

'No. No I don't know what you're referring to.'

'Yes you do. You accessed it from a screen-saver supplier, then after unwrapping it watched the video maybe half a dozen times…'

Abby's posture became rigid, but she nodded.

'Well that was one of ours. You wouldn't believe the library of footage we are building up, and the techniques we are developing, to make our lives more fulfilling.'

'So, you are saying, that video was bait.'

'Well sort of…We are always on the lookout for new members, so I've been sent to sound you out.'

Abby was not at all sure about this, and walked on, looking back only to question another point. 'How do you go about abducting *your* victims?'

'Well it is usually when a person takes steps to abduct and torture others, like you, that we extract them for our entertainment. However, the head of The Clinic sometimes decides an individual, as in your case, has creative merit to be invited on-board.'

'What if this is just a trick and you actually intend to torture *me*?'

'No. The decision has been made to recruit. You'll be well looked after, *and* listened to. We were impressed by the quality of your submissions to the Dark Net.'

'But what would I do there?'

'First you would receive training.'

'Training?'

'Yes. We each fulfil a number of duties, so are trained in surveillance, extraction, computer hacking, and of course torture techniques. But I believe your main duty may well be to be a scout, like me.'

'A scout?' she needed to know more as they headed across the beds of knee high heather and clumps of moss.

'Yeah, that involves tracking people mainly. There can be quite a bit of desk work, hacking into servers and trawling though site search logs.'

'It all sounds highly illegal.'

'Yes, highly, but I really enjoy it.'

Abby suddenly grabbed Gem by the arm, it almost put her off balance. 'You have to watch where you are walking up here,' she said tilting her head with a nod.

Gem looked round over her shoulder at the mat of light green behind her. 'Oh thanks,' she said unsure. 'What is it?'

'Peat bog,' Abby let go of her, with a shove, and Abby put a foot back to balance and went in with a sloppy squelch, up to her hips.

'What did you do that for?'

'Ever heard the story of the Frog and the Scorpion?'

'No.' Gem didn't sound too interested as she looked around for something to grasp, realising she was sinking.

'Well, I don't know how much time you've got,' Abby smiled, 'But the upshot of it is that the scorpion wants to get across this river and needs the frog because he can't swim, and the frog says *okay as long as you don't sting me*. But halfway across the river the scorpion stings the frog, and the frog asks *why did you do that*? He says *because I'm a scorpion*.'

'I don't get it, sorry.' Gem said impatiently.

'That is a shame,' Abby responded with a hint of sarcasm.

'Can you give me a hand out?' Gem leaned forward, only to sink further down.

Abby took a hand and started to pull. 'The thing is, I have a nice young hitch hiker buried alive in my cellar right now.

'I'm looking forward to letting her out into the cellar later this afternoon, just so she'll think I'm going to let her go as long as she promises not to mention anything of it to anyone.

'Then I'm going to drug her and she's going to find herself back in the flagstone coffin, only this time I'm going to be taking a shower as soon as she comes round and guess where the water's going to go?'

Gem noticed that Abby wasn't pulling any more, just holding her. 'Well, *great*. I could join you,' she suggested.

'What?! In the shower?!' She spat with disgust and let go of Gem's hand.

Gem sank up to her midriff. 'No. What I'm saying is that I could watch with you…There's clearly a lot I…We…could learn from you.'

'I dare say there is,' Abby watched her sink a little further, as both their minds ticked over. 'Look I'll go and find a stick.'

'Okay, great. Hurry up.' Gem watched as Abby strode off towards a stand of small trees, which were permanently leaning, indicating how tough the conditions were up there.

Gem tried to move closer to the edge, but that just ended with her up to her armpits. The bog stank with the disturbed rot that lay beneath the pretty green.

As the bog sucked her down she felt the wet moss reach her neck. Gem began to wonder if Abby was actually leaving her to vanish but that didn't make sense as Kate knew where Abby lived. Abby would surely understand that what she had going for her here had now been compromised.

Gem reached for her radio to give a Sit-Rep, but either there was no signal or the water resistant phone was somehow damaged by the bog. Next she reached inside for her gun. She didn't want to scare Abby off, but at the same time she could not let her go if she was not going to join them. But as she pulled on the Sig P266 it got caught on something. In trying to pull it free it slipped from her cold-weakened grip and as she chased it with her hand it sank from reach.

By the time Abby returned the peat was up to Gem's chin and she was very cold. 'What took you so long?'

'Sorry. Couldn't find a branch, but found this.' She had brought a discarded fence post. She swung one end out to Gem, and it caught her at the shoulder.

'Watch out!' said Gem crossly trying to keep her face up, feeling the bog water running into her ears.

'Oops, sorry,' Abby laughed. 'But I need to work alone,' she shoved hard, forcing Gem down.

'No! Wait!' Gem gasped desperately, trying to grab the post, but her wet numb fingers couldn't get a grip. 'We know where you live.' Only her eyes, nose, mouth, and hands were above the surface now.

'Good.' Abby exaggerated her lip movements so that Gem could read them. 'I look forward to meeting the others. I've *so* enjoyed *your* visit.' With one final sustained shove she forced Gem, head, hands and all, below the surface. She pulled back the post and watched for the big bubble of air, before getting back to what she had planned for the day.

Dorothy woke up to find herself in her room, but with her hands and feet bandaged. Then she cried out as the memory returned with trauma aftershock.

When threats had failed she had wrongly expected that it would be possible to simply talk with, and charm, these people. She tried to explain that she saw herself as too long in the tooth for any of these phases of therapy to make any difference.

She had been urged not to prejudge as she did not yet know what Phase Three involved and therefore could be being somewhat overly dismissive of the writing therapy.

When she persisted that Phase Two was not going to teach an old dog new tricks she was asked if she enjoyed playing a musical instrument. Confirming that she rather enjoyed the piano, she had gone on to wonder whether the next form of therapy involved music instead of writing. However, the reason for the question had become clear all too soon as she suffered the long and painful removal of all her fingers, and then her toes.

10

Just after 10:00 on Saturday morning, DI Simon Dunn and DC Rod Watkins arrived at the Best's.

'Hello officers,' said Mrs Best. '*Please* tell me you've found him.'

'I wish we could Mrs Best. But the thing is we need a better picture of your son. That tired look and wonky glasses we were forwarded isn't really working for us I'm afraid.'

'Oh my.'

'Can we come in?'

Mrs Best just stood there for a moment. She still seemed to be taken aback by the news that the photo she had provided the WPC of Ethan somehow had him with wonky glasses.

'I'm DI Dunn, and this is DC Watkins.'

Mrs Best stirred from her daze, trying to gather her wits as she showed them in, repeating 'Dunn and Watkins, Dunn and Watkins,' as she attempted to memorise the names, walking through to the sitting room.

'Do you mind if we search your son's room?' asked DI Dunn.

'Do you have a warrant?'

'A warrant?' he gave her his best confused look. After all, they had been asked by the Best's to find their son.

'Yes you know like they have to have on TV.'

'Oh I see,' he nodded holding his chin thoughtfully, before explaining, 'we only need one of those if the person we're visiting's got something to hide.' He hoped she didn't ask anything else technical. He didn't want to get side-tracked into the details of legal processes.

'Oh, is that right? I never knew that.'

'*Have* you got something to hide Mrs Best?' He hoped his own line of questioning would head her off at the pass so that they could get right on with the job at hand.

'Only the widescreen TV I guess.'

'Oh?' Dunn was surprised by her response. 'Is it stolen?'

'Stolen? No. We hide it every evening because it is worth a *fortune*. Though you know what, it has the same bloody rubbish on that the old one did. Only now, you can complain about it all in 3D.'

'I have a smaller version of it at home.' Watkins put in.

'Does yours have rubbish on it too?'

'Well yes. It has to, doesn't it?'

'Has to?' Mrs Best pondered the idea that rubbish might be a *requirement*. 'You mean like we *have* to have a licence, even if we don't watch BBC?'

'Right…Could you take us to Ethan's room now…maybe?' Dunn tried to bring Mrs Best back to real world.

'Urr, yes. It's just up here.' She led them back out of the sitting room.

Climbing the non-standard steep stairs they found Ethan's room to be a typical teenage boy's room, until you actually saw what you were looking at.

'Aren't these…ur,' Dunn was lost for words pointing at the tank.

'Yes,' Mrs Best confirmed, 'Fish.'

'Piranhas,' Watkins qualified, placing his face close and watching them head-butt the glass, now starving for flesh. 'What do you feed them on?'

'Fish food, I expect.' Mrs Best offered.

'Don't they need meat?'

'Well…Ethan looks after them. Why don't you ask him when you find him?'

'And what's this…a gerbil?' asked Dunn at the new Percy's cage.

'That's Ethan's special hamster.'

'*Special* is it?'

'Yes. If you watch very closely, it changes colour.'

'What…like a chameleon?' asked Watkins stepping across for a look.

They all stared intently into the plastic cage, at the exposed patch of fur in the straw nest.

'I presume so. You can get all sorts of exotic pets these days,' she nodded. 'He had a snake once that could inflate itself.'

'You mean a python? Swallowing animals whole?'

'No. I think he said it was a Coral Snake, because it would balloon up like a puffer-fish apparently, when frightened. A defence mechanism Ethan said it was.'

'And you saw it do it?'

'Well no…I only saw it when it had burst.'

'Burst?' Dunn asked.

'Yes. Ethan said he'd scared it good and proper.'

'But *you've* seen *this* hamster change colour?'

'Well…I've seen it different colours…But not actually changing from one to the other.'

'I see.' Looking across to the desk in the corner Dunn continued, 'we are going to need to look at the contents of the computer. Do you know if Ethan uses a password?'

'I have no idea. Sorry.'

'Well the IT guys will get past it if *we* can't,' said Watkins. 'With teenage boys it's usually something simple like fuck3girls, or fanny4cock.'

'Oh my…' Mrs Best gasped, lifting a hand to her mouth in shock, before removing it to say 'I don't think our Ethan's like *that*.'

'Does he prefer boys Mrs Best?' Watkins pressed.

Dunn gave him a scolding stare. 'I'm not sure that is relevant Watkins.'

'Oh.' He sounded disappointed. 'I was just going to suggest some alternative passwords.'

'Let's not, hey?' Dunn warned, then looked across the room and spotted a video camera on the shelf above the computer. He picked it up, asking 'What does he film?'

'I have no idea.' Mrs Best shrugged her shoulders then explained 'I just dust around his things. I don't touch them, in case they break.'

Dunn opened the LCD panel and pressed play. First he was greeted with an image too blurred to make out, then he realised what he was watching was a hamster swimming, for the best part of three seconds, before being stripped to the bone.

'Hells teeth!' he passed the camera to Watkins, at arm's length.

'Oh my. What is it?' Mrs Best was surprised by the detective's reaction.

Watkins's reaction was different, eyes widening, mainly because the video had moved onto the next clip. 'You know what this means don't you Sir?'

'Yes. We're looking for a very disturbed child.'

'Possibly even the next Fred West.' Watkins handed the video back, still playing.

'The tinned salmon people?' ventured Mrs Best frowning.

Dunn looked back at the screen and did a double take 'Holy mother of...Mr Birdseye!'

Kate Handy sat behind her desk feeling pleased with progress. In her younger years she had never seen herself as a manager of others, yet here she was nurturing her dream; building something epic. Nevertheless, she didn't see herself as the philanthropist she had tried to tell certain others she was.

She preferred to think of herself more like a cross between the characters of Lisbeth Salander *and* Martin Vanger, from *The Girl with the Dragon Tattoo*. When Kate had watched the original film she had experienced a few seconds of intense calm at the end of the movie, as Salander and Blomkvist discovered a large collection of what Kate considered to be very artistic pictures of Vanger's torture victims.

Now, with The Clinic, was her chance to deal with such horrors in the real world.

'What do you mean we lost contact with Gem?' she asked Eleanor.

'She confirmed her arrival at Abby Carlton's this morning. Then we lost her.'

'That's a real shame,' Kate sighed, 'Okay we'll send in a clean-up team. Have Mel and Tina come in.'

'Right away,' Eleanor wasted no time and Mel and Tina soon reported to Kate's office.

'It seems we are down two scouts now girls.' Kate was seriously considering revising the recruitment process to begin with a straight forward extraction. However, she previously considered this would not get them off to a good start with a potential new recruit. 'Clare is still unconscious and a growing source of concern, as she is well past the predicted recovery point, and now Gem has failed to report in.'

'Maybe she's just out of signal range,' suggested Tina.

'Where was it you sent her?' asked Mel.

'Well it *was* the Peak District. But she knows that if she doesn't have a signal she needs to use a land line. No, I think it is entirely possible that Gem may have got in over her head with our Miss Carlton. I've reviewed a satellite feed of the area, and the car is still parked outside Miss Carlton's. So I have to assume that she has got into difficulty inside the house.'

'Okay we're on it,' said Mel.

'Well whatever has happened to her, we can't afford to leave any evidence trail, however small,' Kate bluetoothed the girls the address from her tablet.

Will picked up the courage to walk over to Gina's desk and try again with her. 'I was thinking.'

'Were you?' She looked up and stared at him expectantly with her emerald eyes. She found herself thinking he wasn't bad looking for a jerk.

'I know it's been a couple of days, but I'm sorry I got off on the wrong foot with you before, over the stakeout material, and thought *these* might be more to your liking,' he held two new magazines in front of her, one in each hand, neither Vogue or Marie Claire.

'Wank-mags?!.' Gina declared despairingly for all to hear, looking at the scantily clad girls on the covers of the offered T4 and Stuff. 'So...now I'm one of the lads am I?'

Will quickly pulled them back and moved to his plan-B and offered her a pack of Jaffa Cakes 'For the car.'

'Thanks, but the car's doing fine on biodiesel.'

'I meant for *you*.' His face started to go pink. She was making him feel like a child.

'I know...I was trying to be funny *that* time. I guess I need to be less bitchy.'

'Thanks.' He took that as an apology.

'Well I better get off.' She shut down her tablet. 'Off to another eighteen hour bum-numbing session of watch-for-wifey. I just hope she shows today.'

Will decided to take another chance. 'Maybe if she shows early and you get what you're after, we could...*I don't know*...meet up for a beer.'

'*Yeah*, I don't know *either*.' She didn't want to commit to anything.

Will watched her leave the office and it was only after the door closed behind her that he noticed the number of colleagues smirking at him.

'What?'

Gina didn't like working Saturdays, but sometimes it was necessary to getting the job done. At least it wasn't every Saturday. At least the traffic was a little easier.

It was a relatively uneventful drive down to King's Heath from the city centre. Gina didn't nudge a single cyclist this time. She was all for keeping fit and reducing carbon emissions where possible. Nevertheless, she didn't like the way some cyclists weaved through the traffic as if cars could respond just as quickly.

She was all for separate paths for pedestrians and cyclists. She had even considered starting up a protest group to keep cyclists off the roads completely, called *Friends of the Tarmac* with the strap line: *It's where you're head's at*.

She managed to park in the same spot she had vacated only seven hours ago. She hadn't been there very long when a car pulled up opposite. She saw DI Dunn and his sidekick DC Watkins get out. Neither noticed her on their way in, but Dunn spotted her on the way back out, almost an hour later. Watkins was carrying a PC and some other items to the boot.

'Orangina,' Dunn bent to her window.

'I'm on stakeout,' she warned him off.

'I guessed that. She got you waiting for her psycho son? I kind of think she'll know when he comes home without you keeping watch, don't you? But I guess you've got to earn a living.'

'What *are* you talking about?'

'Ethan Best.'

'Who's he?'

'Only Mr Birdseye's killer, that's who,' Dunn grinned with appreciation of the two cases coming together.

David sat strapped into a wheelchair in Monitoring, waiting. He had just completed his test materials.

'What do you mean, *oh dear*?!' he said coldly, though knowing the reason for the nurse's response to his results.

Even after the trauma of his non-anaesthetised castration, and the pain of his wounds, the images he had been made to watch of torture and death calmed him.

It had however irritated him to see that the nurses were quite obviously enjoying his dilemma, and he knew at that moment that they were no better than him. Why was *he* getting this treatment and not *them*?

'We are just going to have to keep progressing with Phase Three aren't we David,' said the Monitoring nurse with a smile at his cold expression before giving a nod to the two Phase Three nurses.

He resented his helplessness. 'Fucking bitches. I'm going to sue your asses for this malpractice!'

The nurse behind the wheelchair turned it and wheeled him towards the door, as the second nurse picked up a metal case.

As they wheeled David down the corridor he tried to control his pain. He found himself fantasising about what he would like to do to these women, if he could turn the tables, but he just groaned bitterly.

They took him outside, something he had not expected, and this helped distract him from his dark thoughts for a while as he looked around. He tried to get a sense of where this place was. From the sound and smell it seemed to be on farmland. He shortly became convinced that this trip outside was not intended to bring relief when he was painfully wheeled across a rough cobbled yard towards a shed.

'You are going to see some other animals,' said one of the nurses as if talking to a child. It brought to David's mind the expectation that he was about to be shown victims of this barbaric treatment. Victims being made to live like pigs. A warning for him to control his behaviour before it became too late.

On seeing pigs in the pens he realised he was letting his imagination run away with him. Then as they stopped in front of one of the pens with two large pigs squealing with excitement it occurred to him that they might be there to feed them.

The nurse with the metal case stepped round, releasing the case catches, and as the lid opened there was the slight hiss of a hermetic seal breaking. 'As part of your therapy, *you* control how fast we progress by your responses to the material you are shown. But in Phase Three you have further control of rate of progression, through this *feeding of the animals* exercise.'

'What are you talking about?!' he didn't want to understand what he feared was coming.

'In this transplant transportation case, looking like a sausage and two meatballs…' she showed him the contents.

'Fuck, no!!' he cried.

The nurse continued, '…are your lovely genitalia. They have been kept on ice and it is entirely feasible that our very adept surgical staff could replace them if you make progress with the next test,' she offered hope, before quickly closing the lid.

As he was turned and then wheeled away, the squealing of the pigs changed tone to one of intense disappointment.

'You're not getting my balls,' David muttered, willing himself more than ever to focus on being upset and scared by the materials he would be made to view.

However, before they finished crossing the yard he was distracted by the sight of a paraplegic sobbing and pleading as he was wheeled to the pigs by another two nurses with a larger metal case, and David's imagination ran away with him again. Did that box contain this man's limbs rather than his bollocks?

He was soon inside being reconnected to the monitoring equipment then almost immediately was given the same ten minutes of 3D images and video he had already watched. This time he thought to use his imagination to see himself in the place of the victims, but they didn't look or sound like him, and even his imagination wasn't creative enough to cover for his lack of empathy.

All too quickly it seemed his time was up, and he frantically searched his mind for ways he might stop the inevitable as he was wheeled back to the pigs.

The cobbles rattled the wheelchair again, increasing his pain like his need to break free.

Back at the pigs he saw a large patch of vomit on the concrete floor, left by the previous person. They were clearly not a psychopath like David, if they had that sort of emotional response. Was nobody safe?

There was no sign of the paraplegic now, but there were what looked like eight bones scattered about the pen, three of them cracked, looking like they might be tibia and fibula, as well as ulnar and radius bones. One of the pigs was crunching on a bone while the other licked its lips, looking to David for his afters.

The nurse with the case opened it up and unceremoniously dumped his penis and testicles into a large hinged tray. 'Now the way this process works is that *you* have to feed the pigs your body parts all by yourself. We don't do it for you. To do this we untie a leg and you only have to kick the tray forward and it tips the contents into the pen.'

'No.' David refused flatly.

'If you resist David it only makes things worse for you, though much more interesting for us. We are required to warn you not to resist, but we would encourage you to do so for *our* entertainment.

'You see we are equipped to use a number of *inducements* to help you control your behaviour. That's the beauty of this treatment.'

'Oh do fuck off.'

'Language David,' the nurse behind him admonished as the other bent to release his right leg.

As soon as it was released David lashed his leg out, but not at the tray, he was attempting to get away. Unfortunately for David he only got as far as lurching forward and getting his body weight to his right foot. Unable to hop away with the wheelchair bound to him, he fell heavily sideways into the patch of the previous man's vomit.

'Well that *was* silly David. We are going to have to hose you and the chair down before we go back in to Monitoring.'

Both nurses righted the chair, and he was repositioned in front of the tray.

'Just one kick and this part will be over,' prompted the nurse who was now resealing the emptied case.

David remained still, gritting his teeth. He was growing angry. It was no fun at all when the torment was this way round.

'Would you like some *inducement* David?'

He didn't reply.

'We have a number of inducements, not that *you* get to choose, and we always find that *one* of them helps.' The nurses waited for a response but none was forthcoming.

The nurse with the case placed it on the ground and folded her arms to enjoy what was to follow.

David began to pull at his arm restraints as the nurse behind him took a clear plastic bag from a pocket and slipped it over his head, smoothing the polythene down over his face

before twisting the plastic into a seal around his
neck.

11

As she sat waiting for Mrs Folie to put in an appearance Gina had the radio on low and was listening to the local news.

'Boring,' she moaned killing the radio as she realised that the news reader was about to talk at length about the latest football games, at which point she noticed a taxi pull up outside her target's address.

There followed some raucous laughter, like happy gulls at a tip, as two women got out and went to Folie's door.

Squeals of joy filled the street as Mrs Folie appeared at the door, and stepping out closing it behind her. The threesome clattered their shoes down the path to the taxi.

'*Now* it's party time,' there was a distinct sense of relief in Gina's voice as she started the car, and followed.

She almost lost the girls a couple of times once they got into the centre of Birmingham. They got caught at one set of lights with a number of other taxis which then went different ways, like an attempt to switch which cup the pea was under.

However, Gina followed her instinct, and even when they got out by the nightclubs, and Gina needed to park the car she didn't lose them for long.

It was a nice change of scene, to go from sitting on your bum for hours watching nothing happen, she mused, to propping up a bar and watching nothing happen.

The girls really did seem to just want to have fun, dancing and drinking. The only thing that didn't feel right, from Gina's experiences of nights out, was that they seemed to be staying in once place, instead of doing a circuit.

'I'd hoped you would have given me a call when you were done,' said lips very close to her ear.

Gina turned to see Will behind her.

'Yeah well I'm not done!' she yelled back over the noise. 'Have you been following me?'

'No. I felt like getting out and just saw you here actually…So you're still working then.'

She nodded and returned her attention to the three girls.

'Need any help?!'

'You could watch my targets for me while I go to the ladies!'

'Which lads is it?!'

'Girls…The red top, the yellow mini-dress, and then the black sequins, she's the main target!'

'Right…Can I get you another drink?!'

'J2O…Thanks…Orange and Passion fruit!'

'Okay!'

When she got back from the ladies she only had a mouthful of the J2O when Mrs Folie, in her slinky black number, headed her way. Gina wondered if she'd *been made* for a moment, but should have had more trust in her covert activity skills.

The young woman came to the bar, where a tall dark gentleman, possibly the club owner, appeared to have attracted her attention.

Looking at their expressions, they were not strangers. There was no way of hearing what they were saying, but his head flick followed by her turning and signalling the girls on the floor, who laughed and waved back, said it all.

As the two of them went through a door at the back of the bar, Gina turned and yelled to Will 'This could be it!'

'What?!'

'To get some evidence!' she explained.

'Are you crazy?!' He watched as she took her phone in hand.

'100% Proof!' she responded before taking another gulp of the J2O. 'Keep an eye on the other two for me!'

Gina could see that the bar staff were too busy filling glasses to notice, so walked through the door behind the bar with the confidence of someone who had every right to.

She had no idea what was beyond. It could have been a kitchen, an office, or a lounge. She hoped that if she was quick enough with the phone she could video something that would close the case. What she discovered though were stairs up to the next floor.

The thump-thump of the music quietened somewhat as the door closed behind her. She made her way up the stairs, treading at the edges to conceal her approach.

At the top was a door to the right labelled Storeroom and another to the left a bit further along labelled Manager. That door faced down a corridor.

Looking round the corner Gina could see a door ajar at the very end, with a light on, and a closed door to its left with a bar that suggested it was a fire exit.

The manager's office had giggles coming from it. She started to turn the handle, but it only turned a few degrees. It was locked.

Bollocks. Gina mouthed. Then she noticed there was a clear glass panel above the door. She reached up with the phone. '*No* that would be *too* easy wouldn't it Oakley,' she muttered to herself not able to reach quite high enough.

She wondered if there was anything in the storeroom behind her which she could use to stand on. She listened at its door but heard nothing, and there was no light coming from underneath. The handle turned and this door opened. She didn't risk switching the light on, just peered in with the light from the corridor, and spotted a crate. Quietly she lifted it and placed it in front of the manager's door, stood on it, and held up the phone set to video.

Mrs Folie was bent over the side of a leather arm chair, taking it up the arse, and clearly enjoying it. Not Gina's choice of orifices, but hey, each to their own she thought. Then the manager stepped away and sat in the chair, as he brought her round by the hand, where he guided her head down on him. Watching this on screen Gina uttered an involuntary *and* loud 'Ee-yewww!'

She continued to film for just a few more seconds, the occupants still unaware of their voyeur, before the question 'What are you doing?' came as something of a surprise to Gina. She wasn't by any means a jumpy kind of person, but this came pretty close.

Thinking on her feet she continued filming with a smile and said 'Hi, are you John?' chancing a common name.

'No, Finn.' He was built like a tank and appeared to have all the humour of one too.

'Hi. I'm Sabrina…The girls were wondering how Brenda was doing,' she giggled, but noted there was little sense of comprehension in this man's eyes.

He just looked like he was after half an excuse to maim and shame for kicks.

'She really needs to sort her shit out,' she continued, 'seriously. She's grown up on a sad diet of vampire romance. You know the type I mean Finn?'

He just glared.

'To her, *down for the count* means giving Dracula a blowjob.'

'Give me that,' he pointed at the phone.

Gina stepped down and aside from the crate but held her phone out of reach behind her back. 'Sharn't,' she said in a teasing tone, still smiling.

'You *will* give that to me *now*!' he insisted.

She extended her right fist towards his large chest. 'If you come any closer you'll regret it.'

Not standing for it he stepped into her surprisingly fast and hard blow, stopping dead as something cracked. His eyes widened, and his hand reached towards his left breast. Gina gave her Bruce Lee impression of the tiger-cub mew then announced, 'One-Inch punch. Vairwee powafoo.'

His hand came back out of his jacket 'You've bust my iPhone screen…Bitch!'

Gina turned to run. It was all she could do, but it was never easy to run in heels, and Fynn was right behind her in his steroid rage.

At the top of the stairs she changed tactics and curled into a ball, causing him to crash over the top of her as he attempted to grab her by the hair. She didn't wait for him to reach the bottom, just got up and followed him down, only to find that his now unconscious form was preventing the door from being opened.

She raced back up, by which time the manager had come to the door, and tumbled headlong over the beer crate winding himself.

He sprawled over the floor trying to recover his wits, his shirt unbuttoned and his trousers still unzipped. As Gina passed the open door she caught a glimpse of Mrs Folie in the back of the room trying to straighten her clothing and tidy her hair.

'What the fuck's going on?' the manager wheezed.

'A man has fallen down the stairs we need to get an ambulance.' She had no intention of stopping. She headed straight for the open office at the end of the corridor, but at the last moment went left via the fire exit.

'Not that way!' the manager yelled too late.

The fire alarm sounded, and in short order people poured out of the nightclub shrieking as the sprinklers soaked what little they had on.

By the time Gina got to her car, her phone had a text from Will. 'I hope you got what you came for. Do you fancy a nightcap?'

She texted back, 'Another time maybe. I've had quite enough action for tonight.'

Ethan's day had been another long one. It had particularly dragged from the moment that he knew he had a plan. It was a plan that could not start until turning out time that Saturday evening, and although he had been heading south it required turning around and heading towards Birmingham centre.

He still had just enough money for some fast food, thanks to what he had stolen from Bertie, and went into KFC to eat. It filled him for a bit, then he manage to go and see a movie for free by waiting outside of a cinema's fire doors, and after the first few people came out, he went in against the flow mumbling 'Fucking mobile, fucking shallow trouser pockets.'

Once inside the multiplex he only had to read the screens beside the doors to see what was about to start or had just started, then he was lost in someone else's world of make believe.

After the film finished, credits and all, there wasn't long to go before his *mission* really got under way, and he walked the streets to pick a promising pub, after which he slipped into loitering mode.

Luck was with Ethan, if not for unfortunate Paul Hinckley, a forty-something accountant who'd recently been dumped three times, by the same girl. This had driven him to go and suspend his self-loathing in an alcoholic haze.

Paul now wove his way down the street to the corner, where he made a conscious effort to check the name of the road he had arrived at before turning down it, while searching in his pocket with seemingly numb fingers.

He was oblivious of Ethan closing in from behind. Finding his keys and pressing the fob button, there issued the synchronised '*doink-doink*' and light flash, to guide him in to his vehicle.

'I wouldn't do that if I were you sir.'

'I'm not occifer...Ha...ha ha.' He turned slowly. 'How bloody corny is that. I actually said occifer didn't I...Pathetic.'

'I think you've had a few too many.'

'Bugger me, the police really do start to look like boys when you turn forty.'

'I'm not police, just a caring citizen.' Ethan touched Paul's arm. 'Let me walk you home...Leave the car.'

'No, you're alright. I'm stain with a french...I just need to get my overnight bag from the boot and I'm sordid...I'm not driving in this cognition.'

'I should hope not.' Ethan watched Paul open his boot.

'Look, see!' he pointed at a green kit bag, before grabbing it. 'Now it's off to my friend's house.'

'Why aren't your friends with you?'

'Oh, they stayed put,' he said with a laugh, remembering them all decline the offer to join him in drowning his sorrows, once again.

'Are they nearby?'

'Oh yesh...It's Mr Premier.'

To Paul's drunken surprise Ethan shoved him hard backwards and down into his boot. Trying to make sense of this Paul apologised, believing he had maybe slipped, and then thanked Ethan when he tucked his feet in. He just gave a confused smile when Ethan punched him hard in the side of the head to shut him up.

Ethan just looked at the blood coming from Paul's silly smile, where he had bit his lip, and then hit him hard in the eye. Paul just looked back at him and laughed, sort of knowing something wasn't quite right.

Ethan became frustrated, wondering whether he really was that weak. He was *the* school bully for fuck sake he berated himself, as he hit Paul in the temple again and again, making his knuckles ache. Nevertheless Paul continued to laugh strangely like he was still in the process of getting Ethan's joke, while the world span on regardless.

Ethan searched Paul's jacket pockets and his trousers. He found Paul's mobile before locating his wallet, which was what he was really after. Then he grabbed the green kit bag and slung it over his shoulder with the school bag. He leaned in and delivered one last almighty blow to the head, this time with his left fist.

Paul just laughed again, 'You're a good lag.'

Giving up, Ethan threw Paul's mobile and keys into the boot.

'Fangs.'

As Ethan closed the boot and walked away to inspect his takings, he heard Paul call after him. '*Night*…You take care now!'

Still constrained but now in bed, David blinked his eyes which had become dry from staring too long at the ceiling. Even after what he had been put through he didn't want to die. He had submitted to the repeated suffocation and finally kicked his genitals from the tray to the pig pen.

As a result he no longer felt like a real man, but the monitoring that followed his cold hosing down showed no improvement so now he was being given time to think things over, he assumed.

He was bitterly disappointed that things had turned out this way. What kept him going now was his need for revenge, but he didn't see a way of making any of his fantasies possible. He remained helpless.

As much as he considered his escape and then the capture and torture of these women, the image that kept coming back to him was of the pigs turning their snouts up at his *meat* and going back to gnawing on bone.

12

Enter the Dragon sang out for Gina. As she drew the throbbing mobile from her pocket she had a hunch it might be Will. She was close. Looking at the caller ID it was Tom.

'Orangina, we've had a call from a Mrs Best. Says she wants to talk to you about doing a job. Say's that Detective Inspector Dunn gave her your name and the number of DNA. She said that you would understand.'

'Well I don't.'

'Well you better go and find out then.'

'I'm in the middle of…trying to do something *properly*, Tom.'

'Well…When you get a spare moment, her address is…'

'I know where she lives.'

'You *do*?'

'Yeah…Just a few doors down from that shitty cock-sucking slag, whose adulterous ass I've nailed at her so-called girls night out.'

'Right ho. Good to see you're still *passionate* about your job,' he hung up.

Gina turned round to glare back at the looks she was getting in the hush of the Library. 'What?!'

Monday morning Ethan stood in a post office queue, knowing he really didn't need to do this. The idea of it just amused him. He had only wanted the money from Mister Hinckley's wallet. He didn't find the pin numbers for the cards and none were contactless. He knew he would only get three tries to guess each of them anyway.

No, it seemed altogether funnier to use a little of Hinckley's money to post the wallet and cards back to him, second class, to ensure it would arrive well after he'd had to cancel all his cards.

Ethan couldn't forget the man's embarrassed laughs as he kept hitting him, and it struck Ethan *weren't people strange*?

In front of him was an old man, whose whole body seemed to tremble, even though it was not cold in the post office. Ethan hoped he never ended his days that way. He'd rather go out standing on a landmine on some ethnic cleansing mission somewhere.

The next person waiting to be called from the queue had brought a dog in with her, and he knew by the harness that it must be her seeing-eye dog.

He found himself wondering how long it would take for a dog that size to be stripped to the bone, and whether the woman would appreciate quite what was happening to her faithful companion, by sound alone.

He almost turned to share his thoughts with the attractive young woman standing behind him, but decided against it as she looked like the sort of person who would tell him he wasn't right in the head.

Ethan had decided over the weekend that today he would take a coach to Hereford. The rail pirates would have fleeced him for every last penny if he was to take the train. He could imagine the people in charge of rail fares laughing at how people voluntarily complied with their extortion. He guessed it was a more grown-up version of his mugging. People just paid up because they didn't think they had a choice.

It was this worldview of Ethan's; cutting to the quick, that he felt gave him the confidence to be able to make his way in this world. After all, from what he had seen, financial success didn't appear to come to those having a conscience.

Dorothy's bandaged foot hurt so much as she slowly pushed her fingers and toes into the pen for the squealing pigs. They were devoured in seconds and she wept. She had been too weak to face the bag any longer.

She wondered why no one had come to rescue her. Her husband's contacts must have worked out where she had been taken. Maybe Rupert was behind this.

She was taken from the large shed back to Monitoring. Her mind felt numb and detached as she was rigged to the equipment, then she was aware of the exciting images which lifted her spirits. This only led to concern though, as she had the kit removed and heard the verdict.

'Oh dear,' the nurse said with a smile, 'We are a naughty girl.'

Dorothy was wheeled trembling from Monitoring to Assessment. But now she knew this was not for the assessment of anything at all. It was purely a theatre of amputation.

After a long wait for the team to prep and the audience of staff to be notified of more torture for viewing and filming, Dorothy was wheeled in through the double doors and very firmly transferred by four nurses from the restraints of the wheelchair to those of the gurney.

Sandra came across to check on their victim. 'Hello Dorothy. What is it today? Hands and feet?' she asked as if she was only a hair dresser asking about a preferred style where Dorothy would be allowed to decide.

'You have no idea what you have done.' Dorothy stated. '*Your* time is coming...*All* of you.'

'Is that so?' Sandra smiled at the empty threat.

Abby had been waiting all day for her next visitors and was now becoming extremely frustrated. She didn't find out where Gem had travelled up from, so had no idea how long it would take for the others to arrive.

It really was becoming most inconvenient. She could hear the young Dutch woman, Erika, in the basement calling every now and then. It was exciting to hear her distress, but at the same time a tease because Abby would rather deal with any new visitors first, so she could then relax in the shower.

The Prius was locked and the keys had gone down with Gem. She was intending to tell those who asked, that someone had parked it on her drive when she was out, and had first presumed they had run out of fuel and gone to the nearest village to get some.

That would certainly be the story when she later asked the police to tow it away. She could see that it would also lead to a mountain rescue search, which she would of course help with because the inconsiderate walker had used her drive to park near the stile. It wouldn't be the first time.

The search might even turn up Gem by examining the peat bog, but so what. She was a careless walker. The boots would not be traceable to Abby. She had taken them from a previous victim.

Abby knew she would have to make damn sure she didn't lose the keys off the next visitor or visitors, or else her story was going to get exponentially more complicated.

Then she found herself wondering what the end of this story realistically was for her. Would more people come after she had dealt with the next visitors? How much truth was there in what Gem had said anyway? Maybe no one was coming.

Psychopaths and the likes working in a *team*? She knew there'd been the West's, and before them Myra Hindley and Ian Bradey, but that was couples. Psychopaths, in a social group, didn't seem too likely to her.

Maybe she was really just being spun a line by Gem because she was supposed to be *Gem's* next victim, a bit like a Dexter, some serial-killer on serial-killer action.

'Fuck'em!' Abby announced at the kitchen sink, and decided to head for the basement.

Down the stairs she wheeled the sunbed aside and revealed the stone slab with a handle on, and bending slightly she lifted the stone a couple of inches and slid it along a foot or so of its stone trough.

Immediately there came a waft of urine and a pair of hands trying to push the slab further. 'Stay there! You dirty girl,' Abby commanded.

The young woman froze but cried miserably. 'Please let me go!'

'Well you know I can't do that Erika. I have your passport but you had no pass to be in the national park area.'

'But you don't need one!'

'Of course you do you double-Dutch girl. You can't just go wandering around other people's land, without permission...*alone*. Something quite *awful* might happen... Oh look...*It has*,' she chuckled.

'Please let me go! I'll leave the district! I won't say anything!'

'You speak very good English for a foreigner. I like that. It shows you've really tried to be a decent person. Do you have any drugs in your back pack?'

'No...I don't do drugs.'

'Oh, pity, I just thought you might want to do some, if you had. To...you know...help you through this ordeal.'

'Just let me go, please!'

'Well I'll think about it.'

'Thank you.'

'...As I take a shower.' She slid the heavy slab back in place, to renewed sobbing from Erika. She flipped a switch on the wall and the sound of the sobbing was immediately amplified by the speakers in the corners of the basement. This seemed to quieten Erika momentarily, as she became conscious of her own voice, then she screamed for help and heard it cause feedback.

Abby laughed and then it went quiet again, as it dawned on Erika that Abby was enjoying it because she knew no one else would hear. Then Abby pulled on the cord by the shower unit, reached past the plastic curtain and turned the shower on, before slowly getting undressed, listening with expectation for the moment of realisation.

Suddenly, in the darkness below the floor, Erika became aware of a trickle of water by her legs. She knew she had not wet herself again, though this wetness did have some warmth to it. Then she made a connection to the shower.

'Hey! There's water coming in!'

'Don't be so stupid!' Abby spat, while beaming a smile of delight.

'Yes, yes. It's starting to...I think it's leaking from the shower.'

'You know...I think there *is* some sort of leak from the drain,' she laughed as she stepped into the spray of water, pulling the curtain across.

As Erika's wails of panic grew, Abby began to rub herself over with the shower gel. Her nipples were already hard; standing proud to the sound of her victim's terror. Spreading the gel over her breasts and then down her belly she ran her hands over her buttocks then her muscular legs.

As the water level rose, Erika's choking shrieks reached fever pitch, then the power went off. The pump spluttered and Abby froze. Had the generator just failed, or had she got a visitor who didn't care for knocking?

Abby didn't waste time listening, she grabbed the metal bar she had propped in the corner of

143

the shower for such eventualities, and quietly pulled the curtain aside, stepping out.

Erika continued to cry out, but Abby didn't mind, the noise would cover her own movements. She also reckoned that the intruder would look in the direction of the crying first, and she would strike above the anticipated torchlight with her bar.

Dressed in black and wearing GPNVG-18 panoramic night vision goggles, Tina and Mel came down into the basement. Abby saw no torchlight, so reacted to sound instead but Tina saw the blind swing of the bar and side stepped. Realising her first swing had missed, Abby was bringing the bar round when a boot hit her hard in the chest and threw her back on the flagstones.

'Fuck!' Tina gasped as the gel on the sole of her boot had caused her to do the splits, tearing muscle.

Mel quickly moved round Tina towards Abby with her cuffs ready but ended up sliding around on the floor with her, getting kneed and elbowed as she struggled with Abby and her gel. It was like trying to cuff an eel, till Tina stilled Abby with a kick to the head. 'Bitch!'

With Abby secured, their attention moved to the occupant of the pit. As soon as Mel lifted and pulled the stone slab along, a coughing spluttering Erika bobbed up. 'Thank you. Thank you!' she sobbed. 'I didn't think anyone was going to come in time.'

'It's not Gem,' Mel informed Tina before turning back to the still trapped woman. 'Have you seen anyone else?'

'No, no I haven't. Please help me up.' Erika couldn't see who had come to the rescue.

Mel heaved the stone aside and gave Erika a hand out of the water.

Tina threw Erika a towel which gave her a fright, then asked 'Where are your clothes?'

Erika couldn't see anything but a very dim light from the top of the stairs. 'They might be upstairs.'

'Go and get dressed and wait up there.'

'Thank you,' Erika almost sobbed with relief as she gingerly fumbled her way up out of the basement.

Abby meanwhile shivered with the cold as she came back around in the pitch black. 'What do you want?' she moaned.

'We've come to ask some questions.'

'About what?'

'Let's start with Gem.'

'Gem who?'

'Oh that's almost corny. *Gem who*? You didn't even attempt to make your tone of voice convincing.'

'Look…I told her I'm not interested. So if you've come to convince me…'

'No, no. That offer has closed I'm afraid,' said Tina.

'What did you do with Gem?' Mel asked.

'We went for a walk. I said I wasn't interested, and that was the last I saw of her.'

'Okay but I think there's more to it than that.'

'No. She left her car in my drive and went for another walk.'

'You really aren't a very good liar,' Tina pointed out.

'It's true!' Abby yelled, angered by their intrusion.

'Yeah, and you came home for a shower and some potholer who'd lost their way happened to come up under your floor,' Mel quipped.

Abby screamed as without warning Tina snapped her index finger at the second joint.

'You made that look so easy Tina. Can I have a go?' asked Mel.

'Of course you can.'

Mel pulled on the chain of the cuffs took the index of the other hand, and Abby screamed out again.

'Gosh,' she laughed, 'that's given me an idea.'

'Has it?' Tina sounded amused.

'Okay, look,' Abby spluttered fearfully, 'Gem fell into a peat bog, just up on the fell.'

'Mmm…Two uses of the word fell there, yet only one of them sounded correct,' said Tina.

'Okay, okay! I pushed her in.'

'That's more like it.'

'What we need you to do now then,' said Mel, 'is show us where this bog is.'

'Why? She's gone.'

'Well we'd like to see if you could…*retrieve* her.'

'You've got to be fucking kidding. You'd have to drain the bog and dig down to get her body out. She's there for keeps.'

'Now that sounded convincing. You see, you can do it.' Tina turned to Mel. 'What do you think?'

'Tidy up here and go home I'd say.'

Abby still could not make out the two figures but the suggestion that these women might head home relaxed her somewhat. She was going to have to try and sort out what they had done to her fingers.

Tina's nod was immediately followed by Abby screaming and thrashing about as six further fingers and both thumbs were snapped in quick succession. Then as Abby panted desperately against the pain, Tina and Mel removed the cuffs and put her into the watery grave, pulled the stone over her and then thought it a good idea to pull the sunbed on top for good measure.

Abby begged for mercy from under the floor.

'It's a shame you didn't chose the other path this morning, but I hope you make the best of this experience instead,' said Mel.

'Sorry we can't stay to appreciate the ins-and-ins of your little design,' Tina smirked, understanding the connection with the shower, in part because of what they had both heard immediately prior to their descent of the stairs.

When they arrived upstairs Erika was still there with the towel. 'I cannot see anything up here. The lights don't work.'

'I'll sort that.' Tina went and put the mains power back on.

They then heard the sound of the shower pump in the basement, immediately followed by the amplified sounds of Abby's agonised attempts to shift the stone slab.

'Are you just going to leave her die?' asked Erika.

'It would appear so,' said Mel.

'Good.' Erika felt that was justified, but soon, when she had found her clothes and got dressed she considered whether she might be wrong as she listened to the dreadfully loud sounds of Abby drowning.

13

Mr Best opened his front door, took one look at the orange hair and said, 'You must be Orangina.'

'It's Oakley actually,' she corrected, preferring not to allow that nickname to be used by clients.

'Oh. Sorry I was expecting someone else.'

'No…you weren't.'

'Oh I think I was,' he corrected her, feeling another difference of opinion with a woman coming on.

'I *am* Orangina,' she tried to explain.

'But you just said your name was Oakley. You're not from the *press* are you, changing your name to get a story? Something you can misquote, to make out our son's a raving psychopath?'

'What? No.'

'Well what do you want then?'

'You're wife wanted to talk about hiring me to do some investigative work…I'm assuming.'

'Right then, so you *are* Orangina. Come on in,' they moved into the hall where Mr Best seemed unsure where to take her next.

'Is Mrs Best in?'

'No, actually. You *just* missed her.'

'Oh.'

'She was taken away in an ambulance.'

'What happened?'

'After the last visit from the police we realised that our son's pets would probably need feeding by now. We gave Percy some cheese.'

'His *mouse*?'

'Hamster.'

'Right.'

'Then we looked for the fish food, but couldn't find it. I remembered Irene saying that one of the policemen, who took away Ethan's computer, camera, and other things, had said that these fish ate meat. So she went and got a piece of chicken we had left over from the Sunday roast, but they didn't seem too interested. So I said maybe they prefer raw meat.

'I soon wished I'd kept my mouth shut. She only comes back with the best part of my fillet steak. Fillet steak! I mean, it's like feeding gold to goldfish. Ridiculous! Only it turned out to be nothing like feeding gold to goldfish. I've never seen such a commotion.

'I swear those things came out of the water. Irene's thumb and two fingers looked stripped to the first knuckle. She pushed past me, heading for the bathroom, blood everywhere… Look.' He pointed at the bottom of the steep stairs.

Gina noticed for the first time the sizable blood stain on the carpet. 'Shit. Will she be alright?'

'She'll bounce back, I'm sure. She's a tough one, though she did pass out rather unexpectedly before reaching the bathroom. That's why she took a tumble down the stairs you see…Of course I knew not to move her, in case she had a broken neck, and phoned for an ambulance.'

'I'm surprised you didn't go with her to the hospital Mr Best.'

'Well I did say there wasn't much on TV so I could come along for a bit. But she told me in no uncertain terms I could bloody well stay here. *And* that I was to answer *all* your questions when you arrived. She said it was more important that Ethan is found. I suppose she's right.'

'Sure.'

'Do you want to come through to the kitchen, while I put on a brew?'

'Okay.' Gina followed him into the rather cosy kitchen and sat at what she guessed counted as a breakfast bar.

'Regular or herbal.'

'Got any coffee?'

'The percolator is on the fritz. I think someone put something in it that wasn't supposed to go in. It has an odd meaty smell to it now.'

'Oh, regular tea then, and black with one sugar please.'

'Sorry we only have sweeteners.'

'Do people still use those?'

He looked at the large dispenser, for the sell by date. 'Well we *have* had these for some years it seems.'

'I haven't seen any since the nineties.'

'How about milk?'

'Oh well I've seen plenty of that.'

'No I mean do you want any?'

'No, no…So…Can you bring me up to speed with the case please Mr Best?'

'Haven't the police told you everything?'

'I won't know till you tell me, will I.'

'I guess not…Well we've been told that Ethan is not thought to be in the neighbourhood any longer, and that when he *was* here he may have been getting up to some questionable activities. Which I might add, Irene and I knew nothing about.

'But it seems his school were aware of certain behavioural issues. The Head said that Ethan had to learn to deal with them, but didn't want to say what was up in case it affected their next Ofsted report. In fact I really don't think they care too much that he's gone…either.'

The kettle finished boiling and he poured water onto the bag in the pot, watching it spin as it drowned.

'So might he have gone to see some friend?'

'Ethan isn't good at making friends. We did try to get him involved in the Scouts when he was younger. He wanted to join Army Cadets but Scouts were the only option round here.

'But there was some misunderstanding over the discharge of an air-pistol during one of their camp fire sing-songs, in Sutton Park, which injured a cantering horse and sadly he was banned.'

'Does he still have this air pistol?'

'Good heavens no…That went some time ago, as I recall in part exchange for an air rifle.'

'And where is that now?'

'I don't rightly know. He didn't take it to school with him the day he vanished if that's what you're thinking.'

'But he had taken it to school previously?'

'No. It's too big to fit in his school bag. However…those two police officers never found it.'

'Do you mind if I take a look in his room?'

'No, not at all…Though it is in a bit of a mess.'

'Aren't all teenagers' rooms?'

'No I mean after the police tore it apart.' He handed Gina her Tea and they headed up to Ethan's room.

'What the hell did they do in here? I've never seen anything like it.' There were CDs, Blu-Rays, and books strewn across the floor.

'Well the police were pretty keen to find clues.'

'Well there's keen and there keen, but I've never seen anyone take a fucking bed before.'

'No, no. Ha…Ethan sleeps in a hammock,' he pointed at the bundle of netting now draped over the back of the chair at the desk.

'Oh.' Gina continued to scan the room for inspiration, spotting a box set of Bear Grylls Blu-Rays and then a box set of Dexter. It was rated 18. So many parents allowed their under 18s to watch such things, she didn't bother to comment. Then she recognised some of the books. 'He does seem to have a lot of Chris Ryan and Andy McNab.'

'Oh yes. Our Ethan isn't much of a one for talk, but one thing he does like to talk about is how one day he's going to make selection for the SAS.'

Gina wasn't sure from his tone whether Mr Best was suddenly sounding proud, or contemplating the possibility of Ethan getting killed in action. Her intuition suggested this child was not well loved.

'Don't you find that worrying considering his present situation?' she asked.

'I think he can look after himself.'

'Has he ever visited Hereford?'

'Ur...No...With school you mean?'

'Never mind...Have you got any family he might have gone to stay with?'

'None we're close to...*anymore*.'

'Right, well what about someone you are not close to; someone who is a little *mixed up* say, who maybe has decided not to tell you that Ethan is with them right now.'

'Like who?'

'Well I don't know Mr Best. It's *your* family.'

'The thing is, Irene and I were only-children, and couldn't have children of our own. So Ethan was adopted.'

'Does he know that?'

'I think so,'

'You *think* so?'

'Yes. We did tell him, a number of times.'

'And is it possible that he's gone to try and meet his real parents?'

'I don't think so. As far as I understood it his father had died in some bizarre accident involving fruit, and his mother never kept in touch after the adoption. Said it was *for the best*. I don't think she was making a pun, but rather it's what they all say when a child is given up.'

'Do you have any details about her? Like her name?'

'I'll have a look. But I'm not sure it's such a good idea.'

'Oh? Why?'

'She said there would be serious consequences if anyone tried to find her.'

'So you are saying that Phase Two is actually working with Peter then, Eleanor?'

'Yes Kate, it is early days but it would seem so. Monitoring has seen a gradual reduction in his responses to the test materials, and now he's receiving creative writing support from Teri.'

'I must admit the stuff he had been writing had made good bedtime reading.'

'Yeah.'

'But now seems to have been getting a little stale.'

'Yes I've heard similar comment from the other girls.'

'Well let's see where Teri can take him.'

'Okay.'

'Right then…Ethan Best. Where are we with *him*?'

'We've spotted him with facial recognition on CCTV getting on a coach for Hereford.'

'*Hereford*? What on Earth is he going *there* for? I'd have expected London. He must be trying to throw us off his sent. Just keep on top of him. I want him brought in first real opportunity we have.'

'Okay.'

'And how are the plans for the Moldova strike going?'

'Just confirming the logistics, but our girls in Russia are pretty psyched up about this one.'

'Well if it all goes to plan, with the data we have been collating, there will likely be a load more operations abroad on the cards.'

'Good.' Eleanor actually preferred the black-ops side of their business, but then she had been in the services herself.

After a pause Kate asked, 'how is Clare doing? Is there any improvement?'

'None…To make any progress I think she will need to be taken to a hospital.'

'It's too much of a risk. She knows too much, and if she is not in full control of her faculties we could have a problem.'

'So what are we going to do?'

'I guess if she's stable, we give her a few more days.'

'And if her condition becomes unstable?'

'As with any liability, I suppose we may have to consider Phase Four.'

'*Phase Four*?!'

Ethan wasn't sure whether it was excitement he felt as he stepped off the coach at Hereford bus station. He needed a plan but he only had a first step.

He walked into the town centre, looking for a W. H. Smiths. When he found one, to one side of a pedestrianized market square, he went straight to the map section. He picked an Ordnance Survey up at random and checked the back to see where Hereford was and saw he needed map 149. He got one and opened it up. Since the Landranger maps typically covered over 500 square miles, the 149 showed a lot of the surrounding countryside, including Hereford's neighbouring town of Leominster. However, what Ethan was keen to locate was Credenhill.

If the SAS novels were to be believed Credenhill barracks were the home of his heroes. He noticed that just north of Credenhill was a park, with earthworks and more importantly woodland which might offer somewhere to hole up overnight.

Paul's cash had got Ethan to Hereford but wasn't going to stretch much further. He needed more money now to get the sort of kit he would need to keep him warm and dry.

He decided he needed to do another mugging, but didn't fancy trying it on with any bloke in this neck of the woods in case he found they were an off duty trooper. So he decided he would be on the lookout for a woman this time. He made a mental note of the road numbers, though he expected the road signs for Credenhill would be clear enough. Then he replaced the map and left the shop.

It took him just over an hour to get to the barracks. On his way out of Hereford he spotted no opportunities for a mugging and realised it was now inevitable that he would have to return to the city if he did acquire any money and with the time now getting on it would likely mean having to stay in the city the first night.

If it came to that he had already decided to go check out the sewage works that he had noted on the map, which was by the river on the south side of the city. He reckoned no one was likely to come looking for him there.

He decided it best not to loiter as he passed the barrack gates. There were no signs to confirm it was even MOD property never mind home of The Regiment. He was disappointed not to see even one beige beret.

He moved on towards Credenhill park wood following his mental map. Climbing to the top of the hill it took the best part of another hour. Ethan found that though it was a good hundred and sixty feet above the barracks it was too far away and too densely wooded to see anything of the barracks. Besides which, he expected the camp would be designed to obscure view of The Regiment's activities from that and other vantage points.

'Bollocks!' Ethan cursed his stupidity.

How was he to find his inspiration now, he wondered. Not allowing himself the luxury of a sulk he turned his mind to checking out the park for dry hiding places. He did not relish the thought of another damp night if it could be avoided.

Banks and the remains of walls would offer some shelter from the wind, but not rain. There were places amongst the trees he could bed in with the right kit, but on the whole the park was criss-crossed by paths, so he would be spotted by anyone but a blind person walking their dog.

Now deeply disappointed he headed back towards Hereford, taking another peak into the barracks as he passed the gate, to again see nothing of interest.

Nevertheless, much further on he saw an old lady tending her front garden, and decided to take his chances with her.

'Granny!' he called with glee in his voice.

'Tim?' she asked attempting not to get up off her knees too quickly, turning and peering at him as he drew closer.

'Yes,' he smiled.

From the look of her peering up from the flower-bed at the edge of the lawn he expected she might be a bit short sighted. He stopped at the gate. 'I wanted to take a look at something of granddad's, for a school project.'

'Not this evening Tim. You know all that stuff is tucked away in the loft.' This seemed to Ethan like confirmation that the old woman was living on her own, and most importantly *vulnerable*.

'Oh well how about some tea and biscuits then, before I go back.'

'Well I suppose I can manage that…It *has* been a while since you have been round to see me.'

'Sorry about that Granny.'

With a further groan she straightened out as best she could, looking like she needed to keep moving so as not to fall over, and moved inside. Ethan followed, feeling his luck was now on the turn as he closed her gate and then her front door, with a devious grin.

Craig Bosworth finished watching the latest download he had purchased from the Dark Net, and began to review the context and content of the video, having already logged what site it was acquired from in his Word document.

The facial recognition software he had run alongside the video had not identified any known people, missing persons or otherwise, which was not unusual. The next thing he intended to do was delve into the programming of the source file. He wanted to see if any traces were inadvertently left behind pointing to the origin and author of the material.

If he had completed that task he would have determined that this video's origin was Moldovan. However his concentration was disturbed by a noise from downstairs. His detached house on the leafy outskirts of London was equipped with a top of the range security system, and having no pets to trigger it he assumed it might have been something shifting in the dishwasher. Nevertheless, he knew he would not be able to focus unless he at least went to check out the possible cause.

Quietly descending to his hallway he reached for the light switch. It was then that he saw a dark figure near the stairs.

'Who…?' As the light came on he became aware of movement behind, and turned to see a further two armed troopers. 'How did you get in here? This is private property!'

Like many others Craig was surprised by their stealthy appearance, but unlike the others he made no attempt to run, as if he did not register them as a threat.

'I asked you a question!' he insisted, turning to face the first trooper, now taking him by the arm and raising a syringe. 'What the…' he tried to pull away.

The troopers were saying nothing.

'There's no need for th…' Too late to reason further, the needle's contents took immediate effect.

14

Ethan had not slept well. There had been another nightmare about his mother. He thought the content of it had probably been triggered by the actual events of the following evening.

'No Tim. No more cowboys and Indians,' the old woman had protested as he had bound her to a chair from the kitchen table with a length of washing line, as the kettle boiled.

She had put up a half-hearted struggle then gone limp. Believing this to be a ruse Ethan pinched her left cheek as he raised her lolling head, but there had been no reaction.

When he had taken this spur of the moment decision to play *Take Granny Hostage* he had been ready for it to go wrong at any point. He had expected to find someone else in the house, or for someone to return home or visit. Nevertheless, he had not anticipated this. As he quickly unbound the frail old woman she tipped forwards in a dead collapse onto the kitchen tiles.

He felt for a pulse, turning her over and watching her complexion turn grey before his eyes. He hadn't intended this. He had wanted food and money, but had become involved in yet another person's death.

'Stupid old bint!' he cursed as he lifted her and took her upstairs. He expected her to be a deadweight, but she seemed very light, like a withered leaf that had been waiting to fall.

Removing her shoes and her gardening jacket he had placed her body in her bed and pulled the duvet over her, before returning to the kitchen for his cup of tea and a cupboard search.

Far from the cupboards being bare, he had found loads of tinned food and a freezer that was well stocked too, and came to imagine that he might stay here a while.

Having eaten steak pie and chips, he then went on a search of the house and found a stash of almost a thousand pounds inside a teapot in Granny's big china cabinet. He couldn't believe his good fortune; the recent death no longer a concern.

However, when he woke in the middle of the night in the spare room and left for the loo he found the old woman there on the landing. She was just clutching the banister. Ethan seemed to have little control of the scream that came out of him, or her, as both took fright at each other's appearance.

She tumbled end over end down the stairs with some audible cracks which did not sound like banisters or steps. He rushed down the stairs after her to find she had come to an all too sudden halt at the bottom, with her neck at an abnormal angle.

Ethan almost laughed. Then he remembered why he was up and rushed back up the stairs to the toilet. Some minutes later, and a lot calmer, he switched the landing light on and returned to inspect her condition, dead again.

He took her back to her room, but no sooner had he got her through her bedroom door than she was wetting herself. He dumped her back in her bed with disgust, which brought an involuntary shiver as he pulled the duvet back over her.

Now he was worried that he couldn't stay in this house because she would not stay dead. He looked around her room for inspiration, and noticed a long hair pin on her dressing table. Returning to her beside he drove it into her lolling tongue, nothing, he removed it and slid it into her cheek, nothing.

Satisfied, he replaced the pin, switched the light off and closed the door. Turning off the landing light he had then returned to the spare room.

It took him ages to get to sleep, but when he did he dreamed that his mother was a zombie who had dug her way out of a grave and was now looking for him, wearing a gardening jacket and carrying a washing line tied at one end into a hangman's noose.

It was Tom Norton's turn to have Gina visit *his* desk.

'What can I *do you for* Orangina?'

'I need to go over to Hereford for a few days…It's the *Best* case.'

'Glad you think so. It's good to see you are finally feeling *enthusiastic* about one of the jobs.'

'Yes…It seems the police have predicted Ethan will be in London, and have asked the Met to keep an eye open for him, but otherwise are doing little else.'

'Why do you think that?'

'Well there's only so much they *can* do, and…well the lad's not exactly missed by a lot of people, so I guess he's not top of the list of kids to find.'

'So why Hereford?' he gave her a quizzical look.

'Well some say it is often a boy's dream to run away to London, which I guess is why they are watching out for him there, but my intuition tells me that *this* lad's dream lies in Hereford.'

'Your *intuition*? Have you been staring into your dark crystal ball again?'

'What? No…Ethan is keen on the SAS, and I wouldn't mind betting he wants to join up.'

'I thought he was just a kid.'

'He is…Fourteen.'

'Well,' Tom sighed, 'it's just not going to happen.'

'Can't I just go have a look around?'

'No…I mean yes…I'm saying *he* can't get into the SAS at fourteen.'

'Oh I know that.'

'So what would he be thinking to go there?'

'Well I'm guessing he's a bit mixed up right now.'

'A *bit* mixed up?' Tom laughed at her understatement, 'I hear he's hung a lorry driver *and* put his mother in hospital.'

'I know…He likely feels he can't come home, so would go to the next best place he could hope to find comfort.'

'*Comfort*? Do psychopaths do comfort Orangina, do they…*Really*?'

'Okay…For inspiration then.'

'Inspiration?'

'Yes…For what he's going to do *next*.'

'*Next?* Hell, you better get going then.'

Kate sat discussing Craig Bosworth with Eleanor. Watching his room's live feed, reading his body language as he lay on his bunk calmly twiddling his thumbs. Cuffed, and locked in his room, he looked like someone about to be released, or at least holding a '*simple misunderstanding*' card up his sleeve, as did a number of psychopaths. Looking up from her tablet Kate continued, 'So no sign at all?'

'No. As you saw on the Monitoring video, when he was viewing the test material he *was* registering distress. And from what we have found out from what was seized from his property he appears to be an independent researcher and author.'

'A journalist? That's all we need.'

'No. Not a journalist. He writes about serious organised crime and terrorism. A couple of publications of his were seized. He seems to be focusing on how terrorism is being funded through the Dark Net's exploitation of human trafficking.'

'So you don't think that is just his cover then?'

'Cover for what? I don't think he enjoys the materials he works with, just seems driven to make a difference.'

Kate blew air out between her pursed lips as she forced herself to make a decision. 'Right well he's going to have to be taken home, with all his belongings, but not before we have copies of everything.'

'That could take a few hours.'

'Make it a priority Eleanor, he's already been held overnight. But before he goes I want a word with him.'

'Okay.'

That Tuesday afternoon two cars drove around Hereford, each with two women on the lookout for Ethan, but there was no sign of him. After a couple of hours they agreed over the radio to park the cars and meet up for a coffee at Starbucks.

'So tell me, Jane,' Rosie quizzed, 'why *does* Kate want this kid brought in?'

'After what he did to Clare you have to *ask*?'

'Yeah because we are all taking risks with this atypical extraction, so there must be something deeper,' Rosie pressed.

'Deeper than him being a school bully with psychopath written all over his face?' Mel supported Jane.

'Haven't we all been a bully at school at some point?' Rosie argued.

'We've never extracted anyone younger than mid-twenties though,' Tina added.

'Clare's and my surveillance reported that Ethan was a right bastard to other kids at school. And with a number of visits to pet stores he probably tortures animals as a pastime too,' Jane said, turning to look at Rosie.

'Hey, what you looking at me for?!...I never *liked* kittens, okay!' Rosie went on the defensive. 'I'm not the only one anyway. What about miss *Phoenix Quest* here,' she said, looking at Mel.

'I'm not ashamed of getting rid of pigeons and crows. They're vermin anyway. I just wish they'd fly a bit further before they drop, more like real fireworks.'

'So what do you think he was doing on the waste ground that day, Jane?' Tina tried to get the conversation back on track.

'Not sure. We didn't get close enough to him to see what he'd been up to.'

'But close enough for a rock.' Rosie quipped.

'Piss off.'

'So should we, maybe, be looking at areas of waste ground here?' Tina prompted.

Jane shrugged. 'Why come all this way to visit waste ground?'

'Maybe he has relatives here,' Mel offered.

'I doubt it,' Jane shook her head. 'He is adopted so that would suggest he has no biological family ties.'

'How about non-biological then?'

'Yeah, that would be suds law,' said Rosie with a smirk.

Ignoring her, Jane continued, 'I don't think anyone knows for sure why he came here. He was spotted in the high street before we lost him. So I guess we should split up and go looking round the shops.'

Gina arrived in Hereford mid-afternoon and booked herself into a B&B. She anticipated her search could take a couple of days. Within the hour she was walking around the town looking for her own inspiration as well as Ethan. She had never been into Hereford before, even though she had had dealings with them and the SBS during her time with Five.

With no sigh of Ethan she decided to take a break at an Internet café, where she looked up The Regiment and read from their official site for inspiration.

At the end of the hour she had consumed two cups of coffee and come up with only one idea. It looked like a pub-crawl was in order. Who might know better than a squaddie why a young lad would come to Hereford? If she was lucky someone she talked to might even have seen him.

Craig stood before Kate's desk still in cuffs. 'Are these *really* necessary?' he raised his wrists.

'I suppose not.' Kate nodded to the nurse behind him, who stepped forward and removed them. Kate could see Craig was full of questions, but she had her own. 'What do you intend to do with your research Mr Bosworth?'

'Publish a book about how the Dark Net is being used to fund terrorism, to make people aware of the damage it is doing.'

'And what good will come of awareness? These people who watch this material don't give a damn about terrorism. They are not going to stop feeding their needs for some greater cause, especially if it doesn't affect them.'

'So what are you *saying?* That my work is pointless?'

'I am of the opinion that your intended publication will achieve little, but your work on the other hand is not pointless, no. I am interested in a couple of your tracking methods.'

'Why? For your abduction and incarceration?' he almost sneered.

'In part,' she nodded.

'Pulling these people out of society is still a burden on the tax payer.'

'Not necessarily, but what would *you* have us do Mr Bosworth?'

'I'm old-school, eye for an eye, but we have a legal system that does not allow that to happen. We are expected to treat each criminal as a product of their nature and nurture, but there is no cure for this insanity.'

'I'm not sure that is true. We are having a degree of success with our four phased treatment process here.'

'Which involves what?'

'I'm not at liberty to say, since you will shortly be leaving us, and we don't want you writing about our approaches.'

'But *if* they are that affective, why not?'

'Let's say that the process depends upon each client being unaware of what comes next in the process, so that they focus on the phase they are in.'

'Don't they tell one another?'

'No. Each phase has its own wing, and each client has private quarters.'

'*Solitary confinement*?'

'Hardly…There is more than enough interaction with staff here.'

'Okay, but where do these people go after?'

'Some, like yourself, go home on the understanding that they are to mention nothing of The Clinic and its approach, and that we may check in with them from time to time, even if they move.'

'So what part of the government *is* funding this?'

'That's classified,' Kate caught the nurse's eye.

Craig turned to see the nurse holding a syringe like the trooper had.

'Wait! I just…'

David was now numb with trauma, as he looked at his hands and feet in the trough. All he had to do was kick out with his bandaged stump and they would be gone, but he just sat there, knowing what would happen if he took too long.

He debated whether this was all a forgone conclusion, regardless of his test results. He swore he had felt differently about the test materials before they wheeled him out, knowing what was coming only too well, yet the nurse had cruelly given him that 'Oh dear,' of hers, and here he was.

He was starting to wish they would just kill him. What life would he have as an invalid? But they weren't about to just let him die. They resuscitated him when he passed out, and would probably tell him that provided he *turned the corner* he could be fitted with prosthetics for a return to society.

He heard the whisper of the plastic bag behind him. His chest still ached and his nose was still encrusted with blood from the last smothering, in his room. Quickly he kicked out and pain like lightening shot up his leg to ignite the scar tissue at his groin, and he cried out.

But he couldn't be heard over the squealing pigs.

Over the noise he heard the nurse at his ear. 'Spoilsport,' she chided, and to his surprise pulled the bag over his head.

15

Deciding he could not stay in the old woman's house without a decent escape and evasion plan Ethen drew up a shopping list. Although the shopping list did involve some food, it mainly involved a visit to Hereford's *Army Surplus* store. He needed a fully kitted out Bergen to aid his survival better than what he presently possessed in his two bags.

Early Wednesday morning, so as not to be spotted, he left the house through the back door, taking everything of his with him, plus a few extras, in case for some unforeseen reason he was unable to return. It was also important to him not to leave obvious evidence of his presence there. He didn't think he had been followed to Hereford, he had certainly not heard anything on the news about a search for him, but he enjoyed the process of covering his tracks; rubbing down surfaces he may have touched, whilst checking for other signs of his visit.

Later in town he had to fill in time till the store opened so decided to return to the bus station. The only place he could think of going if he had to leave Hereford was the Brecon Beacons, which was where the SAS ran their selection exercises. If nothing else he thought it would be good experience for him for when he got to do selection himself in a few years' time.

The Brecon Beacons were only fifty or so miles away from Hereford so the bus fare would

172

not be expensive, but more important than that it offered a relatively quick way to vanish into the terrain.

After getting a timetable for the number 39 bus from the station, Ethan went on to a Tesco where he bought a variety of high energy snack foods, a roll of Clingfilm, sealable sandwich bags, a twin pack of toilet roll, and two large bottles of apple juice.

He wanted to be prepared for *hard routine* if necessary, to leave no evidence to track him through. This would require him to defecate on a square of Clingfilm and put it, with the toilet paper he would use, into a sealed sandwich bag and carry it with him, until safe disposal was possible.

Similarly he would need to carry away his urine in the bottles he had just bought. Ethan smiled to himself as he passed through the checkout. The juice looked the same now as it would coming out the other end, rather like he had heard said about pate.

Next he returned to W. H. Smiths, where he bought the number 11 Outdoor Leisure Ordnance Survey map. He already owned a well pawed copy, but like a lot of his kit it had been left at home.

He was the Army Surplus Store's first customer of the day. He gave a cock and bull story about going bird watching in the Forest of Dean to the young man there, who clearly didn't give a toss.

He bought the remaining contents of his shopping list. He gathered up the items as he spotted them: A Silva compass, a camouflage jacket and trousers, a pair of size 10 black leather boots, and some green and black face paint.

Placing them on the counter he turned and picked a camouflage Bergen, a green four season sleeping bag, a camouflage Gore-Tex bivvi bag, a couple of microbe filter water containers, a camouflage net and a pair of small green waterproof high-magnification binoculars.

He looked longingly at the hunting knives in the glass cabinet as he paid, but knew he would not be able to buy any of them without proof of being 18+. His school bag already had a number of sharp knives in anyway, taken from the old woman's kitchen.

Gina woke later than intended, with a dreadful hangover, but was in plenty of time for breakfast. As she forced down the full English and worked her way through two cafetières of atrocious black coffee, she thought about the previous night.

The pub-crawl had not proven as enlightening as she had hoped. None of the squaddie *types* she had struck up a conversation with admitted to being SAS. Bar one drunk who turned out to be a builder on holiday.

Three of the men came on to her. Two of them were pretty good looking, but for some strange reason when she began flirting with them she found Will coming to mind, which helped her focus on the job at hand.

None she talked to about possible reasons for a fourteen year old coming to see the SAS in Hereford could fathom it. If it had been part of a TA visit then maybe, otherwise there would be nothing to see really, and the kid would soon realise his error and surely go back home, they thought.

One man however, possibly an officer, did say that if it had been him he would have gone to the Brecon Beacons instead, and attempted Pen y Fan and the other key peaks of the SAS selection course.

She wondered if the man was right, that maybe Ethan had instead gone straight to the Brecon Beacons and not come into Hereford at all. She knew she would have to get across there and investigate, hangover or not.

She took two paracetamols, swilling them down with a glass of fruit juice, which tasted more like vinegar.

Gina had brought most of the kit she would need in the boot of her Tigra, but thinking ahead what she was missing was an image intensifier night scope. Unlike night vision goggles this device did not rely upon infra-red lighting to work well, instead it intensified ambient light. It was intended for viewing at long distance as opposed to close quarters like the infra-red systems. She checked google maps for an Army Surplus Store in Hereford and shortly after breakfast was finished she drove into town.

As she neared where she thought the store should be she couldn't believe her luck, coming towards her but on the opposite side of the road, walking along with a Bergen on his back was a lad matching Ethan's photograph. The traffic was slowing down but there were no parking places on her side of the street.

She needed to turn the car around. She contemplated driving along the right-hand lane past the traffic and cutting down a side-street. Instead she spotted a gap between two cars coming up on the opposite side.

Without thinking to signal she pulled the wheel hard over. The gap was not large enough for her to park in, but she wanted to use it for an emergency three point turn. Unfortunately, she was in such a rush her foot slipped off the clutch and the car mounted the pavement, almost mowing Ethan down.

Ethan's reflexes were given a boost by an unexpected blast from an angry motorist horn just as some crazy woman tried to run him down, and he legged-it off down the street.

Gina desperately wanted to complete her three point turn, but as she threw her gears into reverse whilst winding down the window, she found that the car behind had pulled in too close.

'Ethan! Ethan Best!' she called pointlessly after the fast receding figure.

'You mad bitch!' shouted the driver from behind, 'I almost went into you!'

'You shouldn't have been so close then!' she retorted. 'Back up. I'm in a hurry.'

'Left your curling tongs on the bed have you, *darling*?!'

'Fuck of and do as I say, now, *sir*!'

The last word of forced politeness reframed the perceptions of the angry driver and he reversed, grunting 'Bloody police' through gritted teeth.

Gina shot back down the road, but too late, Ethan was nowhere to be seen. She found a place to park up then walked back again, this time looking into the shops on both sides, but he and his Bergen had vanished into thin air.

'Bollocks!' she turned back towards her car. 'Who does this kid think he is? Bloody Jason Bourne?'

Will sat at his desk staring blindly at the case file in front of him, but wondering how Gina was getting on tracking down her client's son.

He hadn't heard anything from her, but then he didn't expect to. It wasn't like she reported to him; she reported to his uncle.

Then his mind turned to considering the fact that he wasn't wondering how anyone else was getting on with *their* workload. Gina had an attitude that set her aside from the others, a sexy kind of confidence that realistically would not make for an easy relationship, and he began to wonder if in this short space of time he was becoming infatuated with her.

He'd already read her dossier, a couple of times, and she clearly had a lot of skills and experiences, but he couldn't help but feel there was a whole lot more to this woman which he would like to know about.

Nevertheless, he forced himself to focus on the job at hand, a missing person. The client, Roger Walton, did not feel that the police really intended to help, or maybe the circumstances somehow left the police unable to. So he was willing to pay for a private investigation to find out the truth.

The missing person was Jane Newton and she had been reported missing over two months ago. The reason the disappearance had not been in the press, and not investigated beyond initial questioning, was probably because the client had come home to find a *Dear John* letter to explain the disappearance.

The hand writing had checked out as Jane's, as it explained simply that she had been feeling caught in a rut and had now found someone else. The client's brief further described however, that it seemed strange to him that Jane would have taken all of her computer equipment with her and yet left behind a wardrobe full of her clothes.

Because of his concerns he had taken Jane's letter to a handwriting specialist who had said that in comparing the letter with other writing from Jane there was a possibility that the letter may have been written under duress, and therefore added fuel to Roger's theory that Jane may have been abducted.

Will decided it was best to go and visit Roger, and see the flat first hand, even though he was inclined to agree with the police appraisal of the situation.

Even though he did not see this case having a future Will saw that he could, at the very least, see if he could talk Roger out of his downer. Will would keep this intended approach to himself of course. His uncle would not want to see that company time was being spent on offering amateur mental health support whilst letting paid work go unattended. Nevertheless, Will well knew from personal experience that the brain could play funny tricks on a person in attempting to rationalise events and deal with the grief of being rejected.

Gina had quickly returned to her car and then driven round to the bus station in the hope of getting to Ethan before he boarded the bus, but which bus?

Parking up as close as she could to the bus station she went to her boot and switched her black jacket for her green Berghaus Gore-Tex, then went to look at time tables, trying not to rush; trying to avoid attracting attention.

It took five minutes to work out that Ethan would probably be intending to catch the number 39 bus, but the 9:10 was long gone, meaning a wait until 11:40 for the next one.

She sat on a bench away from stand 6, where the 39 would come in, to watch and think. There was no sign of Ethan, though there were a number of people around with rucksacks, none were like his. She considered that he might also be waiting and watching elsewhere so she decided to go look for a café. The one that was closest to the bus station only had a few people in and all of them appeared to be OAPs.

Gina decided not to stop for a coffee because she was sure that Ethan would now be attempting to outsmart her. She doubted that he had the money to afford a train journey, but may have decided to walk along the route of the 39 to catch the bus further along, so she went back to her car and tried to follow the bus route. She referred to the 39's time table and Google

Maps on her phone and headed down Broad Street to join the A465.

She was sure that if Ethan was indeed attempting what she had considered then he could not have got very far. There were set stops for the 39 to check on but there were different routes he could take on foot to get to them for the bus arrival time. If she did not see him on the actual route she would turn back and drive around a bit.

She also decided that Ethan would probably not go much further out than the Tesco at Belmont and if he was there before 11:50, he would likely go to the cafeteria there to wait.

On the way she spotted a McDonalds and pulled in to check it out, but she knew in her gut that, even for a wannabe Jason Bourne, Ethan could not have reached there ahead of her car. There was no sign of him there and she shortly confirmed he was not at Tesco either. She turned back.

She drove around between the bus station and Tesco for a couple of hours using a variety or routes till 12:00, then decided that either Ethan had gone into hiding, possibly to take a later bus, or may even have managed to hitch. She headed back to the Army Surplus to see about the image intensifier.

Ethan kept an eye out for the crazy woman with the Tigra as he headed down the A49 towards the A465. It could just have been an accident, just as it might have been his imagination that he'd heard his name, but after the brush with the law on the waste ground in Birmingham he wasn't taking any chances.

He hadn't long crossed over the River Wye when his hitching paid off and a red Ford Fiesta pulled over. It was a man headed for Swansea. Ethan said he was looking to meet up with some mates at a bunkhouse near Pen y Fan, the man agreed to drop off him at the A470 junction near Merthyr Tydfil but he'd have to hitch again from there, or walk it.

Once the kit was put in the boot and Ethan strapped himself in, they were off.

'So what's your name?' the man asked.

'John Sully,' Ethan replied without hesitation, having been rehearsing a cover story while he hitched.

'Nice to meet you John. I'm Kev Robson.'

'Thanks for the lift Kev.'

'No worries…Do you mind me asking how old you are. You seem quite young to be heading into the Brecon Beacon's alone.'

'Well I won't be alone when we go up Pen y Fan. I'm 17.'

'So why aren't you travelling all together?'

'Me and my friends are from all over.'

'Not from school or college?'

'No, we became friends via Facebook, and most of them will be coming down from up North.'

'Internet friends eh? I didn't have such things in my days. All sounds a bit worrying to me, with what you hear about people on there not being who they say they are.'

'Oh sure, you do need to be careful. I know there are people out there who'd enjoy doing a person over, but I can take care of myself.'

'Well I hope you're right.'

'Oh yes, don't you worry about me…So what are you going to Swansea for?'

'I'm and investigator for the RSPCA.'

'You mean you're a real life Ace Ventura?' Ethan laughed at the thought.

'Not exactly, no. I've never had a case of dognapping. I'm usually involved in gathering evidence on animal cruelty.'

'Like kid's teasing cats?'

'Usually it'll be to do with neglected pets, like dogs left at home crying all day while their owners are away at work, but today I'm investigating pit-bull fighting.'

'Right, but is *that* really cruelty though? I mean, if the dogs didn't want to fight they would stay at opposite sides of the pit wouldn't they? Aren't some animals just natural born killers, being true to themselves?'

'These dogs are usually tormented before they are put into the pit. When they both hear one another barking they respond to the situation as a further threat, but one that they might be able to do something about.'

'What happens to the owners?'

'Not enough. They get fined and the animals taken from them, but then they just get others.'

'Where from?' Ethan didn't remember pit-bulls at Pet Barn.

'Well, it *is* illegal to fight dogs, so all of the breeding and selling of these dogs is an underground activity.'

'So what would *you* like to see happen to the owners?'

'It's not for me to say.'

'But you do have something in mind,' Ethan coaxed.

'Well there is something, yes.'

'Go on, what is it?' Ethan pushed further.

There was a long pause while Kev considered whether he should share his idea, but then he started to think about the pictures of the poor dogs in his case file and said, 'I'd put them down a pit two at a time, to bare-knuckle fight until one of them was dead.'

'That sounds fair, but what would happen to the winner?'

'They would be pitted against the winner of another fight.'

'Would there be a paying audience?'

'Oh no, it wouldn't be for bets like the original bare-knuckle fighting. It would all be about staying alive for another day. And the one who survived the longest of course would become so injured and punch-drunk that in time they *would* fail to survive. All of them would have enough time to think this is what their dogs had been trying to do, stay alive another day.'

'Hell Ace, that's pretty dark for an RSPCA person isn't it?

'I guess, although there are a number of us who do prefer animals to people. The world seems to be going to pot.'

After a moments contemplation of Kev's vivid description, Ethan asked 'What's the weirdest case you've had to deal with?'

'It would have to be the feeding of a massive Burmese Python. The owner claimed not to know it was illegal in the UK to feed pets with live food. I found they were feeding it lambs that they were taking off the hills.'

'But surely that was stealing?'

'Yeah, but get this, they said they thought they had all escaped from a farm so were anybody's.'

'Crazy.'

'One of my colleagues once dealt with a case of a very rich couple who thought it was a neat idea to have their internal door panels fitted with double glazing, only the double glazing was then filled with neon tetras.'

'Neon tetras?'

'Yes, little fish that have neon lights down their sides. They had all died pretty quickly from stress because the only way they could turn around was to swim upside-down back the way they came.'

'Didn't the owners realise, or the person they bought the fish from, mention anything to them?'

'All I can say is loads of money does not guarantee loads of brain cells, and when people have loads of money those who want it don't tend to ask questions.'

'I think too many people see animals as no different to insects. I think we should all be encouraged to treat animals as we would people. I know I do.' Ethan said with a smile.

Jane, Rosie, Tina and Mel received a report from Eleanor that Ethan had been picked up on CCTV getting into a Red Ford Fiesta on the A49 with a large rucksack, and soon both cars made an attempt to catch up with it. However, not wanting to risk getting picked up for speeding, by the time they caught up with Kev, after an extensive length of gratuitous coning, they were just outside Glynneath.

Pulling him over, pretending to be plain clothed police, they asked about Ethan. Kev told them the lad had said his name was John Sully. He had dropped him off at the A470, because he was supposed to be meeting friends at a bunkhouse up in the national park. When Kev had said John seemed such a polite lad and asked what he had done they declined to give details. They thanked him and went on their way.

Doubling back and heading up the A470 they did not see Ethan anywhere, not even at the bunkhouse Kev had heard referred to. This was because, following a quick check of his map after watching Kev go Ethan had headed back up the A465 a little way then turned north, taking his first opportunity to get into the hills, and headed towards Vaynor Common.

The Sit-Rep from outside the bunkhouse ended in some discussion about what Ethan could be doing out here, and Kate joined in with Eleanor, promising to tap into a satellite feed as soon as the cloud cover cleared. In the meantime Kate said she had a hunch that Ethan might be looking to climb Pen y Fan in the next day or so, and so the team were to find somewhere to hide the vehicles and then get up on either side of the peak to wait out for him.

16

Ethan continued on northwards across Vaynor common, but not following a footpath the going was slow because it was rough heather with peat hags in places, and by late afternoon it began to rain to add to the challenge.

He pushed on though, looking for potential shelter in case the weather worsened. The plan forming in his head was to make an ascent of Pen y Fan at night. The western path over the peak was known to be well maintained, with stone steps in places. He thought it unlikely there would be anyone else around at that time. But before he made his ascent he intended to eat and then rest up a while.

Around five o'clock he found a large peat hag which offered shelter under it in the lea of the wind and rain, like a wave of earth with a heather crest. Here he ate some of his cold rations, washing them down with apple juice, before laying out his Gore-Tex waterproof bivvy bag. That done, he decided it was not yet necessary to play it safe with *hard routine* so took a leak straight into a little stream. Returning to his camp he stripped off his waterproofs and shuffled into his sleeping bag. He placed his waterproofs, rolled up, under the bivvy bag as a form of pillow, then tried to get some shut-eye.

Colin Fairfax was a long distance truck driver from Leeds, but he had not set out in life to make a living *on the road*. He was going to be a footballer, once. Like so many other youngsters he had been convinced it would *just happen* and therefore he did not need to make an effort with his school work.

However, he hadn't joined any youth football club either, and as it happened was rarely picked at school when team sides were chosen.

The fact that his near constant kicking of footballs against metal garage doors, at the back of his flats, had not been sufficient to gain him a place in the premier league had bitterly frustrated him. Now, at 48 it didn't occur to him that this deep seated frustration might be why he always got a such kick out of the games he played on the road with his truck; his trusty stead.

He particularly liked playing *duel-carriageway clot*, a game that he knew many other truck drivers played. In fact, unknown to most motorists there were actually league tables.

This game involved pulling out as if to overtake a truck in front, especially when there were cars coming up behind, in order to start a queue. In bringing the cab in line with the other one the speed would be slowed to match. This would then require pretending to invite the other driver to go for a drink at the next services, or to ask directions, by way of hand signals and through the use of Wallace & Gromit style animated lip movements.

It didn't matter what the excuse was, the point was to see if he could get a new record for the number of vehicles stacked up behind. Just imagining their shouts of frustration, and the beating of their steering wheels, titillated him, often making him shift in his seat with excitement.

At the end of duel-carriageways there were arrows which demanded drivers move to the left, and these offered a bonus trick for Colin. He would leave it to the very last minute to slam his breaks on, and then employing the *give-way to the right* rule, would simply drop back and pull in behind the truck he had paralleled, even if there were other vehicles behind.

His high sided truck was excellent for obscuring oncoming road markings as well as road signs, which often meant that the irate drivers behind, who were fully focused on a chance to get past, were often ill-prepared for the quick change in circumstances.

Colin placed little mushroom-cloud stickers to his cab door for each of the accidents his antics had caused. These stickers did of course raise questions from other truckers as to their purpose, which he covered with a shrug saying they were to mark how many Vindaloos his hiatus hernia had survived.

When he was not driving his truck he drove around in his Nissan Skyline, at half the speed limit, again counting the length of the stack he could build, as well as the number of horn blasts he received.

Again it was such a thrill to imagine the anger of the motorists behind as he drove at thirty to forty miles per hour in a sixty zone, in a car that many people would know could do 0-60 in 5 seconds, with a top speed of 190mph. On occasions it made his day when someone from the back of the queue attempted a risky overtake and ended with a total wipe-out.

Colin was not one for washing his car or truck, which was why his number-plates were often difficult to read. As a result he had so far received no visits from the police following up any complaints, so he believed that someone *upstairs* was looking out for him.

It surprised some but not all people to find that Colin not only went to church every Sunday, he was also a member of the Salvation Army. He claimed to be a Christian who was tolerant of all other religions, however, what he could not tolerate were *sinners*.

He was also a member of a local rugby club, but he liked to keep all of his activities separated, so the lads never knew about his work with the *sally army*, and never got invited back to his place for a piss-up.

This was probably wise since another hobby Colin was consumed with was collecting blades. He had over three hundred assorted blades, from swords, daggers and hunting knives, to butchery knives and scalpels.

He had been acquiring these since he was a child, and now had them locked in his basement. The problem was that owning the blades and seeing them lie *unused* was a frustration that he decided, God help him, this needed to be dealt with.

He didn't think it was too much to ask, and prayed to God that the chance would come for him to open up a sinner, maybe just one of course, and just enough to see their darkness within; just enough he thought that they would never mention his hobby to anyone.

He began to put his plan into action by making his house into a honey-trap. He started to leave the front door and windows ajar to attract opportunist burglars.

Hidden under the carpet in the hallway, and by the open windows, he had placed a mass of needles from his diabetes kit standing up like a spear-pit from wooden panels.

Only *he* knew to tread to the sides where the floor was firm and safe. Their tips kept the carpet level with the rest of the floor, showing no sign of their presence underneath, but if trodden on would penetrate the carpet plus the intruder's foot-ware and feet.

This might only have brought about an agonised scream had the needles not been coated with a neuro-toxin derived from the Australian Blue-Ring Octopus, which left its victims totally paralysed but fully conscious, ready for Colin's attentions.

The neuro-toxin was not something a person could simply buy *off the shelf*, and this is where Colin believed the hand of God had acted on his behalf. He had been playing *duel-carriageway clog* next to a foreign truck destined for a medical research centre when everything came together, quite literally.

The arrows were coming up on the road ahead and he was about to brake and pull in when the truck driver to his left, who had not understood his Wallace & Gromit impression, panicked and braked to let him get into the oncoming single lane. Not reacting to this change in game play Colin's own breaking and turning to the left simply brought about a collision with the foreign truck.

The cars behind both of the trucks braked but not quickly enough. As the foreign truck began to jack-knife, those cars which did not plough into the side of it either hit the central reservation barrier or went up the embankment in an effort to avoid crashing. Nevertheless a multiple pile-up ensued.

Colin couldn't believe his luck, he had surpassed himself. As he pulled over just up ahead his inspection of the damage found only a few scratches to his paintwork, while further back down the road the *foreign twat* had managed to turn his vehicle on its side and spilled its goods completely blocking both lanes.

'That'll teach you to play silly buggers with me,' Colin said as he went for a closer look.

He found a mixture of boxes and containers of liquid, many of which carried warning signs. One labelled *Neuro-Toxin highly dangerous* caught his eye.

'I'll have some of that, as payback for the paintwork, you fuckwit,' he called across to the unconscious driver draped through his windscreen.

Colin used the Internet that evening to check out what he had acquired, and started to get ideas for his anti-intruder traps. But first he had wanted to be sure of what the toxin did, so he put some on one of his needles and pricked the neighbour's cat, which was always coming to shit in his vegetable patch.

Pickles, the big tomcat, had been full of energy one minute, weaving its figure of eight round Colin's legs, the next minute he was out cold. Its breathing was very shallow, but it was still alive. It was still lying there by the rhubarb when Colin came back, then next morning.

That day his skinflint neighbour who was known to raid skips and forage for food had asked if he had seen Pickles. Colin had said that it was often coming into his garden so he would go and check. He soon handed its cold limp form back to his neighbour, telling her that it looked as if it might have had a heart attack or something.

Unknown to Colin, what happened next was that his neighbour, in floods of tears, assuming the cat dead, went to the bottom of her garden and buried it alive.

Eager to catch an opportunist thief or some other uninvited visitor, Colin wanted to hedge his bets anyway he could. It was his hope that some of his irate drivers would follow him home to exact their revenge.

Nevertheless, as weeks passed by and nobody took the bait of Colin's *open-door policy*, his disappointment grew more intense.

He was frustrated that he was not getting a *sinner* to practise on with his knives. Eventually, he started looking for alternative entertainment materials on the Internet, hoping to satisfy his cutting fantasies. It was this that led him to what was on offer through the Dark Net.

He had no second thoughts about investing in the software required to view the embedded materials. He was soon enjoying the thrills of real live torture of what he convinced himself were whores, and women drivers, reaping what they had sewn.

Nevertheless, after his third evening of entertainment, which had shown an elderly woman in an operating theatre undergoing amputation without anaesthetic, something unseen was set in motion.

Late the following evening, a black van had pulled up outside his house and immediately disgorged four black clad troopers. They had gone straight over the garden wall, not chancing the gate in case it squeaked, and while two waited at the front the other two went round to the back door.

The front door was seen to be open and this was reported back to control. It was thought possible that Colin had either just popped out, or simply had not shut his door properly, but the decision was made to proceed. Once the two troopers at the back of the house had the kitchen door's lock picked the *go* sign was given. They pulled down their night vision goggles and went in, raising their suppressed HK MP7A2 submachine guns, safeties off.

The first trooper to take the front door yelped into her gasmask as she went inside, and tumbled forwards. The second trooper caught sight of the carpet lifting, stuck to the other's boot, but was unable to prevent herself from stumbling over her. The call went out, 'Trap! Girl down.' but it was all a little too late.

The troopers in the hallway had landed on a pressure sensor, also hidden beneath the carpet, but they did not hear the alarm that was raised. It was alerting Colin via his phone, on vibrate.

The troopers at the back had their own surprise to deal with, when the kitchen door swung open to trigger strobe lights, which were not unlike modern-day flash-bang grenades.

However the girls had received their own special forces training including drills in their own *killing house.* They almost instantly recovered from the visual onslaught with heightened alertness, as the *trap* warning came through on their earpieces.

Behind the kitchen door had been attached an air freshener, which when switched on and then activated by the door opening diffused a squirt of its liquid content. Colin had switched its scent for his neuro-toxin. He had not risked trying it out as he had with the needle, worried that he might inhale it himself, though he was pretty sure that once it got absorbed through the lung tissues it would have the same impact as the needles.

Unfortunately for this security measure the troopers each wore gasmasks, and with the kitchen clear they were straight through to the hallway.

The downed trooper was left where she fell. It was standard operating procedure to call it in but push on. The downstairs rooms were cleared, but the process was now much slower than preferred as the troopers were mindful of traps in the interior. The cupboard under the stairs was inspected and found to contain a Dyson, a stack of shoes, and the mains circuit breaker. The power was turned off.

Heading up the stairs the lead trooper tested each step with the suppressor of her weapon while given cover by the other two following up. The bathroom and three bedrooms were each cleared in turn, looking under each bed, and in the cupboards. There was no sign of Colin, maybe he was outside, the team leader reported in her next Sit-Rep.

Their van driver was ordered to check out the garden, joined by one of the three from inside the house. Acknowledging her order the driver pulled on a mask, pulled up her hood, put on her night vision goggles and helmet then grabbed her weapon. Stepping over the wall to join the trooper now coming out of the front door the driver wondered whether the garden might be mined, or set with trip-wires, and trod with care as they both moved around to the back garden.

Inside the house the team leader was quite conscious that things didn't add up. Not only was there no sign of Colin, there was no sign of his computer or other associated possessions expected to be located on these raids.

The two troopers returned to the cupboard under the stairs, still weary of trip-wires. The vacuum cleaner was removed then the shoe rack. Sticking her head inside, the team leader saw a collapsible ladder then looking up spotted a catch on the ceiling. She lifted the carpet to reveal a trap door which hinged up against the underside of the stairs, to be held in position by the catch. Looking inside the hatch she realised the collapsible ladder was required to descend, and soon descended to inspect what was down there.

Since Colin could not pull the trap door down *and* put the Dyson on top of it he was clearly not expected to be in the basement, nevertheless caution was maintained for what *might* be found there.

'Come and see this,' the team leader called to her associate.

The trooper on her knees at the cupboard floor attempting to provide cover with her muzzle through the hatch, though unable to see much, descended into the basement. It was no less than a museum of knives, glinting green in the infra-red glow. The basement was also found to contain a computer workspace, and what was clearly intended to be a torture workspace, where in one corner of the room sat a dentist's chair, in its own little hose-down area.

Colin had been convinced he was going to be spotted hiding in the airing cupboard when one of the trespassers had looked in, but his bolt-hole, a box made to look like a large pile of blankets, had done its job.

Listening intently he thought he had heard them all go back downstairs. One sounded like they had gone outside, while two seemed to have found his basement. That was both bad and good news for him.

He hadn't expected a *gang* to turn up, or that any would survive his devices. He certainly had not expected his secret basement to be found so easily, but since they were down there he intended to make that work in his favour.

Quietly climbing out of the box, already feeling a little stiffened by its confines, Colin took out his flick-knife and moved downstairs, treading soundlessly on the lower rail of the banister and the skirting board on the opposite side, using the top rail of the banister to control his descent.

Once in the hallway he went to the cupboard under the stairs and closed the hatch, locking it. Then all hell seemed to break loose. He didn't expect the immediate buzz of suppressed bullets to rip through from below. None hit him, as they went on through the stairs and came up through the hallway carpet, but he felt splinters bite into his face and the backs of his legs as he leaped aside leaving the cupboard unlocked.

Avoiding the kitchen in case there were still traces of the neuro-toxin spray suspended in there, he turned to the front door. Only then did he take notice of what looked like an unconscious trooper and stopped there for a moment, confused.

'Who the fuck are these people?!' It looked like the SAS. None of them wore police markings. He didn't recall obstructing any military convoys, but then didn't the SAS drive round in unmarked vehicles?

No time to figure it all out there and then he ran into the front garden. Seeing the black van that half blocked his gated driveway, making a getaway with his Skyline out of the question, he wondered whether the van itself could make a ready means of escape. But then he worried that he might find more soldiers inside. There was nothing for it he decided, he was going to have to go down the street and maybe hide in a neighbour's garden till things cooled off.

The garden gate squealed painfully as he opened it.

'Stop!' a voice warned him from the path that led around his garage.

It sounded like a woman, and this did not instil any *submission to authority* from Colin.

Instead it brought out a rage. Rather than pushing on with his escape plan, he turned and ran at the two troopers, roaring like he thought he was the Hulk.

He came at them so fast and hard that only one of the troopers got a round off, which missed him by a millimetre and put a hole in the van. He took them both down and as they scrambled to recover and grab him he went to work with his knife. He soon discovered how difficult it was for his very keen flick-knife to penetrate their Kevlar.

Then just as one trooper grabbed him from behind to pull him off the one he had climbed onto, he managed to stick his blade deep into the prone woman's throat, thus instigating the trooper's *non-return policy*.

The two troopers from the basement had just shot their way out of the cupboard and leaped over their fallen associate in time to see the extraction target attempt to kill the two troopers on his side path. At the moment the blade thrust forward he was awarded a double tap, which sprayed blood and brain matter onto the wall behind him.

The mission had been recovered, but it was no less a shambles. The neighbourhood had now become aware of the noises, and now lights were being switched on. Quickly the team leader stripped off her mask and goggles and went to the van. She drew out blue lights and placed them on the cab roof setting them flashing, hoping that this might gain them a few extra minutes, but they couldn't be there when police did arrive, as no doubt they would.

The second girl down was coughing on blood as the driver tried to stem the flow with a pad from her medical pack whilst sitting her up and forwards. Another trooper was inspecting and reporting on the first girl down. Returning from the van the team leader brought a body bag and stowed her kill.

Shortly the team leader closed the door to the house, switched off the blue lights and stowed them, then they were off. In the back were: Colin's body, his two downed troopers, his computer kit, and the container of neuro-toxin from the basement. It was hoped it might help inform the medical centre back at The Clinic on appropriate treatment.

However, three needles having penetrated the trooper's foot, their payload of toxin coupled with the distance back to base did not work in her favour. Before they had even reached the M1 she had died.

David sat with his back to the bathroom door shaking, and bleeding from his gums and lips where he had torn the bath plug chain loose. He had attempted to lose it down the toilet, but the chain had proven too heavy for the water to flush away. There was nothing more he could do with stumps for knees and elbows. The treatment he was receiving was simply barbaric, he would have enjoyed watching it all being done to someone else, but he just couldn't cope with it being done to him.

He kept expecting to lose his upper limbs next, but instead the nurses seemed intent on playing games with him now that he could not put up much of a fight.

His stumps were so painful without pain-killers that every movement was like he was being set on fire, whenever he attempted to scramble away. The nurses would laugh as they caught up with him.

There was a sick wickedness in them that he recognised in himself. How was it, he wondered, that they were given free reign, and in a *hospital*? He had to escape, but had no idea how. He did not know enough about where he was to act on any opportunity of escape. Now he felt crippled physically and mentally. He felt different now. It made him so angry, being so helpless.

He heard someone entering his room. He tried to control his breathing, pressing harder against the door. He could not lock it.

'David?'

He held his breath and almost immediately heard the door handle on the other side turn above his head and felt a pressure on the door.

'He's in here,' said the nurse.

'Are you okay David?' the second nurse enquired, her tone a caring one. 'We've come to change your dressings.'

'You don't want to let gangrene set in,' the other added. 'You know what happens then.'

Together the nurses forced their way in, shoving David aside and causing him to cry out. Suddenly he began flailing about, overcome with rage.

'Oh dear, that's no good. Are we getting all hot and bothered again?'

'Shall we run another cool bath?'

The nurses looked at one another knowingly and smiled.

17

Ethan stirred in his warm cocoon and realised it had stopped raining. Unzipping his bivvy bag enough to look out, he saw it was a full moon. He couldn't believe his luck.

'Ideal,' he whispered, and made to break camp quickly and quietly.

The need to be quiet was self-imposed as part of what Ethan now considered his personal training in evasion. His mission was to bag Pen y Fan and then move east to Fan y Big before daybreak. Fan y Big made him laugh and wonder who came up with these names. He looked at his G-Shock and it had just turned 23:00. He considered it tight for time, but doable.

Before he moved out he checked his bearing with the compass and map and headed first towards Craig fan Ddu which he could see by the map was going to lead to a sharp steep ridge before he could join the main tourist route up to Pen y Fan. The going was not as easy as he imagined, even with the moonlight, the ground seemed rougher than it had from a distance in daylight, having lots of deep shadows because the moon was low in the sky. On a couple of occasions he tripped but recovered his balance. It was a challenge not to swear at the dumb rocks and hummocks of earth.

When he reached the ridge at Rhiw yr Ysgyfarnog, which he had found quite unpronounceable, the southwest side seemed surprisingly steep, while the northeast side was more disturbing because he couldn't see much with it being in shadow. He slowed right down, watching his footing.

He hadn't long joined the main footpath, with only half a mile to go before the summit, when he thought he heard rocks falling to the left. He stopped and looked but saw nothing on the ridge to the northwest. Deciding it was probably sheep he pressed on.

It was almost 1:00 in the morning when he reached what he had expected to be a standard concrete triangulation point on his map. Instead he had discovered a small cairn with a slab of rock displaying the National Trust emblem and the name and height of the peak, 886M.

He touched the sloped edges of the slab's top, as if he was expecting to receive a computer-gamers power-up. He took a rest, removing his pack to take a well-earned drink, finishing the last of his apple juice.

It occurred to him that these Brecon Beacons seemed a lot easier going than he would have expected for SAS selection terrain, and what with the number of deaths that had happened in the area he had to question whether the place was dangerously deceptive.

He also wondered if those on selection were expected to come up steeper more difficult routes. He hadn't managed to find the selection course route online. Though there was one that claimed to be, but just didn't look authentic to him.

He thought he could hear movement again, and peered down the path he had just come up.

He was surprised to see two figures coming up. They were dressed in black and he wondered if they might be SAS, but they were not carrying packs which he would have expected.

As he waited for them to arrive he wondered what he could say to two troopers in the middle of the night on Pen y Fan that might sound cool.

As they got closer he could make out that they were wearing night vision goggles, and frowned because he had thought they only wore those on a job.

Then he noticed that one of them was removing something from a side pocket. He could have been mistaken in the moonlight, but it looked like a syringe. What were they going to do with that? Did doping go on in the SAS as well as sport? Ethan was too swept up in his hero-worship of the SAS to register any threat.

Suddenly the two troopers stopped. They turned away to look to their left, towards the north ridge. One spoke, 'Say again?'

'Women?' Ethan muttered, and powered by his recent paranoia he grabbed up his Bergen and swung it over his right shoulder and was trying to get his other arm through the strap whilst stumbling off along the southwest ridge that he had intended to take down off Pen y Fan. He couldn't afford to take his time now, but he couldn't afford to rush either.

Suddenly he slipped, twisted his ankle and fell into the darkness to the left. If it wasn't for his Bergen he could have fallen further, possibly to his death but his pack got wedged in a small dry stream gully, holding him like a tortoise stranded upside-down.

He quickly released himself from the pack. Biting back the pain in his ankle, trying not to make any more sound he looked around and then back up to the peak. He tried to think how he was going to get away now.

It occurred to him, that there in shadow, if he kept really still behind his pack he might actually be safe even from night vision goggles, at least until first light. The two women were not coming after him. As he watched, they now seemed to be fully distracted by the appearance of a third person.

Tina and Jane had not expected anyone other than Ethan and their team to be up on Pen y Fan. Thanks to the clear sky and the satellite feed everything was going to plan, until control informed them that a sixth figure had appeared out of nowhere. Since teleportation was still science fiction they had to assume that this person had been under a reflective sheet, to hide their heat signature.

As this figure approached, it was clear they were female, but clearly not one of theirs, and instead of heading for the cairn she was heading for them, fast. *No worries* they thought as Jane raised the syringe again. However, as Jane stepped forward to put the needle into this unknown red-head she blocked her, planting a boot between her legs immediately followed up with a palm-heel strike under her chin, which knocked her out cold and she dropped backwards, narrowly missing opening her skull on a sharp rock.

Tina tried to deal with this threat to their mission by lunging at the woman, but her leg was still sore from the slip in Abby Carlton's basement, which worked against her. As she punched out she found herself gripped by the wrist pulled onto the woman's back, twisted over and thrown off the hip to land badly on both her knees.

'Fucking bitch!' Tina roared trying to grab a leg but instead received a boot, to the side of her head and the lights went out.

Gina had been aware that there were a further two figures on this peak that appeared to have gone into hiding along the Craig Cwm Sere ridge. Now she was concerned for Ethan again as whomever these people were that was the direction he had fled, but she could see no one now.

Moving carefully off the summit, unsure how long the two women above would remain unconscious, she called out in a loud whisper, 'Ethan?'

Looking to both sides of the ridge as well as further down it, she thought she saw movement in the shadows to her left and descended from the ridge to investigate. She found Ethan lying in shadow.

'Ethan,' she tried to rouse him but his body remained still.

'Too late,' a voice whispered from her right, followed by a needle to Gina's thigh from the left, as two women rose from behind long grass either side of the gully.

Gina struck her left hand backwards across her thigh as she straightened up, knocking the syringe out and clattering down amongst the rocks. Then she followed up with a knife-hand strike with her right into the woman's throat, knocking her backwards gagging.

The other woman grabbed Gina from behind with a firm arm around her throat. Gina tried an elbow strike to the assailant's ribs but struck body armour, then dropped as far as the strangle hold would allow and twisting her torso in the opposite direction she delivered a left elbow strike up and into the woman's groin.

However, even as the woman cried out and bent forwards, loosening her grip on Gina's throat there was no stopping the attack. She twisted back again to plant her knuckles into the side of the woman's right thigh, deadening it and making her fall away to the side, cursing.

Quickly Gina stood up and stepped towards Ethan. There was nothing for it, she was going to have to pick him up and carry him out of there, but it was as if she had got up too fast and felt herself falling forwards in a faint.

Jane came back round to the sound of Eleanor in her right ear. 'Jane, get up, you need to go help Rosie and Mel.'

'Uh?...Where are they?' She sat up, straightening her goggles.

'To the southwest of your position,' Eleanor directed.

'Right okay,' she complied, getting back onto her feet. 'Tina is down.'

'I know, just help the other two to deal with that unknown person.'

'Will do.'

Carefully moving over the turf and gravel down to her colleagues Jane saw the unknown person putting up quite a fight ahead of her, before collapsing on top of Ethan's body. As she reached them, Rosie and Mel were dragging the unconscious figure aside, where she joined them in giving the woman a kicking to remember them by.

'Both are secured now,' Jane gave the Sit-Rep. 'What do you want us to do with this woman?'

Kate's voice replaced Eleanor's. 'Check her for ID.'

Jane searched Gina's crumpled form, but found nothing. 'She's in her thirties I'd guess, but has no ID on her.'

'Okay, bring them both in.'

The next morning, awaiting the return of her team and their acquisitions from the Brecon Beacons, Kate sat in her office looking across her desk at Peter. 'So, how do you feel Mr Trent?'

'Different.'

'How so?'

'A bit numb…empty to be honest,' he shrugged his shoulders.

'Part of that will be exhaustion. It has been an intensive course of treatment.'

'Tell me about it. It seems such a simple thing to do, and yet, somehow it has removed my interest in torture. Wouldn't it have happened in time anyway though, as I watched more of the video's?'

'It would seem not. Simply watching such materials, certainly if you have a propensity for arousal when viewing them, it typically further habituates the activity and need. Whereas the writing task; the expression of desires, as a form of art therapy coupled with low boredom threshold can, as I told you at induction, rewire the brain at an emotional level.'

'So am I free to go then?'

'Not exactly free…You will be kept under *observation*. You are not permitted to speak to anyone of what we have achieved here. Treat this demand like the official secrets act.'

'But why? If you can help people deal with such addiction to experiences of this nature, the whole world should know.'

'Thank you for the complement and confidence in The Clinic, but we will continue to manage *very tightly* how we work. In fact if you *are* found to be talking to other people about your experience here, you *will* be brought back, and Phase Three with be used to bring about a change of mind more acceptable to *us*.'

'So what does Phase Three involve?'

'You don't need to know. You just need to forget your time here. Put it behind you. Get on with your life.'

'So you're just going to take me home, and *that's it*? What do you expect me to tell people about my absence?'

'You can tell anyone who asks that you had an accident involving a head injury and have been in a coma. You were carrying no identification when admitted to hospital so nobody was able to inform next of kin.'

'What if I feel I need to get back in touch?'

'Let's hope for your sake it doesn't come to that Peter,' Kate nodded to the nurse behind him.

'But what if…' The needle went in and his knees buckled.

That afternoon the team from the Brecon Beacons returned looking the worse for wear and the two body bags on gurneys were wheeled into the operating theatre for inspection.

Notified of their arrival by Eleanor, Kate was there to inspect the long awaited catch. Unzipping the bag containing Ethan first, Kate almost smiled, 'That's him…Get him cleaned up and taken to Phase Two.' Then she turned to the other gurney and drew the zip down on the mystery body.

The girls all saw a shocked look come over Kate they had never seen before.

'Shit! It's Agent Orange!' Kate gasped, taking a step backwards. 'Get her out of here!'

'Phase Two?' Tina asked.

'No!' Kate stepped forwards and zipped the bag back up quickly.

'Phase Three?' Tina ventured more hopefully.

'No, no! Get her out of here, as quick as you can.'

'Who is she?' asked Rosie.

'Agent Orange is Ex-MI5.'

'So you want us to put her back up on Pen y Fan?' Jane sounded ridiculous.

'Just get her well away from here. *Things* happen around this woman.'

The girls turned to look at one another, wondering why Kate suddenly seemed to be acting almost superstitious.

Jane made the first move and took hold of the gurney. She had an idea what to do, and thought in Kate's state of mind she probably didn't need to know the details, but it *would* need someone else's attention.

Pauline had a room set to one side of the kitchens for her butchery. As she sharpened her tools again she walked around what lay upon her table. There were no legs or arms, just torso and head. Having said that, the head no longer contained teeth or eyes, and the torso had undergone a double mastectomy.

Most people had suffered heart failure well before this point in the process, so they were generally speaking dead by now. Occasionally people did make it this far alive, holding on to their fantasies of revenge, but this only served to heighten Pauline's own pleasure as she brought about what she liked to refer to as their final *disorganisation*.

'My you are a tough old bird.'

18

Gina woke up feeling groggy and aching all over. There was a salty smell in the air. She tried to get up but banged her head. Her knees were bent and her lower legs were raised. It was as if she had fallen between seats in a dark place. She tried to make sense of her position, and remember what had happened.

She felt around her and was sure she could hear voices carried on the wind from some way away. Then as she more carefully righted herself she became aware of a slight rocking motion. Her intuition told her she was on a boat. Memories of the *Wave Forge* came back to her and she was seized by a desperate need to get out.

There was a waterproof cover tied down on all edges. She felt her pockets for a knife, but she had nothing on her. She remembered leaving all her kit in a hurry on the side of Pen y Fan.

There was nothing for it, she began pushing on the tarpaulin and shouting. Shortly she heard French voices sounding alarmed, saying something that sounded like *'immigré stupide'*. They went away possibly to get help.

Quite some time later people returned and began tugging at the tarpaulin rope. When she got to see the light of day, she found she was facing a channel ferry Captain and his security officer.

When Ethan came around he tried to figure out where he was. He was on a bed, wearing hand-cuffs and what looked like a hospital gown; His clothes and kit gone. He appeared to be in a padded room with windows.

Limping across to them he found them all to be fitted panes. There would be no way of getting fresh air in, or him out. They looked out on a big lawn with woods at the back. There was no sign of anyone out there, not even a road or a path, just a rabbit.

Ethan would normally have considered things he could have done to amuse himself with the rabbit, this time his imagination was engaged with more serious matters.

He turned his attention to the door. There was no handle and when he tried to get a grip on the padding at the edge and pull he had to conclude it was locked.

He turned around and his attention was taken by the chair at the desk. Grabbing it and lifting it above his head, attempting a fast limp he rushed at the windows and threw it with all his might at the largest one. It made a loud bang but bounced off.

It was coincidence that the bang covered the sound of the door opening.

'If you're quite finished Ethan…' said Eleanor.

He whipped his head round.

'…We shall begin your induction.'

Ethan did his best to charge at Eleanor roaring like a wild animal, but she side-stepped at the last moment and then he was out of the door, but not free. His bandaged ankle gave and he crashed into the opposite wall of the corridor thanks to a well-placed foot from a waiting nurse. Turning, he placed his back against the wall and drew his leg in to his chest giving an extended series of pain-filled gasps, sucking the air between his teeth.

'Who do you think you are,' asked the nurse devoid of sympathy, yet smiling, 'Peter Griffin?'

'It's my bad *ankle*!' he almost cried.

Deciding that they would have to use the wheelchair, Eleanor helped the nurse secure Ethan into the chair then wheeled him to Kate's office.

Along the way Ethan attempted to take in as much of his surroundings as possible. He considered that the place looked more like a hospital than it did a police station. He was distracted from his observations however when the nurse guiding his chair banged his injured foot into Kate's door, in the process of opening it.

'Hello Ethan. I'm glad you could finally join us,' Kate greeted.

'Who are you people? You're not police.'

'Very astute of you Ethan...Sorry about our little ruse,' she smiled. 'You are in *The Clinic*, and we are here to make your stay an *interesting* one.'

Eleanor laughed.

Ethan turned to look over his shoulder. 'If you hadn't made out you were police I probably wouldn't have thrown that rock.'

'Yes well, Clare is still in a coma,' said Kate.

'*Really*?' Ethan sounded impressed.

'But that's not the reason you are here.'

Ethan's eyes seemed to search for a reason. 'That guy in the warehouse was suicide. I was only there checking out my traps and happened to have my video with me.'

'I don't know anything about that Ethan.'

'Well what then?' He began to wonder if this had actually got something to do with Bertie.

'Let's say I have plans for you.'

'Which are?'

'You will find out in due course, depending on how well you do with your treatment.'

'I don't need *treatment*. I want to go home. My parents must be worried.'

'Yes they must be. But I would have assumed you have already given them years of worry, so a little more won't hurt.'

'What are you going to do?'

'It's what *you* are going to do.'

'You're not making me do anything. I know my rights.'

Kate pointed out of the window. 'The windows of The Clinic are mirrored so no one on the outside can ever see what goes on in here. And do you see down our gravel drive, those nice big security gates?'

'What of em?'

'Well your rights are just out on the road, waiting for you.'

'Bitch.'

'I've been called worse. Now today we are going to start you on writing therapy.'

'*Writing*? I can't be *arsed* with that.'

'Oh go on give it a go. I want to see how dark your thoughts are.'

'Ha…Darker than you can imagine lady.'

'I'll have to see then won't I.'

'Yeah you will. I'm going to write down exactly what I'm going to do to you bunch of mothers.'

Will finally confirmed with his client Roger a time to meet about the *missing* girlfriend Jane, who had dumped Roger for someone else, a couple of months ago.

For someone desperate for *the truth* Will's client was a difficult person to nail down. It still felt like a foregone conclusion but he had to go through the motions.

So he arrived at the address he had been given and rang the bell. There was no answer. He rang again a few minutes later in case Roger had been on the loo when he rang the first time, and just maybe had then promptly forgotten that the doorbell had rung.

With still no answer Will lifted his hands in the air and shook them, then in a ghostly voice he said, 'Oh, maybe he's been abducted too.' Switching to another silly voice he continued, 'It's no joke. They've taken my girlfriend away, and I really *really* love her, and I…'

Will almost jumped out of his skin as a gasping voice came from directly behind him, 'Sorry I'm late. Taking an afternoon off I still had to get things straight before I could leave the office.'

'I didn't hear you coming.'

'No? Maybe 'cos I've had my shoes resoled.'

'Right,' Will didn't sound convinced but stepped aside to let Roger get his key in the door. 'New lock?'

'No?' Roger seemed surprised by the question.

'So you haven't changed your locks in case the people you believe took your girlfriend come back?'

'Would they do that?'

'Who knows?'

'What if Jane manages to escape and gets back only to find I've changed the locks?'

'I expect she would assume you had done that in response to her letter.'

'Oh right.'

'Let me look at the door,' said Will as he followed Roger inside. 'Mmm…No sign of forced entry through *this* door…Either they would have come in another way, or Jane *let* them in.'

'The police already checked for forced entry and said that there had been none.'

'None that *they* could detect,' corrected Will.

'Right. None that *they* could detect.' Roger repeated, beginning to sound hopeful that here was *someone* who might actually fight his corner.

'How much have you moved,' Will gestured with his finger, 'since you first found her gone?'

'Oh a few things here and there, what with house work and all, when I can manage the time.'

'And was there sign of a struggle or things out of place when she was gone?'

'Not a struggle so much as her computer equipment missing, as I said to the police.'

'Okay, can you take me through each room and point out things of hers which have been left behind, please?'

Roger pointed out a print hanging on the wall in the hall. Deciding it was ghastly and saying so, Will discounted the fact it was left behind as irrelevant.

In the lounge there were pictures of Roger and Jane on holiday, and at a Christmas party, pictures she also would not want to take if she was done with him. Then he noticed a photo of an old couple.

'Your parents?' Will hazarded a guess.

'No. It's hers actually.'

'Oh. I take it she had others?'

'No…she wasn't fostered was she?'

'Other photos of them,' Will pointed.

'Oh. Not that I was aware of. Maybe in an album, but I doubt that because I never saw her with an album, and to be honest I don't think she got on well with her parents.'

'Okay, so it might not be relevant that she left that behind *either* then.'

Through into the kitchen Roger pointed at the coffee percolator. 'That was a leaving gift from her last job. It's one of those *really* expensive brands, but amazingly this one *actually* makes a pretty good cup, with the right beans of course. She even brought it on holiday with us once because she did not trust hotel coffee.'

'Yeah well hotel coffee at best is only bitter hot *stain* isn't it. If it wasn't for milk there'd be no goodness there at all.'

'I'm not sure Jane was into goodness then,' Roger joked. 'She used to say she liked coffee and tea as dark as her men.'

Will was led upstairs. The bathroom had all of Jane's toiletries still in place, which seemed a bit odd. Then in the main bedroom there were Jane's clothes in the cupboard and draws.

'Was Jane the sort of girl who couldn't cope with wearing size 20 because she saw herself as a size 10?'

'No.' Roger frowned, confused by the question. 'She was, *is*, as size 14.'

'So, it wasn't size that was a reason to leave these behind,' Will said, checking a few labels and confirming they were as Roger said, only size 14s. 'Maybe they were a few weeks out of date.'

'Oh I don't know about that.'

'Me neither…Did you buy her clothes?'

'Never, well, did it once. She binned it I believe, so never again. She's quite a strong minded person. Knows what she likes.'

Will noticed a load of jewellery on the dressing table and assumed it was not Roger's, so that seemed an odd thing to leave behind, being easy enough to pick up even if in a hurry.

He pointed at the jewellery, but predicted a similar response to what had been said of the clothes, 'So what about the sex?'

'What?' Roger gasped.

'Sorry, just trying to ease you into the more difficult questions now, to get a better understanding of the missing person. How many times did you do it?'

'Two or three times…' Roger gulped, his throat suddenly dry, his face turning red. He was feeling so flustered by the intrusive questions, and the images they stirred up, that he omitted to qualify *a week*.

'Well that could be her reason for going Roger. You see, despite what people say about men needing it more than women, there's been shown to be no difference between the genders, and some women need it more than the men they are with. I think she just needed it more, don't you? And found someone who satisfied her.'

'Oh…' Roger half sobbed and sat on the corner of the bed to deal with Will's bluntness with the possible truth.

'Sorry Roger. It is a rather unromantic world we live in. Society has come to realise that everything is up for grabs, so the takers win it all.'

'You know, she went through a phase where she wanted to beat me with a stick.'

'No I didn't know that.' Will made it sound as if he was someone who was supposed to have known Roger for years. However, it came across as insincere and he made a mental note that he needed to work on that.

'It turned me off. So we stopped with all that.'

'Don't blame you,' Will had a thought. 'When did Jane get this computer kit she took with her?'

A look of dawning came across Roger's eyes. 'Actually, come to think of it, it wasn't long after she stopped beating me. But she said it was for work.'

'What does she do?'

'She's a nurse.'

'Are you sure?'

'Yes. The hospital rang a few times the first week to ask why she hadn't come in. I made excuses for her at first, but by the end of the week I told the matron she was missing.'

'How did she take that?'

'It was the oddest thing. I'm not sure I remember her exact words but it was something like *that's strange, another one.*'

At that moment Will's mobile rang, and checking the caller ID, it was Gina. 'Excuse me Roger I just need to take this.'

Roger nodded and put his head in his hands.

'You are where?...Did you find the lad?...You've been *abducted*?'

Roger looked up and he and Will just stared at one another in disbelief, the world had gone mad.

Gina felt like a down-and-out as she made her way into the city. She had suggested to Will that he order her a train ticket from Dover Priory to get her to Pentre-Bach station in Merthyr Tydfil. When he asked why she explained that she had to return to the scene of crime and check Pen y Fan for clues as to her abductors. He had said that he didn't think his Uncle Tom would sign off for rail fare, so she was to hold tight, he was driving down for her.

The problem, as Gina saw it, was it was a good four hours till he arrived and then another six to get back to the Brecon Beacons, by which time the evidence could have been taken or tampered with by tourists. Nevertheless, she waited for Will.

She cursed herself for not keeping her purse in her trouser pocket, only it was uncomfortable there in that sleeping bag in her observation post. Now her stomach was uncomfortably hungry.

She wandered around the supermarkets checking for free tasters at the bakery and delicatessen counters, but came away disappointed.

The looks she was getting from people weren't exactly helping. Even though she had taken the time to clean herself up on the ferry back to England, her general posture, and the condition of her face gave an indication that she now possessed some broken ribs. That was in addition to a fat lip and black eye, not to mention an assortment of cuts and bruises on her arms and legs from the kicking she had taken on Pen y Fan.

The ferry Captain had urged her to go to the hospital and said he would be calling the police, but Gina had said not to bother them, she was with MI5 and this was not a local issue but national security. They would handle it, but thanks for his concern.

19

'What the hell happened to *you*?!' exclaimed Will as Gina slumped into the passenger seat and put her head back closing her eyes for a moment, grimacing with the pain from her ribs.

'Did you bring any food?'

'No,' he realised he'd been thoughtless, again.

'Thanks Will.'

'Hey, I got here as soon as I could.'

'Right well,' she said opening her eyes to look down the road, 'we need to go get some supplies, food and medication, and then we need to get over to Wales ASAP.'

'Right.'

'Once I've had a rest I'll try and explain.'

Gina gasped as she pulled the seatbelt round and clicked it home.

'You okay?'

'Did you say it was a degree you did at university?'

'I'll take that as a yes then.' Will put the Astra in gear, checked his mirror and pulled away, thinking he'd never expected his degree in criminology was going to lead to a case that was this exciting. Then he told himself to calm down that he was behaving like a kid when in fact he was a year older than Gina. He'd checked.

David struggled as the nurses moved him from the constraints of the gurney.

'No more amputation,' he demanded, at a loss what else to do or say, but his voice betrayed the fact that his spirit was still not broken.

'No not today, David,' said Monica. 'I'm just going to take a look at the damage you have done to yourself. It would seem that you have not been looking after your teeth lately, and we can't have that, can we.'

The nurses strapped him firmly into a dentist chair.

'No!' he struggled pathetically. 'Leave my teeth!'

As Monica lifted a spring device that was clearly intended to keep the jaws apart, David clamped his jaws shut, biting back on the pain of his cracked teeth and torn gums.

The staff made no attempt to force his jaw open. The jaw muscles were the strongest in the body though there was a pressure point at the back of the jaw which could loosen the muscles.

'We haven't got all day David, and you do have a full set of teeth to remove.'

David shook his head, moaning, with his eyes tightly closed.

'I promise I won't be sticking you with any nasty needles,' Monica said stifling a laugh.

David continued to clamp his jaw closed.

Monica looked at the nurse behind David and with a knowing smile, having been here dozens of times before. 'Would you like some *inducement*, David?'

A leather ligature was swung in front of him, matching marks he already carried round his neck.

Heading east on the M4 Gina woke with a start and a snort.

'Lovely bedside manner dear.'

'What?' She looked around bleary-eyed to work out where she was. 'Oh.'

From his peripheral vision Will watched her rub her sore face. 'Was that a good nap?'

'As good as I can expect right now I guess…,' she sighed. 'I nearly had him Will. I was so close.'

'So what happened?'

'Do you want the long version or the short version?'

'Let's start with the short version.'

'Okay, I fell on top of him and blacked out.'

'Excellent summary,' he laughed, wondering whether that was payback for his earlier quip. 'I see I'll be needing that extended version then.'

'The police had responded to a call from Mrs Best that her son was missing. They interviewed her and took Ethan's computer, video equipment and phone away, but found nothing to suggest where he was. They presumed he had headed to London.

'Not satisfied, Mrs Best contacted DNA on the suggestion of DI Dunn and asked for me to help. But as it turned out, I had to interview Mr Best because by the time I got there Mrs Best was in hospital with Piranha injuries.'

'*Piranha injuries*?!'

'Yes it would seem Ethan likes to keep exotic pets. I say keep in the loosest sense. I have my suspicions he enjoys animal cruelty.'

'So a sick little bugger then.'

'Not so little. He's a tall fourteen year old with a reputation for bullying at school.'

'So you'll be reporting him lost and leave it at that then?'

'Actually no. The reason I need to get back up Pen y Fan is because I have reason to believe that Ethan like myself was abducted, and unless he has been dumped somewhere like I was, *they* still have him. I had the Captain search the other lifeboats…'

'Lifeboats?'

'Yeah. Someone had smuggled me aboard the Dover-Calais ferry and shoved me in a lifeboat, tying the tarpaulin down. I thought Ethan might have been put in another because he was not with me, but the others were empty. I told the Captain I was still working with Five, and I needed his crew to check people disembarking at Calais to see he was not being taken to France, and again at Dover in case the search had made Ethan and his abductors double-back. But we turned up nothing.'

'What do these people want with him?'

'I don't know, but I intend to find out. There were four of them in total, reasonably well trained and well equipped, certainly not members of his *Parents and Teachers Committee* on a revenge mission.

'They were using syringes of what must have been anaesthetic. By the time I had fought my way to Ethan they had already knocked him out, as they then did me. They obviously gave me this payback kicking after I was out.'

'They did quite a job on you. It's a wonder you're alive.'

'Yes, that is odd. They could have left me on Pen y Fan, dead. But not only did they keep me alive, they took me with them to Dover. They must have taken me on the ferry hidden in a car which must have meant they were on board with me for the journey, but I didn't recognise anyone's faces.'

'Maybe they got someone else to do that for them.'

'You could have a point there. As I was attempting to creep up on two of them out of the shadow they both turned to look in my direction as if they knew I was coming, and one of them said *Say again*, which suggests they were in touch with others. That could have been the other two I ran into shortly afterwards.

'Though potentially more worrying, is the thought that they could have been guided by a control centre with satellite back-up. It was a clear enough sky for it.'

'So what you're saying is that this could be a government operation?'

'That sounds too much like a wacko conspiracy theory, but my intuition says it could be someone with *access* to certain systems and data.'

'Just to nab a school bully?'

'I know, I know. We need to find out more before it'll start to make any sense. I want to see if they left any syringes up on Pen y Fan that we can take prints off.'

'Not likely. I would think tourists would have taken off with those by now.'

'Well we *have* to look.'

'I'm on a bit of an odd case too, though I doubt there is any connection.' He described the case of the missing nurse and the comment from the matron to the nurse's boyfriend that she was not the first to disappear.

Kate walked in to Monitoring where the nurses were just finishing up with Ethan. Even though he was cuffed they still had him strapped into a wheelchair.

'Do you mind if I take him away from you for a few minutes?'

They shook their heads. They didn't question where the head of The Clinic was taking him. They just waited for his return.

'I want to show you someone.'

'Is it going to be a surprise?' he asked sarcastically.

'Probably not.'

'So it might be my *mad* mother.'

'What makes you think that?'

'This is the sort of place I'd expect my mother to end up, and then it might make sense why you brought me here.'

'I rather think you are here on account of your unacceptable behaviour, as a *client*, not simply an unwilling visitor, Ethan.'

He was wheeled into a room with a woman in bed, on life support. The monitors she was connected to each gave the impression the patient was stable but unconscious.

'Do you recognise her, Ethan?'

He attempted to lift himself a little higher in his seat for a slightly better look, but shook his head, 'Nope.'

'*This* is Clare. She has been in a coma since the day you hit her head with that rock. She may never recover.'

Ethan sat back with a shrug of his shoulders.

'What have you got to say to that?'

'Lucky shot.'

'*Listen*,' Kate span his chair around to look into his cold eyes. 'She only wanted to bring you here, to *help* you.'

'I don't need anyone's help.'

'You do *now*.'

In the car park below Pen y Fan, parked next to Gina's Tigra, she was clearly in a lot of pain.

'Look Gina, I'll go up and look around. You are in no state for that climb.'

'I've had worse.'

'You sound like that knight out of the Holy Grail.'

She smiled at the idea. 'Anyway, look the peak is in cloud now, and you'd need me to show you where it all happened.'

'Okay, but we'll take it easy.'

There was no argument there. They took the path from the wide strip of lane which was a poor excuse for a car park considering the popularity of Pen y Fan. Almost immediately, Will suggested they take a break to go look at a waterfall, making it sound as if his real concern was that Gina take plenty of rests. The truth was he was not used to walking far and the thought of having to walk up a mountain when he could not even see the top was a bit daunting.

It took almost an hour to reach the summit, with Gina leading the way. They passed two walkers and one cyclist. She slowed towards the top, not because of the pain and exhaustion she was enduring but because she was looking more intensely for anything that might be a clue. The first two women she had taken down may have picked up the syringe they intended for Ethan because there was nothing, beyond a couple of marks in the turf as signs of a scuffle.

Will tried to help, looking around the cairn. There was nobody else there, and with his jeans now soaking he didn't see why anyone would want to be up there.

Gina joined him, reaching into the shopping bag she had brought with her she took out an aerosol of dry air, for cleaning photography equipment among other things. She blew the moisture from the top edges of the slab and used lengths of Magic Tape to see if she could lift any prints.

'You don't expect to get prints off of that do you?'

'Maybe, maybe not. I've seen people touch the tops of cairns and triangulation points on reaching a summit. So it's worth a try.'

'Right.'

She placed the collected strips in a few sealable sandwich bags. That done she moved on towards where she recalled the final scuffle had taken place.

'Are you sure it was down here Gina? We've wandered off the path.'

'Yes I think Ethan must have fallen in trying to get away. He was lying in that gully there,' she pointed ahead.

Surveying the scene she could see nothing, but thought to go further below and then look back up. It was then that she spotted the edge of a syringe plunger in the long grass to one side, in what would have been deep shadow last night. Taking another bag and reaching in she had a sample now that was more likely to provide a clue.

'Excellent!' Will cheered, less for the case and more for the prospects of going back down. However, as he followed her back up and over the summit she veered off to the right. 'We came up this way,' he said pointing towards clear the path.

'I know. I just need to see if any of my kit is still where I left it.'

To Gina's surprise, there, under a camouflage waterproof sheet, still pegged down, was her reflective blanket, bivvy bag, phone and most importantly her purse. 'What are the chances of that?! I won't need to cancel the cards now.'

'Yeah, I'd have expected someone to have nicked off with your stuff at first light.' Worried that his comment might have sounded sarcastic he quickly added, 'Mind you, someone could have taken all your details and replaced your purse so that you wouldn't cancel it before they bought a load of stuff online.'

'Thanks for that Will. Now you can carry my kit down to the car.'

Gina and Will had driven back from the Brecon Beacons in their separate cars. Will went straight home. He felt shattered. Gina however, though also shattered, went to see DI Dunn.

'Shit Orangina, what happened to you?'

'Let's just say I've been getting quite a kick from investigating that case you passed onto me.'

'Ethan Best did *that*? I thought he was a bit of a psycho, but…'

'No, it wasn't him. It was his abductors.'

'*Abductors*? Neighbourhood watch finally caught up with him?'

'I have no idea who they were. That's why I need a couple of things from you.'

'Name it.'

'I need these checked for prints,' she said, holding out the sealed bags.

'A syringe?'

'Well spotted. And Magic Tape. I tried to pull prints off a cairn.'

'A what?'

'A rock.'

'Couldn't you have just bagged that too?'

She shook her head. 'I don't think the National Trust would have been too pleased.'

'Right,' he frowned, none the wiser.

'I'm hoping for a positive ID on Ethan. I'm convinced it was him I saw at the scene, but it *was* the middle of the night.'

'So where was he?'

'Pen y Fan.'

'Penny Fan? What a pub lock-in?'

'No a mountain.'

'Oh, how…never mind. Is it just Ethan's prints you are checking against?'

'No. More challenging than that, I want the evidence checked against missing persons.'

'Okay.'

'His four abductors were female. I think they are involved in something covert. I'm going to see what my ex-boss at Five thinks.'

'But why would these women be missing persons.'

'I have a hunch it is to do with another DNA case.'

'Right well I'll get these across to the lab then.'

'And one other thing…I need to know what was on Ethan's phone and computer?'

'Since the case is not closed they have to stay at the station, but I can give you a copy of the forensic report. I'll get it for you now.'

20

It wasn't easy for Ethan to sleep with cuffs on, however, sleep did come, but then so did the nightmares.

His biological mother looked smartly dressed, like a young company executive, and he found he was oddly attracted to her. Ethan felt himself questioning whether this *was* his mother. He did occasionally have other dreams that did not involve her. She was excited about something, but seemed to be having difficulty getting his father's attention. He was hiding behind a large newspaper.

'I adore being a Solicitor,' she said. 'It's so easy to make loads of money these days, thanks to the Americans showing us how to sue effectively. I just love finding up-and-coming writers and lyricists and finding potential to sue them for every penny they will *ever* earn. It's such a thrill to ruin lives for money, it feels kinda *dirty*.'

'I guess that's why they call it soliciting dear.'

'I even go ahead and sue when a potential client claims to see no grounds to take offence. In those cases I get to keep all of the money.'

'Isn't that a form of fraud dear?'

'You better watch what you're saying. I'm not above suing you.'

'Yes I always thought you were a bit of a gold-digger dear.'

'If my sources are correct our son has recently started writing. He has been writing such disgraceful things about people, soon he won't have a leg to stand on.'

Tom rested his chin between both of his fists; his elbows planted either side of the tablet, reviewing DNA's financial situation. His eyes swivelled to his nephew to Gina and back again. 'No.'

'But Tom, we are on the verge of something big here. The police report said that Ethan had been accessing materials from the Dark Net, as well as starting to film his own snuff videos. Then we find he gets nabbed by some sort of paramilitary extraction team.'

'I know. I *was* listening the first time. Look DNA is not in the newspaper business. You are not journalists chasing a story. You are private investigators trying to fulfil a client brief as efficiently as possible, so that we can make enough money to sustain this company. Jim Devereux would tell you the same.'

'I know, but…'

'Look. This receipt alone is for three hundred and twenty quid, not to mention the claim for other more *justifiable* items.'

'I needed that image intensifier to find Ethan in the dark,' Gina argued.

'But we already have a couple in the kit room.'

'Yes but I didn't know I'd need one till I was down there.'

'If you continue running up the costs at this rate the client will not be able to afford to pay their bill, and you will have created no benefit from our investment.'

'But we are talking about a young lad's life here Tom,' Gina tried to play the ethical card.

'I don't mean to sound callous but I have to run this company, and I have the last word. You both have new briefs to review on your desks. Leave this with the police now. They have the prints and know the last sighting. They can deal with it.'

'This is bigger than the Best boy. Something else is going on here,' Gina pressed.

'Based on what?'

'My intuition,' she said as if he would gain confidence from that, but reading his face she added 'Imagine the publicity and work that will come our way if DNA are the ones to crack it wide open.'

Tom blew exasperated air out between his teeth as he rolled his eyes, convinced he was going to regret this. 'Okay. If you both want to keep working this case fine, *but* you have to do it in your *own* time.'

Robin Faddon had considered himself a normal guy as he grew up. Sure he had fantasies that involved school uniforms, but he was convinced that most men did, otherwise the old Britney Spears video would never have been such a hit.

However as the years passed by he began to grow somewhat more concerned. He had a wonderful wife, son and daughter. He and Judy had married at nineteen and their future looked bright, but at thirty Judy just didn't have that youthful appeal to him anymore. His problem frustrated him, yet to his way of thinking he dared not say anything about it because women were all so insecure about their looks.

It wasn't like there was anything wrong with her, she was still an attractive woman, and thirty was not old. However, she was a lot more mature in her ways as a mother, and often tired, but he didn't consider that this was any excuse for him not initiating sexual intercourse as much, so he decided something must be wrong with *him* and must be done about that.

He found himself preferring to watch programmes with younger females in like the soaps and kids TV, but then he began to worry that he was turning into some sort of paedophile.

Next he began worrying over how he felt about his daughter who was becoming more attractive and reminding him of Judy when she was younger. Most dads worried about what others might do with their daughters, but Robin began to grow very anxious about what *he* might do.

Trying to find a better way of coping he started watching porn-am on his tablet when he had time on his own, and imagined the girls he watched were Judy.

He didn't want to be calling out the name of another in his hoped for heights of passion with his wife, or in his sleep. Watching porn on the Internet seemed to calm him for a while, and improve his and Judy's sex life, but eventually what he was watching did not provide the same arousal that it first had, and he moved on to stronger material.

It was a slow journey of exploration because, as he saw it, he wanted to be a good person and some of the materials were too hard-core for him, at first. Nevertheless, the day came when the slippery slope brought him to the Dark Net.

He had been prepared to claim that the money he spent from their joint account was subscriptions to magazines *if* Judy noticed anything. *He* did the household accounts so that was unlikely. Judy didn't like dealing with that end of the financial process, she just wanted to know she could buy whatever she wanted.

He tried to use gardening to distract the growing compulsion. This particular Saturday he was down the bottom of the garden, appearing to be planting seedlings when he gave in to the urge and decided to grab a quick gander at his latest purchase off the Dark Net again.

He went back into the shed closing the door after him. Taking his tablet from the garden centre bag he had hid it in, he placed it on his lap and switched it on. He only got as far as watching the laborious start-up sequence and putting his password in when there came a knock on the back gate.

No one ever came to the back gate. He and Judy only used that gate for putting the wheelie bins out. Reasoning that it must therefore be the council, Robin placed the tablet back in the bag, leaving it to go to sleep, while he left the shed to investigate.

To his surprise he saw a dark Range Rover parked behind his fence and a woman to either side of his gate. They seemed to be smiling, but he didn't recognise them. However, they could have been some of Judy's friends who he had never met, he supposed.

'We would like a word with you Mr Faddon?' said the woman to his right.

'What about?'

'Shall we say it's about your Internet provider?'

'BT?' he frowned.

'Only if that stands for *Brutal Teacher*.'

Robin gasped. 'I don't know what you mean. Is this some sort of wind up?'

'I'm sure you wouldn't want your family to find out about your *interests*,' the woman to his left put in.

This was fast sliding from awkward to nightmare, and Robin turned to go back into his garden as if he could run from it all. However, the young woman to his right caught his arm and in a soft voice said, 'Just come and sit in the back of the car and calm down. We can explain what is going to happen next.'

Possibly seduced by the voice, Robin relaxed a little and they escorted him round into the back of the car. When he emerged a short while later, he had tears in his eyes and a letter in his hand. Without escort he returned to his shed, placed the letter on the bench and picked up the bag with his computer kit.

Gina tried to get in touch with Penelope Ryder, her commanding officer at MI5, but was told she had left. Not left for the weekend, but gone. She then rang Dave Fendor.

'Hello Dave, it's Gina.'

'Agent Orange. How are you doing?'

'A little worse for wear…Listen I have a few questions for you. I tried to ring Penelope but she's gone apparently.'

'Yes didn't I tell you? She left not long after you. Some said she was unhappy about having been told to dismiss you. You know with the scapegoating, and being seen to have *done* something. Others said she may have had a big win on the Euro Millions, which I find more believable.'

'Right…Well DNA is working a couple of cases which might be related, involving missing persons. Has Five noticed an increase in missing persons?'

'You always were perceptive. We were in a meeting about this just the other day. Yes it seems that there has been an increase in disappearances. The one common factor is that many of these individuals leave unexpectedly taking only their computer equipment.

Our present theory is that they may be terrorist sleeper agents, so we are preparing for an imminent attack, target unknown.'

'I guess there could be something in that. The four people I've had a run in with up on Pen y Fan looked well equipped and relatively well trained. But they were abducting a fourteen year old, who didn't look like he wanted anything to do with them. *And* I swear they had military support, possibly even satellite guidance.'

'Sounds like an entirely different situation to me.'

'Maybe…Do you have a report on these missing persons? Is there a general profile?'

'I'll check it out and get back to you.'

'Thanks.'

21

Chișinău, Moldova.
Alexander Novovitch looked at the new furnishings for his next film set as his crew positioned it all as per his instructions. There were no traces of what had been filmed in the previous scene to give his next victims any clue, just how he liked it, for maximum shock appeal.

He turned to see his right-hand man, Paulo, who was bringing a man across the studio to him. He walked off the set to meet them.

'What is it?'

'Sorry Alexander, the trafficker has just explained that there was a hitch with the Nigerians we had asked for, for tomorrows shoot.'

'I heard that Donnie's camp was totally destroyed, but are you saying there are *no* other Nigerians to replace them?' he looked at the trafficker fiercely frustrated.

'No,' the man replied, shaking his head and raising his hands. 'Not by tomorrow.'

'This is no good. It screws with my schedule. It's bad for business, and if it's bad for business, then it will be bad for *you*, my friend,' he looked sternly at the trafficker.

'Yes.' The man bowed his head fearful of this powerful figure.

Alexander gave a dismissive wave of his hand, and both men began to walk away, but he called Paulo back.

'Yes?'

'Have our twins arrived yet?'

'They will be here within the hour, Alexander.'

'Good. And they believe they are being filmed for Moldovan TV and that they are being interviewed in competition with one another for a single post at a law firm in Russia?'

'Yes, yes, they have been primed, just as you scripted. Each of them is desperate for work.'

'Good.' He turned and pointed behind him, 'I want all these tools cleaned up and out of sight before they arrive. I can't afford to let the cat out of the bag too soon.'

Four troopers strode across the Russian runway as the engines of their IL-76 came to life. They walked up the tailgate to take their positions either side of the fuselage, as directed by the flight crew, then securely stowed their High Altitude Low Opening kit, until it was time for pre-drop checks.

As the three doors which formed the tailgate sealed, and the plane began to taxi, one of the troopers offered out fruit gums to help deal with the changes in air pressure they were going to be subjected to, but the other three shook their heads. They were fine, though one of them looked a little nervous. Beyond training she had only done a HALO op twice before and on one of those missions a team-mate's chute had not opened properly.

They had been practicing for the last week in Russia with a mock-up of the target and were as prepared as they could be.

As the plane climbed on a south-southeast heading the sky through the windows grew darker.

The twins arrived at the studio in a black limousine with tinted windows. They were both so excited. As if the offer of work was not enough now they were to star on a TV show where they would be interviewed about how much they wanted this law-firm job.

They considered themselves under no illusions about this being a *reality TV* shoot. They were anticipating it to be quite an emotional roller-coaster as they would be expected to compete with one another to show who deserved to get the job most.

They had both agreed to be happy whoever turned out to be the winner and had decided to ensure that the competition was down to wits and personality, so did the stereotypical twin-thing of wearing the same outfits; black sequin mini-dresses.

They were shown into what they were told was the green room. There was a TV and a drinks cabinet, but they were told not to drink as they had to go to make-up shortly. They were both disappointed by this, not just because they considered their make-up was fine, but because they did not like missing out on freebies.

Make-up seemed to take an age. The women dealing with them removed all of their good work and seemed intent on making them look more innocent. They didn't dare complain though they felt rather annoyed, for fear of losing the career opportunity.

Then it was back to the green room where they had to wait again for ages. No one told them why there was a delay.

The trip on the plane was a little turbulent, but as it eased out one of the flight crew came along and gave the troopers a Drop Zone weather report and told them they were about half an hour out.

The troopers rarely enjoyed the outward flight to a DZ. It was like waiting for a kettle to boil. They just wanted to get on with the job. It wasn't that they wanted the job over with; it was about working as part of the kill team, knowing that with them their blood-lust was acceptable, and encouraged.

The twins were given the cue to walk on set and were greeted by the host who directed them to sit together on the sofa, as the cameras rolled.

It felt odd to the girls because they had expected applause, though they knew the only audience were going to be the studio crew. They looked around as they tried to settle down, but they could not see much because the stage lighting was so bright, so turned their attention back to the host.

The host welcomed them both and asked them to tell the camera with the red light on, their name and age. That done, he asked what their hopes were? This was very important for what was scripted to follow. They both said they *had* to find work. The only way to get a better life in, or better still outside of Moldova was through the money that a good job would pay them.

Next the host asked to what lengths they would go to get work? They both frowned and looked at one another, unsure what to say. The host rephrased his question to ask whether it would bother either of them if getting the job caused the other pain. Naively, they responded that they knew they were there to compete for the job and that the loser would understandably be upset.

The host shook his head and said that maybe they would understand better if they played a little game. Lifting up a cloth bag from beside his chair and pulling its drawstring open he drew out a cat-of-nine-tails, a whip with nine tassels, each with a sharp metal claw at the end.

The girls gasped as he handed it to one of them. She was reluctant to take it but he was insistent and she complied. Next he told them both to stand up and told the one without the cat to stand at the end of the sofa and bend over the arm. She wasn't comfortable doing it, but it was a reality show and they both knew from watching plenty of TV that guests were expected to do stupid things, so she complied also.

The girl with the whip was told that if she wanted the job she had to flay her sister. She made a less than half-hearted attempt and did little more than brush her sister's legs. The host said that wasn't going to get anyone the job that it needed to leave a mark.

Unhappily the girl struck out at the legs much harder and her sister jolted with the pain. The host agreed that this showed more commitment. Then he told the girls to swap places. They looked into one another's eyes as the cat changed hands.

Now the host told the twin with the cat that to win this game she had to leave a bigger mark than her sister had given her, or forfeit the job offer. She complied and her sister cried out.

They were told to swap again, but this time the twin with the cat was told to pull her sister's dress up over her head, to bear her back and buttocks, and leave her mark in both places.

She was angered that her sister had whipped her legs so badly, she didn't want to lose the job to her now, and whipped the back hard and immediately followed through with the back swing across the buttocks. Her sister cursed her, but the host told her to try again as she had hardly broken the skin. She complied, and her sister screamed.

The twins were made to swap again. Then after two return strikes to the back and the buttocks powered by the need for revenge the twin with the cat was told to draw more blood. However, she came to her senses, and refused. She expected the host to announce that the job had been won by her sister, but instead he commended her resistance and declared that they were now both through to round two.

The twin on the sofa got up, pulling her dress down; the material brushing her raw flesh painfully. They had no idea what was coming next as two muscular, bare-chested, men wheeled massage benches onto the set and both girls were told to strip off and lie face down.

No longer happy with what was happening they both wanted to run but could see they were surrounded by men.

They were both shaking; terrified, as they were forcibly stripped. They continued to resist but were rewarded with heavy punches. They were soon being bound face down onto the massage benches, with cameras coming in underneath for face shots, and they both began to sob.

There would be no running now. Whatever they had got themselves into, in believing a job was on offer, there was no way out of this. The next hour was scripted to be a crescendo of pain that would begin with salt being rubbed into their wounds and end in a blood-bath for both of them.

The troopers and flight crew put their kit on, checking their breathing apparatus was functioning before the tailgate was reopened and the cabin pressure equalised with that of the high altitude outside. Then the troopers carried out their final weapons check, before strapping on their helmets.

Kate was in their ears confirming that the clear night was giving them *eyes-on* for the x-rays, and that the black-op was a *go*. What they needed were the additional *eyes-in*, but that was part of their mission, to get down there, compromise the enemy security and place infra-red cameras before progressing with the full attack.

No-one knew for certain what was going on at the studio, only that it was in use, and Alexander Novovitch was present.

As the troopers moved down the ramp they could feel the vibrations of the engines through their boots increase the closer they got to the outer edge. They watched the red light until it turned green and they stepped into the blackness without hesitation, dragging their packs on cords behind them.

Arms by their sides they fell at an incredible rate through the thin air. Their plane out of sight in seconds, their attention was taken by their instruments, both to guide them in and to initiate the low-opening of their chutes, reducing detection by radar.

Kate was not in her office to oversee this op, but down in the control centre, surrounded by screens and staff. A number of screens repeated the same view, but once the cameras were in place the spare screens would carry their own vital information.

The heat signature of each trooper was only slight, almost ghostly, but on screen each carried a red number tag. With chutes opened they glided in as soundlessly as owls. Almost as one there was a splutter of their suppressed AK47-Ks and four guards collapsed from head-shots, even before the troopers and their packs touched down.

On the roof of the old part of the studio building, which had castellated walls and a higher vantage point, the troopers stowed their chutes quickly, removed their breathing apparatus then prepared their abseil lines.

Kate passed the troopers over to their designated handlers who became personal eyes-in-the-back-of-their-head. Communicating what they were seeing with the *eyes-on* and soon to be active *eyes-in* screens. In addition to which the four-lens GPNVG-18 panoramic night vision goggles they were now pulling into place also carried a trooper-cam.

Two troopers abseiled all the way down to the ground and got sight of two guards out of view from the eye-in-the-sky, confirming this with control. With the two left on the roof in sight of two other guards patrolling the outer fence control called it and the four guards crumpled down dead. Everything seemed to be going smoothly, so far.

There was no intel on how frequently the security reported in, so the team had to work to a tight timeframe of five minutes so as not to raise an alarm.

The two troopers on the roof abseiled down to the more modern roof of the studio to place fibre-optic cameras through vents at each corner, in order to view the scene below. The fibre-optics could carry light as well as images, working like an endoscope, and the cameras could be remotely switched between infra-red and full-spectrum by the control centre, which also had control of their destruction when the extraction was over.

Meanwhile, the two troopers on the ground immobilised vehicles by puncturing tyres, before turning to the generator shed at the rear and placing a pack of C4 and a remote detonator there.

Then they split up to cover the main and side door, and wait for the *go* signal. The troopers on the studio roof came round to one side where there was an inspection hatch for getting up onto the roof. The hatch was opened with a metallic squeak, which was covered by the sound of screams from inside. Together they calmly moved in, onto a gantry looking down on the grim scene below, and split up to take sniper positions at either end.

Alexander Novovitch was just thinking how well everything was going when there was a sudden boom and the lights all went out, plunging them into near pitch black, bar the green glow of the fire exit signs.

The sound was unlike a light blowing, it had sounded like something more sinister had shorted the circuit. As he moved towards the side exit Alexander shouted for the back-up generator in the studio to be started up. Then he heard a phutt and a clunk then another phutt and clunk as the generator was put out of action, as then were the two of his men fumbling their way towards it.

The side door opened in front of Alexander and the last thing he saw before he was awarded his double tap for film production was a soldier. Unfortunately it was time enough for him to press the alarm on a chain round his neck, which went unheard for those within the studio compound.

The main door opened and with six more double phutts from different directions the studio fell quiet except for the sobbing of the twins. It was a success of sorts, no troopers injured this time, but the twins were in bad shape. The troopers cut them loose from the benches but as they were helping them get dressed in the dark, attempting to reassure them that they were safe now; that it was all over, control warned of incoming hostiles.

Two troopers quickly closed and locked the doors, while the other two took the twins to the back and into the green room, where they told them to keep quiet and stay close to the ground, no matter what happened. Then the troopers all climbed up into the lighting gantries and took up sniper positions.

Four T-98 SUVs turned up in response to Alexander's signal, but when the gates were not opened for their arrival they simply rammed their way in. This was the local mafia, who provided added protection and other services to Alexander if and when required, but they had arrived a little too late. Nevertheless they would make good their agreement whether he was alive or dead, as Alexander was part of something much bigger.

Even before the T-98s had stopped moving the men were pouring out. Each of them was heavy set and tattooed. They all looked ex-military and were heavily armed. There were close to two dozen of them; overwhelming odds. They fanned out to secure the perimeter first before they began to tighten their noose, closing in on the studio from all sides. They noted the dead bodies as they did so, inspecting their wounds to inform them of what and who they may be dealing with.

They understood from the head shots that this was a professional hit and the initial attack had come from above. The signal was given to take cover, but none of the attackers could be spotted on the roof. In the continuing silence the next question they asked themselves was, were there any of the opposition left inside?

Moving quickly to stand aside of the main and side doors on cue they opened them wide, two of them calling inside. There was no reply and the lights were all out. They could not see far into the dark studio unit so they switched their weapon lights on and peered back round the door, scanning the interior for signs of life, but all they saw were dead bodies.

The warning call was repeated but again there was no response; not a sound, but deciding this could be a trap the command was given to put on gas masks and throw in tear-gas. This operation had to be concluded quickly. Some key members of the police in this part of Chișinău were on the mafia pay-roll, but they would not hold back for long, and the mafia couldn't afford to be here when they arrived.

Kate had been watching the proceedings pleased that everything was going to plan when the mafia had turned up in force with the girls still in the studio.

'Okay Blue team you are clear to go.'

Watching the satellite feed the men by the doors were seen to raise their canisters of tear gas just before they were dropped with their brain matter reaching the ground before their heads did.

As the men came under attack, the immediate reaction was to step back from the doors, thinking the attack had come from within, but the trajectory was wrong, and the men on the outer edge were still dropping and the realisation dawned. They had been ambushed. Quickly the men were told to take cover inside.

Blue team, working in pairs on two neighbouring roof-tops either side of the studio compound, slung their sniper rifles over their backs and abseiled down to the street. Their boots pounded the concrete as they charged the studio but by the time they entered it they found all of the remaining mafia were dead.

Red Team descended from the lighting gantries. They all had to work quickly now to get what they came for and get out of there. They could not afford to be caught in Moldova.

Not only were the police not to be trusted, their home governments would deny them support if captured by the authorities, because for once they *really* wouldn't know who they were.

So, with that foremost in their minds the troopers searched the pockets of certain individuals for phones among other things, and the two laptops they found were quickly unscrewed to remove hard-drives.

The local police took their time in getting to the scene. To the legitimate and less experienced officers the delay in response seemed to be understandable. The report had been that something big was going down and they all had to have their body armour issued and weapons checked while the Commander agreed the plan of action with the Captain.

They turned up in force, lights flashing sirens blaring, and cordoned off all of the streets around the studio. Nothing else was getting in or out.

With the studio surrounded, they went in weapons hot and trigger happy, but they were met with a scene of a massacre, the likes of which they had never seen before. Moving on inside by torchlight, stepping through pools of blood they moved towards the only sound they could hear. There were sounds of sobbing females coming from a room at the back of the unit.

The door to the green room was locked, but the police broke the door down, to find ten frightened women looking like they had all been abducted from a night out. Two of them looked pretty badly hurt.

The Captain radioed in for two police vans to come pick up these women. They would need to be questioned. The rest of the officers were to keep looking for the killers. They must be hiding elsewhere in the building. They couldn't just vanish like ghosts.

The twins were traumatised. They comforted one another the best they could, and though they needed their cuts and bruises treated they were more concerned over where they were being taken to now.

They had learned not to trust the police, and the fact that their van, and the one following, seemed to be taking a long time to reach to the police station did nothing to quell their growing fears. They kept looking at these women who they had seen strip off their battle gear to reveal a mix of party dresses, blouses and jeans. These women said little, but gave reassuring nods and smiles.

The twins had so many questions, having understood little of what had happened. Like the big bang out the back of the building before these women locked themselves into the green room with them. But no one was about to explain that had been all their kit being destroyed next to the generator shed with the last of the C4. The biggest question was what was going to happen to them all now? This last concern was half answered as they were driven onto an airfield towards a waiting IL-76.

The Red Team leader in front of the twins asked them whether they would like the driver to take them home, or would they both prefer to be found a job within their organisation? If this evening had taught them one thing it was not to trust job offers, but somehow they both felt that working with these women was a different sort of opportunity.

That would prove to be an understatement.

22

Birmingham.
DI Dunn had been quick to get back to Gina, reporting on the evidence she had provided. 'They found a partial print of that Best lad on the Magic Tape, and the syringe had three sets of prints on it.'

'Three? That was careless of them.'

'Only two prints have been identifiable though, and they do belong to missing persons.'

'Do they now?' Gina said with a tone of *I knew it*.

'Yes, a travel agent from Manchester who disappeared about three years ago, called Melanie Bainbridge, and a nurse who went missing two months ago, called Jane Newton.'

'That's the case Will is working on.'

'Right.'

'Is any more known about this Melanie's disappearance, like whether her home was just abandoned with belongings? And whether there was a computer left there or not?'

'Sorry the report didn't cover that.'

'Okay, well thanks for getting back to me so fast Sigh.'

'No problems Orangina.'

After the call Gina started to consider whether human trafficking and brainwashing could have something to do with all this. She made a mental note that when she got home that evening she would delve into the human trafficking question further. She would have to tell Will about the lead on Jane. However, until they knew more she would advise him to say nothing about it to the client. For now though she had to focus on the unengaging job at hand, a man who was claiming someone was stealing fish.

'Sorry about that Mr Holborn, a *serious* case I'm working on.' She put away her mobile and followed the impatient man further down his garden path towards the ill-fated pond. 'So how many of these goldfish have gone?'

'Goldfish? *Oh* they are *not* goldfish.'

'They aren't piranhas are they?' she ventured, her mind making a tenuous connection.

'*Piranhas*? No.' Mr Holborn couldn't believe he was considering paying this defective detective. 'They are prize-winning Koi Carp.'

'Oh.' She was none the wiser.

'Worth a great deal of money,' he elaborated, now considering having words with the *friend* who had recommended DNA to him.

'*Ohh…*' the penny was dropping. Reaching the pond Gina tried to sound a little more knowledgeable by enquiring 'Could it have been a Kingfisher? I've heard…'

'No,' he cut her off irritated. 'They're much too big for a bird.'

'Right…A heron then,' she offered, but saw what was in the pond. 'Fuck me…Maybe not…' The red and pink blotched giants looked like goldfish fed on steroids.

'Now do you *see*, Miss Oakley?'

'Can't really miss'em can you, although I guess you *are* missing some.'

'Too many.'

'How old are they?'

'Some of them are in their teens.'

'Could some of them have died of old age and be on the bottom somewhere?'

'No.'

'The water does not look particularly clear, so forgive me but how would you know?'

'Because when fish begin to decompose the gases in their gut make them float.'

'I see…So how would someone get them out?'

'The same way I do for the shows. I have a sort of little crane which fits into that mounting point there,' he pointed at the metalwork to one side of the garden path where it joined the path around the pond. 'A net lifts them out and then I place them into a transport tank.'

Seeing as he was not in the best of moods, Gina decided to restrain herself from winding him up further by asking whether *Annette* was always in control of the crane. Instead she asked 'They enjoy going for a ride?'

'I don't follow.'

'Well they must do, to swim into the net.'

'Don't be stupid,' he found himself growing even more irritable with Gina, who clearly wasn't taking this seriously. 'I have to use food pellets to lure them in.'

'So what we are dealing with is someone with food pellets who brings the crane here and removes your fish.'

'Yes, yes I expect so.'

'Is this sort of crane easy to get hold of?'

'No they are bally awkward. I have to use a trolley.'

'Not what I meant, but still useful to know. So who makes these cranes?' she rephrased her question.

'Actually, I made it myself,' he claimed with pride.

'Right…Have you considered setting up a camera to catch the thief?'

'Oh yes. The police didn't do much following the first theft but then suggested that I set up a camera after the second one went.'

'And what did you find when the third one was taken?'

'I found that they'd stolen the camera too. It was Bluetooth, and my Internet hub has never been right since. Technology, you can't trust it.'

'So tell me Mr Holborn. Do you have a family?'

'I'm married, but these Koi are my only children.'

'And does your wife feel the same way about your fish?'

'Not really, my dear wife is far more interested in her expensive jewellery.'

'Do you see where I'm going with this Mr Holborn?'

'Not really, no.'

Allah's Fist, as he *still* demanded to be known, saw himself as having become possessed by the spirit of Osama Bin Laden since Zero Dark Thirty. An assassination which had interfered with the intention of bringing misery to Christian and Muslim folk alike. The label of Holy War/Jihad, in God/Allah's name, had been a thinly veiled excuse for the pure enjoyment of bloodshed for both sides over the centuries, and Allah's Fist saw no reason to stop now.

He couldn't understand why, when the world was in such a state of disrepair and despair, that people could not appreciate that he and those he funded were doing common folk and infidels alike a favour by killing them. And so he had had to remain in hiding, rather than be the TV celebrity terrorist he had always wanted to be.

He had considered the saying that *lightening never strikes the same place twice* as a good rule of thumb and had put in an offer for Osama's previous residence to be used as his safe-house. However, to his dismay had found that it was already making money as a serious tourist attraction, with audio guides in ten different languages.

He appreciated that *money talks louder than respect*, as that was one of his own edicts. Nevertheless, inspired by the spirit of his hero, Allah's Fist wanted to hide right under the enemy's nose, so presently resided in a penthouse suite across the Thames from the MI6 building in London.

He felt quite secure in the UK, thanks to its legal system, and preferred the English temperament of *stiff-upper-lip in the face of misery and all that what what*, especially when he got to see that his barbaric actions could get that lip to tremble.

He had been educated in the USA, so considered that he was well versed in the ways of the world. He did not however like the arrogance of the Americans. They were all too quick to bomb other people, and fund others to do so. Who did they think they were? That was *his* job.

No one knew his whereabouts thanks to the onion ring router and network system he had set up, making him appear to be anywhere in the world at any time.

He intended that his followers hold him in awe, like an omnipotent presence, as he turned his attentions from al Qaeda to guide the development of more extreme jihadists instead, from everywhere at once.

Nevertheless, it was not easy earning that kind of respect. It had been achieved by channelling government and industrial funding into training camps, acquiring weapons, and devising new ways of bringing shock and terror to common folk, and occasionally even his loyal jihadists.

It seemed no longer possible to shock the military or intelligence agencies, and without shock where was the fun? Respect also required a degree of keen housekeeping, which meant maintaining watchfulness over his own flock. Disrespect could not be tolerated, unless it paid very well, and unknown to his followers he regularly hacked into their communications as freely as he did those of his enemies.

Allah's Fist had not minded it when he had found reference to himself as The Puppet-Master, but the man who had referred to him as Buda's Palm, in comic reference to the film Kung Fu Hustle, had gone too far and had to be made an example of. Allah's Fist diverted supporters funding intended to arm troops in Syria to have a 1,000,000:1 scale fist imprint chiselled out of a prominent hillside in Pakistan.

The man in question was then to be slowly crushed to death under a steam-roller, in secrecy then placed in the middle of the giant imprint, in a shallow depression created for the remains of his body.

This was then to be photographed, tweeted and retweeted carrying the man's identity and crime.

Unfortunately, the workers had only just finished excavating the knuckles of the index finger when the man in question vanished, along with his computer equipment from his uptown home in New York.

It had been rumoured that some sort of SWAT team had been seen entering his house in the middle of the night. Yet the NYPD knew nothing about it, neither did Homeland Security for that matter.

This was not the first time that Allah's Fist had had his intentions thwarted. The latest frustration was that his film studio in Moldova, a key funding source for *his cause*, had been shut down by *persons unknown*, described as *Ghosts*. He didn't believe in any of that sort of nonsense but would get to the bottom of it. He put his physical and cyber feelers out. He did not expect the answer to be long in coming as he had moles in most governments and security services.

Gina had spent a few hours reading documents she had downloaded from the Internet describing the rise in human trafficking and the measures in place to control it. The National Crime Agency reported that while the larger percentage of people trafficked in the UK were illegals from abroad there were also cases of UK citizens being trafficked.

Trafficking was associated with a number of serious organised crimes typically involving prostitution and abuse, though there were some cases of domestic servitude as one-offs, either way it was still slavery.

Gina wondered how this related to the missing persons she and Will were tracing. According to the report which she had been copied by Dave Fendor, computer equipment was being taken during many of the more recent abductions. This put her in mind of a link to cyber-crime or even cyber-terrorism.

She needed to talk with someone who knew this subject area better even than Five. Eventually she found a name, someone who appeared to be knowledgeable of both human trafficking and terrorism.

She phoned Will to give him an update, only then did she look at her watch and realise it was gone one in the morning. She almost hung up, but then he answered with a bleary 'Yeah?'

'Sorry Will. Did I wake you?'

'Just a bit.'

'I thought I should let you know I might have a possible lead on our missing person cases.'

'That's nice.'

'Sorry, I shouldn't have phoned so late.'

'What time is it? *Oh…Don't you sleep* Gina?'

'I got caught up in reading about trafficking and terrorism, anyway I found someone I'm going to talk to down in London, and just thought I'd let you know I'm heading down there tomorrow…this morning.'

'On a Sunday? Cant it wait till Monday? You need to rest. You can't be over Friday's battering yet, surely. I know I'm not.'

'I'll be fine. Anyway Tom said we had to do this in our own time.'

'Okay look, let me come with you.'

'You don't need to.'

'An extra set of eyes and ears could be useful,' he argued.

'I don't even know if this guy will talk to me. I could call him later.'

'Yes *later* might be advisable.'

'But I think talking face to face would be better.'

'Okay. So what time are you leaving?'

'I was thinking seven o'clock.'

'Seven?'

'Yeah. I thought I'd try and catch him before he goes out.'

'Oh right...well wouldn't six be better. Give me your address and I'll come and pick you up.'

Ethan lay awake. He had not had a good day. His last nightmare had left him anxious about his future.

He knew it was only a dream, and yet during the day he had found it difficult to write down his fantasies of torturing Kate and her nurses.

He found himself questioning why he was writing *any* of this down at all. They didn't seem at all shocked or angry with what he was writing, though he wasn't sure they were even reading any of it.

This therapy seemed odd; writing for himself. It was nothing like doing homework, not that he did any of that. At least with that he was certain he was disappointing teachers expectations of him. Here though, he really didn't know what was expected.

At the end of the day as he continued to struggle, he was told that in the morning he would get to meet the lady who gives creative writing support. He didn't see how that was going to help though.

Ethan's fantasies turned from revenge to a means of escape from The Clinic. Considering that there was no way of escaping through a window, it was clear that he would need to acquire one of the nurses security cards for the swipe locks on the doors. It also occurred to him the cards might have different access levels, and the one he would need in order to be assured of escape then was Kate's.

23

'Hello Ethan,' said Teri as she entered his room.

He turned from where he had been standing looking out of his window since he had finished breakfast, but he was not looking at her face, he was looking at her security card swinging from her belt loop.

'I understand that you were told yesterday that I would be reading through your previous work, just to see how I could help.'

'Did it *shock* you?' he asked with a grin.

'Not particularly, no.'

Ethan's lips straightened. He really didn't appreciate her ambivalence.

'So what we are going to do today will be some exercises. I'm not going to ask you to write any more stories as such but get you to describe details of particular scenes you have already written. To start writing them in more depth this time by thinking about those involved as *people*.'

Her words were almost sounding like *blah blah blah* as Ethan kept thinking about the security card. It had a plastic tubing covered metal cable loop, like a miniature bike lock chain, connecting it to her belt. He had no way of cutting it loose, and the closer glances he was able to take as he was directed to sit at his desk suggested it would not be easy to unclip from the belt without detection.

'I want you to consider what would be going through the victim's mind, as well as the perpetrator's.'

Maybe he needed to strangle Teri quietly and take the card, but he expected he was being watched so would not get far. The killing would likely bring about a game change. That would suggest he needed to force Teri to open the door and then use threats to her safety to ensure his release, but where would he go that they would not recapture him?

'Then I want you to reflect upon these and other exercises today and to consider how *you* feel about what you have written, Ethan.'

The escape plan would need a lot more thought if it wasn't going to conclude in an epic fail.

'Ethan?!'

'Yes. Okay!'

He decided he needed to be mindful of what he wrote about. He didn't want to be giving away any part of his plans. At that moment Ethan had a sudden realisation about his situation and what he had been writing since he had been brought there. He actually enjoyed planning what he was going to do with and to *people* far more than he had ever enjoyed planning what to do with *animals*. Animals were history. Thanks to this treatment, people were to be his new focus, or would be as soon as he got out.

Gina sat with Will in the Astra, waiting. They had been to the address that Dave had given them *off the record*, but the man they wished to talk to was out, though his car was there on the drive. Either he had left quite early, or he had stayed out the night before. This led to some consideration as to whether he was away for the duration, and then agreement that Gina really should have phoned first as she said she was going to. As they broke out the elevenses further discussion led to ironic speculation that this man might have been *taken*.

They sat with the radio on low. It was getting to that point in the stakeout where there had become insufficient stimuli to keep the boredom at bay.

'So,' ventured Will, 'Who *is* Gina Oakley?'

She turned to just stare at him for his rather odd question.

'I mean I know you worked for the police and MI5 and that people say you might be…you know'

'Dangerous?'

'Jinxed…But what is your real story?'

Gina sighed, and he worried that he should not have used the word jinxed or that maybe she had taken his probing as a request for *overshare*. Nevertheless, it was inevitable that the two of them would begin to open up and get to know one another better working on the same or related cases, especially on their own time.

'From the beginning?' she asked.

'If you like.'

'I was born and raised in Edinburgh, but only till I was seven, when my parents moved to Birmingham.'

'So you're a Scot? You don't sound it. But then you don't quite sound Brummie either.'

'No, well my dad was from London and my mum was from the OC.'

'An actress?'

'No, just a resident of Orange County. Anyway, on the evening of my 21st birthday, on the way to my party, they died in a freak car accident.'

'Freak accident?'

'Yeah…My dad drove around in a Hummer. Said it was the safest vehicle on the road, and I guess he was right about the *road* bit. Anything colliding with it would have been like driving into a tank.

'Anyway, that evening he swerved to avoid a dog which had run out onto the road according to the eye witness who had called for the emergency services.

'The problem was they just so happened to be on a canal bridge at the time. The car smashed through the stone wall and went straight down into the narrow canal. It was so narrow the doors couldn't be opened.

The fire crew who turned up twenty minutes later said one or both of my parents might have been able to get out, if it hadn't been for the barge that couldn't slow in time and got stuck on top of its chassis, holding it upside-down.'

'That's a dreadful story.'

Gina nodded, reliving in her mind the moment at her birthday party as the bad news came in the form of two police officers she initially assumed were there to complain about the noise.

'Do you have brothers and sisters Gina?'

'I *had* one of each. My brother we stopped talking to when I was nineteen for his unforgivable interests.'

'Oh God, he wasn't a paedo was he?'

'No, *no*. It was more of a Breaking Bad scenario, which resulted in the *accidental* deaths of two teenage girls.'

'Oh…And your sister?'

'No, not my sister. Why would he kill her?'

'Sorry, I'm just asking how she is?' he guessed this might not be good either.

'Saffy died just a couple of years ago.'

'Oh no.' Will shook his head, wishing he really hadn't asked.

'She was on a night out with the girls, hoping to get lucky. However, by that point she had probably had too much to drink. Apparently, as they stopped at a kebab takeaway one of the high heels snapped and tipped her backwards into the path of and oncoming double decker bus, which…'

'Okay, you don't need to give the details.' Will could see the tears welling in Gina's eyes and wanted to hug her close, but decided to just go with taking a hand and squeezing it. 'Life hasn't been good to you Gina. I'm sorry for your losses.'

He didn't feel he could ask any more questions for fear of bringing more pain to the surface, and he realised why there was a bit of a hard edge to her. There was a long pause and then Gina turned the attention to Will.

'So how about you will? How come you've only just finished your degree? You look around the same age as me, or is that what the stress of university life does to kids these days?'

271

'Ha…I was a mature student. Started when I was twenty eight when I finally knew this was what I wanted to do. I went to university at Huddersfield.'

'So what were you doing before that?'

'I worked for social services for a while then became a prison officer and I guess I just got interested in how criminals think when I was there.'

'Didn't you want to go back?'

'I thought about it. It was an okay job, but I wanted something different and when I graduated this offer of working for my uncle came up.'

'So I'm guessing your parents are Welsh, since you and Tom sound Welsh.'

'Yes, they still live in Rhyl, where I grew up. I used to knock about with a gang of lads who did a whole load of stupid dares, rather like that Jackass programme.

'One of the dares which went on for a while was touching jellyfish. I don't mean their caps, I mean the stingers. I guess it was a sort of rites of passage kind of thing with us. It could be quite painful, though sometimes there was no sting at all. A bit like Russian roulette I suppose.

We were never sure the difference between the jellyfish. Not that they all looked the same of course, some looked really quite different. I guess we just weren't that interested in what they were. We just knew lots of them got washed up along the beaches.

Then the dares progressed from touching the stingers with a fingertip to allowing stingers to be draped across different parts of the body, and often, even when the pain and swelling went down we were left with marks. We called them scars of honour…Idiots.'

As Gina watched, Will pulled up both his sleeves to reveal scarring on his inner forearms, looking like constellations of pale stars. She shook her head. She had had her suspicions about his intelligence, but hadn't quite taken him for a cretin.

'Anyway one day this big pink and blue one washed up with extremely long tentacles, and a lad who was keen to be accepted by the gang was dared to kiss it.

It's a dreadful thing *peer-group pressure*. I can still see it now, without hesitation he got down on his knees, and then came all the screaming and screaming.

At first we thought he was just acting up. His screams were just *so* over the top, we'd never heard such a carry on, but then we noticed his face puffing up so fast it scared us enough to go get help. He had to be rushed to hospital.'

'I heard that some jellyfish can be really toxic Will.'

He nodded sheepishly.

'Did he live?'

'Yeah, but to this day he looks like he's fallen victim to some Botox malpractice. It must have destroyed the nerves in his lips because he has eating and drinking difficulties. His lower lip droops down so far it exposes his teeth and causes a constant string of dribble to soak his clothes. I feel really bad about that.'

'I should think so Will but *he* was fool enough to take up the dare.'

'Yeah I suppose, but it was me who had noticed and pointed out what turned out to be a beached Portuguese Man-of-War.'

Patricia Stevens was no longer *all there*, in either sense of the phrase. Just a couple of days back she had still been capable of ruing that fateful day patrolling the streets, but not now because the trauma had brought her to the edge of close-down.

That afternoon she had been doing well with the day's parking violations. She had taken great pleasure in issuing a ticket for an invalid vehicle parked on double yellow lines outside a doctor's surgery. She had been not at all put off by the copious amount of blood on the driver's seat that trailed from the car door to the surgery entrance.

Her patrol had eventually brought her to a car park where she found a vehicle that she took an instant disliking to. While it was parked on tarmac, and was not causing *any* obstruction, it was not in a *designated* area.

She loved the power the rule book gave her, knowing the irritation and often misery she could bring. Admittedly the white marking on that car park were old and difficult to see in most sections, but to her mind the owner *should* have checked.

Her dislike intensified as she ran a check on the plate number and it came up as *unknown*. She decided to call the police, and was raising her mobile when the back doors of the black van opened to reveal a number of black clad troopers.

'I really wouldn't do that if I were you,' one of them warned.

Patricia wasn't about to be *warned* by anyone. The military were not above the law, and she wasn't going to be swayed in her decision because the warning had come from a young woman either. They could be MI5 or SAS for all she cared. This was going to make a great story back at the council office, so she continued to dial for the local police, even as she was lifted off the tarmac and into the van and introduced to a terrible darkness.

The first two times that she tipped her body parts in for the pigs she had taken in the whole barbaric experience, sobbing and screaming and saying she was sorry. But as her lower limbs now lay ready in the trough she couldn't even register that they had been hers, never mind raise a stump of a knee to tip them in.

'Would you like some help with that Patty?' a nurse asked with a laugh.

Patricia had been driven mad by the mental and physical torture; being made to watch images which she found mildly amusing only to find herself dismembered bit by bit. Kate knew that Patricia was not the normal client for Phase Three and Four, but she was prepared to turn a blind eye to keep her girls happy.

Craig Bosworth was exhausted as he cycled up his drive past his Volvo S40, round the back of his house to dismount and place the bike against the wall under the kitchen window. Fumbling in his bum bag for his keys he opened the back door and went straight to the downstairs toilet. When he came back into the kitchen he had quite a start and was glad he had already just taken a leak.

Standing there in the kitchen doorway was a woman whose face was cut and bruised, who had recently been crying by the looks of her running mascara. He was dumbstruck by the stranger's unexplained appearance.

'Doctor Bosworth?'

'I'm not that sort of doctor. Let me call you an ambulance.'

'No, no, it's quite alright. I'm sorry to intrude but I have a few questions about the *kidnapping*,' she explained badly as the word *trafficking* eluded her through tiredness.

Quite caught off guard by his own exhaustion, and then with Gina's appearance *and* condition, Craig blurted, 'I know I was told your team would be keeping an eye on me after you kidnapped me, but I thought you would give me some warning rather than turn up out of the blue. You almost gave me a heart attack.'

Gina wasn't sure what Craig was talking about at first so simply apologised, 'Yes, sorry about that. We've been waiting to catch you in all morning.'

'We?' he said expecting to see another woman, but spotted Will looking at his bike. 'Who are you?'

'Gina Oakley. I'm working with MI5,' she stretched the truth again, 'concerning a number of missing persons.'

'Oh…I see,' he responded rather slowly, trying to get his head in gear, remembering he had been warned not to talk to *anyone* about

276

The Clinic, and wondering what he had already given away.

'You said that *you* had been kidnapped Dr Bosworth. By whom?'

He struggled with how best to answer this, he'd clearly already said too much.

'Nice bike,' Will said as he stepped into the kitchen.

'Thanks, it's a…'

Gina raised a hand to Craig to stop her line of enquiry getting further derailed by cyclist technobabble. 'Who kidnapped you Dr Bosworth?'

Craig really didn't need the stress, and surely the warning wouldn't apply to MI5. 'It was a team of women. I don't know much about them. They didn't tell me much before they brought me back here.'

'What did they want with you?'

'They seemed interested in what I'm investigating on the Internet.'

'Human trafficking and terrorism?'

'Yes that's right, but specifically Dark Net usage. Surely you know about these people. They appeared to be some government department run unit.'

'No…So what did they ask you?'

'Strangely not a lot. They took my computer equipment and copied all my content for their cyber-forensics girls…'

'Girls?'

'Yes I'm assuming so. I never saw a single man while I was at The Clinic.'

'*Clinic*?'

'Yes, it was a clinic. They did some test on me, making me watch materials similar to what my research has been finding on the Dark Net. Then decided I was clear to go.'

Gina seemed to go a funny colour.

'Are you okay Gina?' Will looked at her concerned.

'Yeah…I think so…It's just I think Dr Bosworth has just broken a dream.' She could hear Penelope Ryder saying '*It's Agent Orange. Get her out of here.*' The more she thought about this it was as if she had been in a hospital when the anaesthetic was wearing off.

'A *dream*?' asked Craig.

'She was kidnapped too,' Will explained for her. 'They left her on a channel ferry. Where did they leave you?'

'They brought me back here, with my computer equipment. Listen, what is this all about?'

'That's what we are trying to find out.'

'I just need to call Five,' Gina mumbled as she walked out into the back garden, leaving Will to follow his own line of questions.

Gina looked through her phone list for Defendor and dialled.

Dave was pretty quick to answer. 'How's it going?'

'Just found someone who almost became a missing person. Interviewing them now. Listen Dave, can you access a picture of Penelope and send it straight over, please.'

'Penelope Ryder? Your commander?'

'Yes.'

'What do you want with a picture of her?'

'I'll let you know later if there is a connection.'

'A connection between Penelope and these missing persons?'

'Maybe, yeah.'

It took a few minutes for Dave to send an image to Gina's phone, during which time Will had managed to cover what had been described to Craig by his abductors about what they were doing at this clinic.

Craig had told of a rather clandestine approach to acquiring clients for what had been described as a four phase therapy process, which they were not about to give away, but it led him to assume it was intended to treat frequent users of the Dark Net.

When Gina returned to the kitchen she was holding out her mobile in Craig's direction. 'Did you happen to see this person at this *clinic*?'

'Yes. That's Kate Handy. Head of The Clinic.'

24

'How's it going?' Dave responded, having checked his caller ID and seen it read Agent Orange.

'A surprising turn of events, actually.' Gina explained as she followed Will down Craig's path, back to the Astra.

Craig was left feeling rather anxious, having been instructed by Gina not to mention this visit or discussion to anyone.

'The person I've just been interviewing has positively identified Penelope as heading up some special unit. So I think we are going to have to tread carefully with this one. I need to know what happened with Penelope. Did she really quit, or was she moved on to some black-ops unit?'

'Penelope isn't the sort of person to do anything untoward. If you *are* right and she *has* had this boy brought in, it must be for questioning. She will have her reasons. He'll turn up soon enough.'

Getting into the car she shook her head. 'No, the man I have been talking to describes being taken against his will to some sort of clinic, giving me the impression that something may be happening to a number of missing persons. My intuition says I should not let this one go till I get to the bottom of it. So I really need to know where Penelope went when she left Five.'

'What if no one knows, or admits knowing?'

'Then we will need to set the image recognition onto the satellite records and see what we come up with.'

'That could take weeks to work through hundreds of days of data, and that's only possible *if* there's a computer spare.'

'Use one of the back-ups from storage.'

'There's an idea.'

'See. There's always a way. Just call me as soon as you have anything.' She broke the connection, so as not to let Dave consider further concerns. Nevertheless, she wasn't sure how much help he could be, realistically. She suspected Ethan didn't have weeks.

Will sat in the driving seat watching her. He hadn't started the engine, so as not to interfere with her call. 'Do you have anything to rush back to Birmingham for Gina?'

'Why? What do you have in mind?'

'I was thinking, with it being a bank holiday tomorrow, maybe we could head into the city centre and catch a meal then see where the evening takes us.'

'Well I suppose it might be handy being close to Five in case Dave turns up something to look at.'

'So what is your preference?'

'Yes, stop over, book a room.'

'Oh right, okay, great...But I was asking what type of food you'd prefer to eat.'

'Oh ur Thai.'

'Excellent choice, in fact I know just the place.'

As Gina waited for her rather un-Thai *death by chocolate* to arrive, Will, who didn't fancy any of the desserts on the menu, broached the subject of relationships.

'So are you and DI Dunn an item?'

'What? No…Not anymore…When we were partners yes, for a while, but it was over with Sigh before I left for Five.'

'So it's done with Dunn?'

'Yes that would never have worked out.'

Will wanted to ask why not but instead asked 'What about your man at Five?'

'Yes we had something for a while too, but I guess I just never date the right guys.'

'*Never* is a bit pessimistic don't you think?'

'Well maybe what I mean is that in these fast moving times most people change one way or another, so it is difficult to build any sort of commitment on quicksand.'

'More pessimism,' he pointed out.

'Not really. I believe in living for the present, and having no regrets…So what about you?'

'Oh I have plenty of regrets.'

'No, I mean are you involved?'

'No. Though there is someone I have my eye on.'

'Oh do tell,' she leaned closer.

'Not much to tell. I haven't known her long. It didn't get off to a good start, but when I see her now I feel excited. She's a bit of a mystery.'

'Oh you want to watch out with that sort. They can be unpredictable.'

Jane, Tina, Mel, Rosie, and Sandra stood around Clare's bed. She lay unmoving under the sheets, eyes closed, breathing very shallow. In fact if her monitors had not been reporting her vital signs as low but stable it would have been easy to believe her dead.

'It's been days now. How much longer will she be kept like this?' Jane asked.

'Your guess is as good as mine.' Sandra said. 'Tending to brain injuries needs better facilities than we have here.'

'Can't we move her to a hospital?' asked Mel.

'Kate believes it is too much of a security risk,' Sandra explained.

'What, *more* of a risk than her possibly dying here?' Jane wasn't happy with that decision.

'The hospital would ask questions on admission, and there is a risk that when she started to come round she could start talking, and things might start to unravel. We can't afford to risk anyone finding out what we have set up.'

'I heard that Kate has even considered sending her to Phase Four,' Said Kayleigh, joining them from her own bed, bandages still covering the stitches to her flick-knife wound to the throat.

'You're kidding.' Jane grew even less happy.

'You're not helping matters,' Sandra warned Kayleigh.

Suddenly the women started wondering to what lengths Kate would go to keep everything secret. They knew some staff that had proved problematic in the past had left The Clinic without a word, but had they *actually* left alive? Jane might just have to have words with Pauline.

Will hadn't been sure whether he was going too far, too fast, as he stood with Gina in a hotel reception and booked a double room. He watched for a reaction from her, but there hadn't been a flicker. He hoped that was not down to the number of beers they had both consumed. It had only been a few 750cl bottles, though he understood that not everyone's alcohol tolerance was as high as his.

'Did you bring an overnight bag in the car?' Gina asked, as Will headed for the lift.

'Sadly no. I had no idea we'd be stopping over to be honest.'

'Me neither. Never mind, I'm sure there will be a load of complimentary toiletries in our room.'

Our room. Will liked hearing her say that.

'Pauline?'

'Yes Jane? ' came the curt reply as Pauline put the cleaver she had been using on the butchery table and reached for the saw, to continue with her latest Phase Four victim; a male.

'Has Kate ever brought anyone to you herself?'

'She's introduced me to new team members.' Her response sounded a little evasive to Jane.

'I'm asking whether she has brought you anyone for Phase Four and said to keep it between the two of you?'

'Well if I told you that, it would no longer be between her and I then would it.'

'So she has brought you people.'

'I never said that.'

'Were they staff?'

'You need to be careful Jane.'

While Gina was in the bathroom taking a shower, Will had stripped off ready to take his straight after her. He sat on the end of the bed with a towel around his lower half, flicking through the TV channels when he heard Gina calling him. He poked his head around the door and through the steam of the bathroom he could see some of Gina through the frosted glass shower.

'Will?!'

'Yes.'

'Be a dear and pass me another of those diddy shower gels will you.'

'Okay.' He stepped inside the bathroom closing the door behind him and checked through the assortment of toiletries by the steamed up mirror. Finding the gel he moved over to the shower and slid the door ajar extending a hand inside. 'Here y'go.'

Gina took him by the wrist, opening the door wider, and pulled Will inside.

'Hey,' he laughed with surprise before her wet lips were on his.

She closed the shower door and pulled him tight against her gelled body, pulling the towel loose to soak further in the shower tray.

'Oh…' he murmured, with a realisation of *this is what she meant by unpredictable*.

David was exhausted. His jaws and gums ached terribly. He just wanted sleep to take him away. There was blood on his pillow cover. Some of it was where he had dribbled, but most of it was from where the nurses had taken it in turns to hold the pillow down over his face. The plastic cover under the pillow case, which served to stop blood penetrating the pillow, had made too good a seal and he had passed out a few times despite the pain keeping him lucid.

Now he felt a change coming over him. His fantasies of revenge were being replaced by something *he* found darker. He was starting to wish he were dead, that it would all just end, and he would not wake up to more of the torment. Life had lost its meaning for him, as it became more difficult for him to imagine ever getting given prosthetics or any level of independence following this treatment.

The door opened up and two nurses came in.

'Supper time David.'

'Not hungry,' he mumbled.

'Oh but you've got to keep your strength up,' the one holding the piping hot soup said with a smile.

'Please. I just want to go to sleep.'

The second nurse stepped closer revealing what she had behind her back. 'Spoon…or funnel?'

Blissfully unaware of the goings-on at The Clinic, Will lay beside Gina tenderly running his hand over her shoulder down to her elbow before crossing her waist to her hip, as he smiled into her emerald eyes. They had both learned in the shower it was not easy doing what they wanted to do when she had a number of cracked ribs. Still, Will made to move on top of her but she placed a hand against his chest.

'I think it might be easier for now if I go on top.' Her gentle pressure rolled him onto his back and she slowly straddled his hips.

The suspense of having her breasts slowly lowered onto him in order that she steal another kiss was unfortunately accompanied by the theme to *Enter the Dragon*.

They froze as if stillness would make it go away. It went to voicemail, but the moment was lost, now Gina needed to know who it was.

The phone said missed call from Defendor. There must be a problem she thought and rang him right back, though she continued to sit astride Will.

'What's up Dave?'

'I set the search going, starting from the date Penelope left and just checked in before I headed home and I think we've got something.'

'Already?'

'I know…It seems that just two days after she finished working here, four black vans came to her flat, and took her and *all* of her belongings away.'

'Black vans?'

'Yes, not a single removals van, but four black transits.'

'Where did they take her?'

'That's the odd thing, I don't know.'

'You lost her?'

'No. The place they took her to looks like some sort of agricultural research complex from the satellite shots, but there is no address. I went and Googled it and there is no information. Not even when I looked at the road leading past it with the three-sixty camera views. The front gates have no sign, name, or number. There's not even a post box or a security buzzer.'

'How do visitors get in then?'

'Beats me.'

'Another thing. I used CCTV footage to run the plates on the vans. None of them are registered.'

'So it sounds even more like black-ops then Dave.'

'Yeah. I think you better leave it alone.'

'No. Send me the GPS coordinates, and before you go home can you see if you can find any construction plans for that place on the local council data-bases, please.'

Hanging up, her full attention returned to Will.

25

Two nurses arrived for Ethan and one announced, 'Time to go to Monitoring.'

'There's no need for the wheels anymore. I won't make a fuss. It's pointless,' he tried to sound more mature about it, stepping forward, glancing at their security cards and having decided he needed to start playing it cool if he was going to catch them off guard at some point.

'Okay then.'

As Ethan limped along the corridor, knowing the way now, the wheelchair was brought along after him just in case.

After an early breakfast, Will had driven them west into the Chilterns, where the satnav, primed with Dave's coordinates, brought them doubling back eastwards on the final leg of the journey.

The unnamed establishment lay behind high security fences that looked more Ministry of Defence than Ministry of Agriculture. Gina had instructed Will to drive past at forty-something, while she faced away using a mirror from her bag as if adjusting make-up in order to covertly observe the building and fence.

There were security cameras, but just as Dave had said, there was no way of getting in contact with the mysterious occupants. Either you were expected and the gates would open, or you stayed outside.

Just beyond the grounds the road turned slightly to the right and went up an incline where there was a small layby with big pot-holes on the opposite side of the road. Gina signalled for Will to pull in, which he did. Turning across the opposite lane he almost wrecked the suspension before coming to an abrupt halt with three out of the four wheels in holes.

Gina bit her lip against the pain the sudden stop had caused her ribs. She got out and went to the boot, to return with binoculars. Looking across at the building it was clearly modern, with its mirrored windows, but nothing about its design gave a sense of its function. There were no vehicles in sight, quite probably because it had underground parking Gina thought.

She phoned Dave. 'It's just as you described.'

'What?'

'The building. No signage whatsoever and no movement.'

'Sorry, I was having a lie-in. Yeah, so you're there now?'

'Yes, with eyes-on.'

'Right.' Dave was heard moving around. 'I'm just getting my tablet switched on.'

'Have you had anything back about who built this place for whom?'

'That's what I'm just checking,' his fingers could be heard tapping impatiently as he waited for the 4GHz processor to start up. He was heard to mumble 'There's no excuse for this.'

'I happen to think it's quite important Dave, even for a bank holiday.'

'No sorry. I'm moaning about this bloody tablet, it's *so* slow. Top-of-the-range too. Unbelievable.'

'They're using mirrored windows.'

'Is that what it is, a new operating system?' Dave sounded confused.

'No. The occupants of this building clearly don't want visitors or surveillance of what goes on inside.'

'Right yeah. Now we're cooking on gas. Here we go, just sign into my account, open this report, and…'

'And…?' Gina prompted after a long pause unsure whether the phone connection had been lost.

'Nothing. It looks like records have been erased. Not even an application for planning permission.'

'A thorough cover up then.'

'Looks that way.'

'What about services then?'

'Nada. Only the storm drains and sewage system running the length of the road outside. There appear to be no phone-lines, or power to the site. Probably has its own generator, and mobile mast.'

'Yes I can see a communications mast. Okay, I will see what I can dig up with the local council tomorrow morning myself. Someone must know something. You can't build something like this without someone noticing and asking questions.'

'Right well let me know how you get on.'

'Will do. And thanks.' She broke the connection still observing at the grounds through the binoculars. As tempting as it was to barge in uninvited she knew that would lead to more trouble than they could handle.

'So I take it that was not good news?' Will concluded from Gina's side of the conversation.

'Not particularly. But we haven't got to a dead-end yet. We are going to have to talk Tom into giving us some immediate leave. This is too hot to drop till next weekend.'

'Are you really sure that Ethan is in there? I mean look at the place?'

'If he isn't in there, then there's something up with my Spidey-senses.'

'Okay Spidergirl I believe you. But short of parachuting in I don't see how you would get in there.'

'Oh *there's* an idea...Look!'

Will looked expecting to see a parachutist, but noticed a black van leaving along the gravel drive. The gates opened, it turned right on the road.

'It's coming our way.' Gina stated the obvious.

'Do you think they've seen us?' Will was wishing he had not parked in pot-holes.

As the van came up the incline towards them it began to slow. Quickly Gina grabbed Will and pulled him onto her, and ignoring the pain in her ribs she began snogging him. He found her lips to be a good distraction from the threat of imminent abduction, but it was over all too soon for his liking.

Allah's Fist didn't believe in holidays as days of rest, the term had originated from holy days and therefore believed that it required him to create more misery and mayhem.

However, he intended to do this in style, managing his emails with plenty of Turkish coffee on tap. He sat in his lilac caftan with his heels resting on a foot stool with his top-of-the-range tablet on his lap, cursing Microsoft for being so slow, inclining him towards taking his revenge someday soon.

Nevertheless, he could not believe his good fortune when he received an encrypted report from his mole in the British Government, to say there was a high level of probability that the people he was looking for had just been unearthed by Agent Orange and Defendor.

He was disturbed by this last part of the report. Was he supposed to know who these characters were? He shot an encrypted reply back to cover this point.

The black van was heard to accelerate past then Gina released Will.

'Do you know how to tail a vehicle without being spotted Will?'

'Sure. Always keep three to five vehicles behind.'

'Okay then, let's get after it.'

Will started the car and played with the clutch.

'What are you waiting for?'

'Oh you know three or more cars to pass first.'

Gina's puzzlement turned to disbelief.

'I'm *trying* to shift the car out of the pot-holes,' he explained.

Gina bailed out of the car.

'Get back in, you're not that heavy!' He called after her.

She pulled his door open, but was distracted by what he had just said. 'What's that supposed to mean?'

'I dunno. With you getting out like that I assumed you might be one of those women who are convinced they have a weight problem, and had thought you were stopping the car from moving.'

'You are *so* in trouble. *Out*!'

'Why?'

'I'm driving.'

Gina had the Astra back on the road in no time, though probably killed anything perched in the hedgerow with the flying gravel. They sped to catch up, but there was no sign of the black van.

'It must have turned off.' She pulled over, grabbed the map, and let her intuition tell her where the van had gone. Turning the Astra back and then turning south she drove even faster through the lanes.

'Colin McRae was this fast and he's dead now.' Will prompted her to consider slowing down.

'He didn't die in a car crash though did he,' she stated, not slowing.

'How did you learn to drive like this? Twocking?'

'No, MI5 training.'

'Of course. I feel a bit safer now,' he lied.

'Didn't stop me from causing a multiple pile-up on the M25 though,' she admitted.

'Great.' He took hold of the handle above the door, to stop his head repeatedly hitting the window on the sharp bends.

After a few hair-raising overtaking manoeuvres Gina slowed down.

'What's the matter?'

'I've lost them.'

26

Allah's Fist had barely slept, such was his excitement. His stomach was in turmoil, though this was in part due to his craving for onion marmalade at such times of action, in rallying the troops.

He leaned onto his right buttock and let out another loud trump like an elephant's war cry and sniffed deeply making an appreciative sound with a nod of his head. For Allah's Fist this was the smell of battle.

He considered the information provided by his British Government mole, concerning the *previously* secret establishment in the Chilterns. It was insufficient to confirm that these were the people who were interfering with his funding of jihadist extremism. He had simply chosen not to concern himself with such details.

At the very least what he considered to be his counter-offensive, if wrongly targeted, would be explained away as a dry run for the real thing to follow. Not that he was about to share this point with any of his people, even if he knew that most would happily throw themselves to their deaths in front of public transport if they were told it would help sadden the Infidels.

The real point of this jihad was to entertain their God with misery and death, and for Allah's Fist it all made good propaganda to raise more money. He loved money, for money *was* power.

There was a time when his actions would have rallied the troops of al-Qaeda, but the recent cleansing actions of IS that he had helped fund in Iraq and Syria had been seen as too bad-ass even for them.

A growing number of Muslims had the affront to declare that he and his terrorists were not following the word of Allah. Allah's Fist saw this as a sign of weakness, losing faith since Osama's death, but it hadn't stopped *him*.

Whilst a child of God still lived there was abuse and murder for him to dish out from *his* God's bottomless pit. Like his followers, he couldn't see the lack of internal logic in his own thinking, considering the problems to lie elsewhere in the world.

For what he had planned he knew it did not have to make sense to anyone else, his combined might of *money and fear* was all he needed to direct his horde. He had made transaction after transaction to terrorist groups and lone assassins. Each had been told where to get to, but none had yet been given their final orders.

Already the forces were amassing, by plane, train and automobile. Even by boat, his horde was on the move. Many of his people dropped everything and headed to England though some were already there.

He was aware that the security services knew something big was going down and that they had maxed-up security at ports and airports, but nothing would stop the sheer numbers involved in his plan. This was beyond anything Britain had previously experienced with the thousands of immigrants trying to enter the channel tunnel.

Even if a point came when no more were able to set foot on British soil, there were all of his brain-washed students living in Britain being mobilised to his cause as back-up. The world would have seen nothing like this. He leaned onto his left buttock this time and with a smile pumped more gas loudly into his penthouse.

Tom looked up to see his nephew enter the office with Gina in tow. Instead of going to their separate desks they came straight to him.

'Morning Tom,' they chorused.

'Morning,' his voice held a tone of trepidation. 'What's up now?'

'We need to take two day's holiday,' said Gina.

'It will all be sorted in two days,' added Will.

Tom noted the way these two looked at one another. Something had changed between them. 'We are not talking wedding bells are we?'

'What? No!' Gina looked at Tom as if he had lost the plot.

'More like alarm bells.' Will explained. 'We have found out where Ethan Best is being held.'

'Great. Tell the Best's and the police where he is and hand Mrs Best the bill. I have more work for you both.'

'I don't think it's going to work that way Tom.' Will said, shaking his head.

'I need to get him out of what appears to be some sort of unlawful secure unit,' Gina tried to explain.

'*Unlawful secure unit*?'

'Dave. It's Gina.'

'I know.'

'I need you to sort me some bits and bobs.'

'*Bits and bobs*?'

'Yeah, a parachute and a flight over…'

'I'll stop you there.'

'What?'

'We are officially in lock-down mode.'

'Lock-down mode?'

'Yes there is a major terrorist attack imminent our sources say. Thousands more illegals than usual are trying to get into Britain as we speak, from all directions. You're not going to get a plane up until all this blows over.'

'Damn. So what is going on?'

'That's the problem. No one seems to know. Not even the people we are bringing in for questioning. Those who we have cracked say they were told to come here and await final instructions.'

'Bad timing then,' Gina sighed.

'You could say that,' he sounded tired too.

'Okay then, plan B.'

'Plan B? We're not about to see another Agent Orange incident are we?'

'Have faith. Now I'm going to need you to borrow night vision goggles and a re-breather from the SBS, and I'll need a size sixteen dry-suit. Any chance of a hand gun?'

'I doubt it.'

'Okay. I'll arm myself some other way.'

'What *are* you going to do?'

'Well since the top-down approach is now out of the question it looks like I'm going to have to try bottom-up.'

Gerald Forte was taking a leisurely walk in the park with Joe his dog, or at least he was trying to. He was a little tense and his twelve year old Jack Russell could sense this. As much as he enjoyed all of the Dark Net materials Allah's Fist had made accessible to him, he was somewhat unnerved by what was now happening at the British borders since he had told Allah's Fist what Agent Orange and Defendor had discovered. It could just be coincidence, but he worried that it was not.

Suddenly he was brought out of his thoughts as Joe pulled at the lead and went for a passing Alsatian, most unlike him. The Alsatian was quick to turn, and bit at Joe's head, but Joe was too quick for it. The Alsatian completely missed clamping down on its attacker's skull. Instead it gnashed down on the old lead, cutting right through as if it had sharks teeth. Joe was now loose. With a change of priorities he abandoned his owner. Gerald, apologising profusely first, then went in chase.

For an old dog it was fast enough on its feet and made it into the bushes well ahead of Gerald, ignoring his calls to come back.

Gerald was somewhat out of breath by the time he got into the bushes or as far in as he could. The bushes were quite thick.

He had to go round the back of some and bend down to look underneath. Getting back up every few metres was making him dizzy. Then he realised that he couldn't hear any barking never mind snuffling over the sound of the blood rushing through his ears. This was when he got what he thought was a thorn in his leg, until he stood up straight again and saw a woman holding a syringe with two other women behind her, and a black van parked just beyond the railings.

'Not *you* people,' he exclaimed as he collapsed.

'That was different,' commented the woman with the syringe as she put it away, leaving the other two to lift Gerald. 'They usually ask *who are you people*?'

The body bag was slung into the van beside the dead dog and they were away in seconds.

To say that Will was not happy with Gina and her Plan B would be an understatement. He initially refused to go with her in the hope that it would change her mind. She was in no condition for covert activities which held any possibility of fighting. Nevertheless, since she seemed prepared to go without him he thought it would be better that he was on hand to help, if he could. So they had driven most of the way in silence to the Beaconsfield services on the M40, where they were to meet Dave.

Waiting in the car park Will wondered whether Dave stood any more of a chance of talking Gina out of her mad idea. He didn't have long to wait to find out. Dave was able to park two bays along and Gina wasted no time in going to inspect what he had for her.

She had initially got Will to take her back to her place for a few important items, but without critical equipment from Dave the mission would have been a no-go. Dave opened his boot.

'Thanks for coming Dave. I know it's been a tight timescale.' She put the re-breather down on the tarmac.

'Just take care with that. The scrubbers in those things need next to no excuse to leak and corrode the skin off your bones.'

'I know. I *have* trained with them,' she reminded him, lifting out the green dry-suit with yellow trim, and showing it to him as if he had not actually seen it. '*Seriously*?'

'I know you asked for size sixteen but I had to go to a dive shop and they only had size fourteens.'

'It will be a tight fit, but that will probably give my ribs more support. But that *wasn't* what I was referring to. I take it they didn't have *black*?'

'What does it matter? You'll be down a drain, and by the time you're not, they'll smell you coming before they see you.'

'*You*, I know you!' Gerald exclaimed as he was revived for quick processing and shown into Kate's office where he was prompted to sit for his induction.

'Unfortunately for you, yes.'

'You won't get me to talk you know,' he declared with pride.

'This isn't about getting you to talk, Gerald.'

'Oh I see what you're doing. Reverse psychology. But you will get nothing out of me I tell you.'

'Oh you'd be surprised what we can remove from people here.'

302

'I will take what state secrets I may know to my grave.'

'I expect you will. I'm really not interested in what you know. I have a crack team of hackers who are probably more up to date with intelligence information than you are.'

'You won't get away with this for much longer,' he chuckled like someone expecting to be saved by the bell.

'Then I believe your stay with us will be a short one.' Kate nodded to the nurses accompanying Gerald. 'I think we can progress Gerald straight to Phase Four.'

'Pauline will be in for a treat.'

'Here somewhere…Look *there*.' Gina said, turning from her phone's GPS map as they approached via back roads from the east. Gina pointed across the road into the verge just ahead of them.

Will slowed and with no traffic about veered across the opposite lane and pulled up on the grass. He reversed up till the boot was close to where he had remembered seeing a concrete rectangle with two steel covers on.

Oakley was fully committed. Getting out of the car and opening the boot she removed her shoes and began pulling on the dry-suit, forcing her feet down to the ankle seals, before pulling on each of her yellow dive booties. She smoothed her fleece trousers down so as to avoid any uncomfortable constrictions as she pulled the suit up to her torso. Tucking her top in, with Will's help, and pulling her cuffs down to the end of each sleeve, she noticed Will smiling as he helped her get her head through the neck seal and then zipped and sealed her in.

'What?'

'Nothing. It's just that you look kinda sexy, or would do if you didn't look so much like that character from…'

'I know what you're going to say, just don't. Okay?'

Will couldn't help smirking, but said nothing as he helped her on with the re-breather and the rest of the kit.

As Gina tucked her hair into the hood and finally pulled on the yellow gloves, Will took the hook rods from the boot and handed one to Gina. Then as they stepped each side of the manhole he said, 'What's the betting that after you've got all dressed up, we can't open the drain?'

'I know you don't want me to do this but it's the only option open to us.'

'I don't agree.'

'I know you don't.'

'We don't really know that the lad is even in there.'

'I do. I can feel it.'

Will sighed. He wasn't sure what to make of Gina's feminine intuition. It was all a bit *Jedi* to him.

'Look, Will, there is a chance that I will only be able to get part way, and then have to abort. But I need to know I tried.'

'Okay.'

Together they lifted the steel lids aside.

'Phwaa!' they both turned away gagging, taken aback by the evil smell, considering they were out in the middle of nowhere, not in the middle of some housing estate.

'I don't know what is passing through here but it's a good job you thought ahead to bring that disinfectant spray, towelling and bags,' he laughed.

'Ha yeah…You'd have thought I'd done it before,' she said as if she had.

Popping her mouthpiece in, pulling her goggles down and then lowering her kit bag ahead of her, Gina descended into the sewer.

'Good luck dear!' he called after her, feeling it should have been him doing going down, but glad he wasn't. He was somewhat claustrophobic. He replaced the lids, plunging Gina into darkness were it not for her infra-red lighting.

There were a lot of steps to the bottom, and by the time Gina was down, Will was already back in the car and driving to the layby with the pot-holes, intending to park better this time.

It was a half mile walk for Gina, bent over to avoid the tunnel ceiling before she reached what had to be the outlet for The Clinic. Her legs were already aching, not to mention her ribs from her poor posture.

She crouched aside of the outlet, it was much smaller than the main drain; not as big as she had hoped. She knew she needed to make her way up it, but she could not get in with the re-breather on. It was barely wide enough to crawl up it without the extra kit. She began to question her decision-making.

What actual proof *did* she have that this was even the right drain? She couldn't even discuss it with Will. There was no longer a signal down there. Gina just had to trust her intuition.

As if in answer to her doubts she thought she heard a scream. Her heart began to race and she tried to control her breathing, which was noisy through the mouthpiece.

Then as she listened intently, holding her breath, she heard it again, eerie and harrowing. Quickly she removed her re-breather from her back, keeping the mouthpiece in. The only way forward now was to use the cave diving technique of pushing her kit ahead of her.

As she lifted the re-breather up, to the sound of more screams, she noticed a trickle of what could have been blood coming from the outlet.

27

Brian Levenholt had fished in the English Channel for thirty odd years, in all weathers. In that time he had never seen the likes of what was taking place now, on this otherwise calm day.

He could only see a fraction of what was going on all around Britain's coastline. Nevertheless, over the last few hours he had noted a very unusual increase in traffic heading across the channel to England, both on the sea and in the air.

It was almost like an exodus from the continent, or even an invasion, but none of the craft were military; they were all civilian, which made it all the scarier. Brian's instincts told him to get his nets back in double-quick, and get back to the harbour.

A number of Royal Navy vessels were out providing support to dozens of Royal Marine launches which were intercepting boats of all sizes.

Brian caught what sounded like machinegun fire. It started some way off, sounding like it was hand weapons. Then there came much deeper; larger calibre weapons fire accompanied by the clatter of rotor blades.

Two helicopters followed by another two sped across the horizon launching their attacks. No air sea rescue craft these, but gunships. However, the boats and planes just kept coming, none turning back.

Then Brian spotted a number of Eurofighters. It was clearly suicide for these people to keep coming, but on they came. It was like Britain had suddenly taken a very hard stance against illegal immigration. Light aircraft were turning into fireballs and ditching into the sea, one came down on a yacht. Two speedboats were reduced to matchwood. Whatever was going on? He wondered. Had the world gone insane?

Progress for Gina was slow in the sewer pipe. It certainly didn't help that the caterpillar motion she had adopted was grating the cracks in her ribs.

If the exhaustion from the pain in her chest was not enough to make her quit and turn back, the exertion of having to push *and* pull her kit along should have been, as it was making her dry-suit decidedly wet inside with sweat.

She hoped her phone would not be destroyed by the moisture building up in her fleece top within the suit. Although there would be no phone signal down there, she could do with some friendly banter.

The only partially positive thing she could think about, other than that every shuffle she made brought her another few inches towards her target, was that at least it was not her on the receiving end of the torture being dealt out up ahead.

She had initially assumed that the sewers would lead to some sort of bathroom or toilet area, but had come to wonder if it actually led to some sort of interrogation facility. She hoped she would not find, after all of this struggling, that the screams had been Ethan, and that she was too late, but she didn't think it was. As the screams of utter agony slowly drew nearer and clearer they seemed more like those of an older male.

Eleanor entered Kate's office.

'It would seem we have company coming Kate.'

'What do you mean?' Kate had the unnerving feeling that the unimaginable was about to happen.

'That Gerald Forte has been singing for his life, as some do, but we have checked out his claim that Islamic State is coming, and he could be telling the truth.

'There appears to be an invasion happening as we speak. The services communication channels in and out of the UK are hot with chatter. People coming to England every which way they can.

'Their direction of travel, once they reach our shores from France, Holland, Ireland, it doesn't seem too off the mark to conclude they are coming here.'

'How is this possible? This whole place is off the radar; black.'

'It would seem that that woman who was brought in with Ethan Best has worked out where we are and…'

'Hell no, not Agent Orange! She should never have been brought back here! But why…How has *she* organised all these people you say are coming? That isn't like her.'

'I don't believe she has.'

'So it's coincidence?'

'No we think it is the work of Allah's Fist.'

'I don't understand.'

'It would seem, from what Forte has given us that Agent Orange has been working with Five and he has passed this information on to Allah's Fist, who has rallied his IS troops to avenge our black-ops successes.'

'But this can't be happening. I…we…have taken such care. How can Agent Orange have worked out where we are? She was heavily sedated when she was brought in.'

'Maybe not that heavily sedated. Looking over the reports of the Pen y Fan extraction team, it would appear that Agent Orange may not have received the full dose.'

'Blast! But still, how did she manage to find this place again?'

'It seems Five traced you leaving your apartment the day you moved here.'

'But that would mean she knew *I* was involved.'

'It would seem so.'

'Damn her. She always was too intuitive for her own good that one.'

'So what do we do now, Kate?'

'Get any units we still have in the field back in now.'

'I think it might be too late for that.'

'Okay then…I want a complete lock-down. You need to prep everyone for possible attack. And if anyone out there finds Agent Orange…'

'Kill on sight.' Eleanor nodded.

'No not kill on sight! Bring her to me. I need to know what she knows first!'

'Sorry, yes.'

'And another thing…Have that Best boy brought to me right away.'

'Ethan?'

'*Yes.*'

'Oh okay,' Eleanor frowned, not seeing why the lad should be key to any of this present situation.

Allah's Fist was hammering both his fists on the table top either side of his tablet making the fan buzz unhappily. Where had his mole gone?

Of all the times for Gerald Forte to vanish off on a jolly, now was not a good time. Allah's Fist needed more first-hand Intel from Five to inform his attack.

He was getting feedback from those who had been successful enough to penetrate Britain's border security and military defences. He had his less well trained people heading into London as his decoy distraction while his highly trained men and women were heading to the Chilterns target area with all speed.

However, both groups were clearly gaining some attention of the police. Nevertheless, this did not worry Allah's Fist much as his horde continued to gather. He would win by numbers. He just needed to know when the best time to attack was going to be. For that he required some idea of what was going on inside the target building, which he understood Agent Orange to be working her way into at that very moment, as his unwitting ally.

Ethan Best, his wrists still cuffed, but no longer bound to a wheelchair, was shown into Kate's office.

'That will be all,' Kate dismissed the nurse, but the nurse just frowned. She had never been asked to leave a *client* alone in Kate's office before. Kate waved her away. 'It'll be okay. I've got this.'

'Okay,' she turned for the door.

'Go and prep with the others.'

'Yes, will do,' the nurse replied before closing the office door after her.

'Ethan?'

He just looked at her, as if sizing her up.

'Sit down.' Kate gestured to the chair in front of her desk, and watched as he sat without argument. 'It is time we talked.'

'Talked again,' he put in pedantically.

'Talked *differently*,' she suggested.

'*Differently*? Would that be in silly voices or…?'

'Don't be stupid now. I have something very important to discuss with you.'

Ethan said nothing.

'I have been watching your progress with Phase Two, and it has come time to decide what to do next.'

'Next?'

'Yes. When a client's monitoring shows that they have responded well to the writing therapy, they can be returned to the community.'

'Community?' he sneered at her choice of words.

'They can be sent back home,' she rephrased. 'But when someone has not responded well to Phase Two we have to try something else. And in your case…'

'I haven't responded well,' he guessed.

'No.'

Ethan's mind began to calculate how easy it might be to overpower Kate and take her security card, and possibly her life. The problem was, she was sitting the other side of the table and he had not seen her security card yet.

'When Phase Two fails the client is moved out of that wing and into the Phase Three wing, where tougher measures are taken. In simplistic terms it might appear that we try to bring about the desired result through a change of mind in Phase Two, while in Phase Three the focus is upon results through a change in body.'

'Eh?'

'I know people might argue that in view of what Phases Three and Four are really intended to achieve it makes Phase Two appear rather pointless, but I rather like the fact that Phase Two throws both hope *and* disappointment into the mix, for all concerned. It keeps life here less logical, and so much less *predictable*.'

'I don't understand *what* you are talking about.'

'Writing about ones thoughts and feelings and reflecting upon them has been shown to alter certain people's self-perception, similarly the removal of body parts has been found to bring about change through a loss of self.'

'Loss of body parts?!' he looked more concerned now.

'Yes. As people lose their body bit by bit, they lose their independence, and come to question who *they* are and what sort of life they have left to live.'

'Hey, you are not chopping *me* up!' he stood up and stepped forward aggressively.

'Sit down! I haven't finished!' she shouted to hold his attention, then softened her voice and with a smile added 'besides, there is nowhere for you to run.'

Ethan remained standing, his eyes searching for the card.

Kate could see he was looking over her desk, so she turned her tablet face down then continued. 'It would seem that people in Phase Three often believe that if they lose their need for causing and viewing pain and death then they will go from Monitoring to be fitted with prosthetics and be allowed to leave.

'At times we may even seed such ideas. But the truth is Phase Three is the heart of what all this is about.' She spread her hands to what was around them. 'Nobody leaves here alive once they enter Phase Three. Everyone working for me has been diagnosed as either a psychopath or a sadist, as are the majority of clients.'

'But…'

'The way I control the loyalty of those chosen to join us is through the manipulation of their dark needs, making them feel accepted, by providing them with a constant supply of *live entertainment*.'

Gina stopped for another rest. She had passed a number of smaller pipes emptying into the one she was shuffling along, so that was confirmation enough that she was somewhere under the building now. She struggled to turn on her side, blocking the rivulet of gore with her shoulder as she reached for her drinking bottle.

She was *so* thirsty, but the challenge of cleaning the bottle when her gloves were so filthy and to then drink from it was all too much. Gina almost sobbed as she began to wonder why she doing this?

The lad she was hoping to find and rescue was to the best of her knowledge a hated school bully. Whilst it seemed fair that everyone should get a second chance, hadn't Ethan in all probability given *the finger* to a ton of second chances?

So if Gina was not doing this for Ethan, then was she doing it for the principle of it? She came to the realisation that she must be putting herself through this because she had to know that she still had it in her to be MI5 material. It was becoming her personal *selection* test.

Looking over the re-breather unit, she thought she could see light up ahead. She lifted the night vision goggles slightly to see with her own eyes. It was a dim light, but it was there.

She lowered the goggles and pressed on. The pain of injuries always felt worse after a rest, but she knew if she just kept going it could ease a little.

Eventually she could see the light was coming from above the tunnel, just a few metres in front of her. But she also noticed two things which made her less happy: First, the tunnel was now at an end with a right angled vertical bend, up which she would need to make her way out. Secondly there was something suspended from the roof of the tunnel just before the turn. She edged closer for a better look.

It was entirely possible that it was some sort of motion sensor defence mechanism. Considering this she decided that if it was detecting motion it would surely have already alerted those above her, but she heard no alarm or activity, beyond the pitiful screams of the still conscious man.

Moving very slowly, knowing that if instead this was some form of weapon that each shuffle could be her last, she tried to make out what she was looking at.

It appeared to be a couple of packages inside a metal cage which was screwed at either end to the ceiling of the tunnel. The two packages had a small device separating them, which was possibly a control device of sorts.

Then Gina had one of those camera zoom-out moments of realisation, *and fear*.

The cage contained what appeared to be two explosive breast implants, connected by an electronically controlled valve trigger unit which protruded into each bag of liquid.

Gina had flashbacks to the *Wave Forge* going up, and felt panic coming for her. She was not claustrophobic, but a tense situation like this could give it to anyone.

Was it possible that Penelope could have taken a couple of those breast implants from Five's evidence-room and had them placed here? But why?

It would be more than a counter-measure; it would be more like self-destruct. Gina knew she had to keep her calm if she was going to survive this situation.

She pushed her re-breather as close to the cage as possible without putting it underneath, then edged herself on top of it, squeezing as close as she could towards the device, to get the best possible look at what she was dealing with.

She decided that the control device had no visible motion sensor, or trip laser, but then it *could* have a trembler switch. The pipes puncturing each of the implants had made a tight seal. There was no sign of leakage.

However, as soon as one or both became detached from the trigger device they would leak immediately. What could she do, other than abort her mission and back all the way out? She knew from personal experience that these two liquids must not come into contact with one another. They would react so very quickly and violently that she probably would know nothing about triggering the explosive, if it came to it. Nevertheless, she was not ready to die today.

She shuffled backwards off of the re-breather and turned over onto her back and removed her filth streaked gloves for greater dexterity. It was the only way she was going to manage what needed to be done next.

She took her black Swiss-army knife from the tool pack on her belt. Then she turned onto her front again and slowly extended her arms over the rebreather and under the cage. Using one hand to maintain upward pressure on the cage, she used the other to unscrew one of the fixings.

The man, no more than a couple of metres above Gina, began his blood curdling screams again. This was not conducive of keeping a steady hand, but Gina had to try and focus. With one fixing loose she swapped hands. Maintaining the upwards pressure was her first priority before tackling the second fixing.

Thankfully the man fell silent and the terrible strain seemed to lift for Gina too. She made good progress and soon the fixings were no longer attached. Now she had to lower the cage millimetre by millimetre, keeping it level, to check out the upper side of the trigger device.

What she was hoping for, but intuition told her would not be there, was an off switch. What she saw, long moments later, was a blank LCD screen. Suddenly the man screamed like he was being disembowelled and Gina flinched. The timer started counting down.

28

The countdown had started at '999' like some sort of sick *call for help* joke. Then it began to strip away the seconds.

By Gina's calculations that meant the device had been set to a delay of just over a quarter of an hour, but what on Earth was the point of a delay? She wasn't about to give that question further thought right there and then though, she had to disarm the device first, and if she was lucky could come back to that question later.

Now that the timer was already triggered she didn't need to take quite the same level of care with the device.

Quickly she placed it onto the re-breather unit, shuffled backwards and turned over. Reaching back into her tool pack she took out two sealable plastic dive-bags which she had kept spare for her phone or anything else she found a need to keep watertight. She had considered finding memory cards and other evidence during her mission but not these breast implant explosives.

Returning her attention to the streaming numbers she inverted the cage and pushed out the trigger and its two tightly packed implants. Then she pulled one of the implants off and put it straight into one of the bags, clipping together the compression seal and turning its two toggles to *lock*. The contents were leaking inside, but provided they stayed in there, and did not react with the dive-bag it should be fine, she hoped.

Wasting no time Gina decided against removing the trigger from the second implant in case its residue came in touch with that of the first. She placed both remaining parts of the device into the second dive-bag and sealed it.

As luck would have it there was enough room in her tool pack to take one of the bags. The other she quickly placed into her kit-bag which she had been dragging behind her all the way.

Now she just had to get out of the drain to stand any chance of putting a stop to the trigger, which would allow the fluid residues in the device to come into contact. There was probably enough left in the trigger device to kill her in this confined space.

There was no longer any sound coming from above which meant no cover for any noise she might make. She tried to keep her movements quiet, but could not afford to take it slowly now.

She moved the re-breather into the bottom of the shaft, shuffled forwards and looked up to see a steel drain cover with liquid still running in. It splashed her goggles but she kept them on for now in case there was bleach or other chemicals in the mix which she could not detect through her mask.

She started to lift the re-breather unit and shuffle into the bend, pulling her kit-bag after her. The bend was a tight squeeze and her ribs complained. As she got her feet under her to try and push up, her knees grated on the inner edge. It was obvious that she wasn't going to get through that way round. She slipped back down and turned around then pushed up with her legs behind her.

Although this felt more awkward it did the trick and as she began to stand she felt the re-breather unit come into contact with the underside of the drain cover. All she needed to find now was that the cover was screwed down. If it was, she would have no way of reaching it.

She would not be able to get the re-breather past her body to stand on and reach the cover. Her only option was to push the unit against the cover as a test of how it was fixed.

Gina pushed, but she could not see what she was doing. She had to judge by feel, and with every push vital seconds were lost.

The cover seemed solid, but then it gave and popped up, as if it had only been glued in place by the residue of torture.

Gina's sigh of relief was almost a sob. She moved the unit in a cyclic motion, up-back-down-forward, inching the cover aside as quickly as she could. Thankfully it did not seem to be drawing any unwanted attention.

Then she was pushing the re-breather out of the drain, as high as she could till it fell aside. Pulling her now aching arms down to her sides she executed a quick chimney ascent to escape. Her hands and boots slipped a couple of times on the filthy walls, but she made it out.

Gina had exited into what looked like a butchery room. She removed her goggles then the mask and mouthpiece and abandoned them both on the tiled floor. She pulled up the kit-bag and replaced the drain cover, then detached the tow-line from her belt.

She still had to deal with the explosive, but first she had to check out her situation.

The table to one side contained a disembowelled torso, and next to it a head. Gina thought she recognised the face. She could have been mistaken, because the eyes and teeth where missing, but it looked like someone she had seen at some of the meetings at Five. Gerald Forte.

Then she noticed the trays with digits and limbs and it became clear what she had been hearing. This was no interrogation room. Who were these people? Was Ethan still alive?

Gina caught herself. This was no time for pondering any questions. She opened the door slowly and looked outside. This was a large kitchen area, as might be found in a hotel, but oddly there was no one there. There were things cooking but no other sign of activity. A point in her favour she thought as she returned to the butchery room, opening her tool-pack as she did so.

She removed the dive-bag, unclipped it and then gripping the breast implant inside the bag pulled the trigger free. She placed the trigger on the table, re-sealed the implant in the dive-bag and returned it to the tool-pack on her belt. Then she placed the trigger inside Gerald's gutted torso.

Even though she had disarmed the explosive she didn't want to be around when the trigger unit detonated, and had no idea when people would return either, but she could not leave as she was. She had to clean up and sort out her weapons, quickly. She saw a showerhead and hose and began washing her suit and kit off.

Meanwhile Will, who had been growing more and more tense, hearing nothing from Gina, noticed a police car in his rear-view mirror. As it passed him by he noticed dents in the back end as if it had been in a recent collision. The car drove down towards The Clinic and slowed as it neared the gates. Then Will noticed another police vehicle come from the other direction to join it, this one a van.

The gates didn't open and as if impatient for attention and entry the red and blue lights came on. When the gates still remained shut the sirens blared. Nothing moved on the grounds, but Will noticed more movement in his rear-view mirror. It was a bus, but this place was not on any bus route.

Pauline was first back from the emergency briefing. She had missed the beginning just because she didn't feel she could leave Gerald's side, unopened.

She had heard enough though to get the gist of the message. There were expected to be some unwelcomed visitors, but that just meant extra playtime to her.

When Pauline got into the kitchen, above the sound of things cooking, she could hear the shower in the butchery room. She knew she had not left it on, so went straight through to investigate. Having just been warned about uninvited visitors, though not believing for one minute they would come just for a shower in her kitchen, she had the forethought to pick up two meat cleavers on her way past.

The door opened wide and both women looked at one another with a degree of surprise. Pauline did not wait to ask who this unknown woman was.

She threw one of her cleavers at Gina's chest for the best chance of bringing her down. Gina did not wait to finish her shower but dived aside, hearing the cleaver clatter against the tiled wall behind her. Getting up off the floor she saw Pauline coming at her swinging her remaining cleaver about wildly.

Pauline, red-faced with rage, didn't look like someone who would hear reason, and being unarmed Gina grabbed the nearest thing to her, her re-breather.

Bringing it up like a shield where she stood, the cleaver came down hard and got stuck. Enraged further Pauline grasped the unit then pulled the cleaver free, just as Gina delivered a heavy kick into Pauline's stomach, which knocked the air out of her and doubled her over, head-butting the re-breather unit which Gina still attempted to shield herself with.

The cleaver slipped form Pauline's grip as she raised both of her hands to her face. The screaming began. She had cut into the unit's scrubbers.

The caustic powder within had bellowed out as she yanked her cleaver free. The powder was now in her eyes, her mouth and even her lungs as she had gasped it in. Gina watched as Pauline fell away, her flesh visibly fizzing.

Gina had no firearm to silence Pauline so grabbed the clean cleaver, dropped earlier, and embedded it in Pauline's skull, cutting short both noise and movement.

She quickly returned to her kit-bag, opening it back up and armed herself, before rushing from the butchery room. She was almost out of the kitchens when two women came in. At first they looked shocked but then they both laughed.

'Who are you supposed to be?' one said as both looked up and down Gina's green dry-suit with yellow trim. 'Kick-Ass?'

'No…Hit Girl!'

They laughed, still thinking it a joke.

'Where is Ethan Best?'

'Who?'

'Wrong answer,' Gina gave her only warning.

Both women understood this was their moment to act and rushed her.

Standing her ground Gina reached behind her and drew from a harness two black nunchakus. The metal bars on chains became a blur of motion as they rotated one way then another, clubbing the women senseless, before coming to rest under Gina's armpits.

The bus did not slow like the police cars had, it turned at the last moment ploughing between the two police vehicles at an angle and through the main gate. It did not get far down the gravel drive however, as the metalwork jammed under its chassis and slewed it onto the lawn. People carrying guns of all shapes and sizes poured off the bus.

Will wondered how the police would deal with this, but as he watched the situation develop, the men from the police vehicles actually joined the people from the bus.

As if this was not shocking enough, Will then noticed loads of people coming from every direction. Not just from either end of the road, they seemed to be coming across the fields and out of the forest like some flash-mob zombie apocalypse. He had to try and warn Gina. As he fumbled with his mobile a big bang came from The Clinic.

Gina was looking through window panes in doors as she quickly made her way down the corridor. She heard an explosion. It hadn't come from the kitchen, though it was about time for the detonator, so what was going on?

That question like many others was shelved as four troopers suddenly appeared round the corner ahead of her.

'Well look who it is?' declared Tina.

'Agent Orange,' said Jane.

'No, no, I think it's...Kick-Ass,' said Rosie.

'Don't,' warned Gina, striding closer.

The women all laughed.

'Where is Ethan Best?' Gina demanded.

'I think you are a bit late Agent Orange,' said Mel. 'I hear Kate is having her wicked way with him right now.'

'What?'

Gina's question went unanswered as the four women launched themselves at her, raising their side-arms. The nunchakus became a blur once again, just as her phone began ringing. She had no way of answering it, what with it being in the pocket of her fleece, inside her dry-suit, and of course being rather preoccupied. Nevertheless, the irony of the loud ring-tone playing *Enter the Dragon* as she swung her deadly nunchakus in The Clinic, was not lost on her.

She smiled as she put one woman down after another, in rapid succession. The battle armour seemed no match for the metal whirlwind, especially when brutal contact was being made with wrists, necks and faces, as payback for the broken ribs and the black-eye Gina was still sporting.

'Stop!' Jane pleaded, disarmed, and nursing a possible broken arm. Stumbling backwards, she was now the only one of the four troopers remaining conscious.

Gina expected this to be a ruse, so remained prepared to deliver her final blow.

'I can take you to Kate,' Jane offered. After all, that is what they were told Kate wanted during Eleanor's briefing.

'Go on then.'

Jane led the way.

As they drew close to the centre of The Clinic two armed men rushed round a corner straight into Jane and Gina.

The men knew from hearing the ring-tone that they were about to see someone else to shoot, so they already had their weapons raised. What they had not expected was one of the women to be already injured. They had presumed that they were the first to get this far.

The other thing that was unexpected was the way Gina wrapped a nunchaku chain around the barrel of a semiautomatic rifle and pulled it aside as she swung her hip in, lifting her leg for a roundhouse kick that caught the man low on the jaw and wrenched his neck sideways with an audible snap.

The second man got a round off as Jane tried to jump aside. The bullet passed through her already injured arm, and she cried out in disbelief. The man aimed for a kill-shot but never got his chance as Gina's second nunchaku caved the back of his skull in.

'Who are *these* people?' Gina asked Jane, now that it was clear that The Clinic was under attack.

'Islamic State.'

'Right then come on.' Gina helped Jane back up, taking the risk of giving her one of the men's AK47s, and they ran on to the sound of *Enter the Dragon*.

Will was getting very concerned now. Gina wasn't picking up, or couldn't pick up yet. Leaving a message seemed pointless so he just kept ringing. More people were coming, from goodness knows where, some on bikes, but now many were on foot. No one seemed at all interested in him. He might as well have been invisible.

As he got out of the car, the idea came to Will of joining the ranks as a way of getting inside The Clinic.

'When I won many millions on the Euro-Lottery some years ago,' Kate explained to Ethan. 'I hatched out this dream, and used my cyber-forensics knowledge of Internet crime to begin redirecting mafia money and terrorist funds into a myriad of accounts of my own, to fund the development of my own network.

'I thought at first that I could involve men and women alike. But the men almost always wanted to take control and I couldn't have that. So most ended up in the pig farm.' Kate explained.

'Pig farm?'

'Yes. Everything we remove from Phases Three and Four ends up feeding the pigs. You see it is literally *My Way or the Sty Way*.' She noticed that her attempt at humour brought out a smile. 'I do have a few male operatives working with us on certain black-ops where necessary, but mainly, as you will have seen, it is women.'

'I wouldn't have thought there were this many like-minded women.'

'Surprising isn't it Ethan.'

'So why are you telling me all this?' He was wondering where this was leading. He didn't fancy the *Sty Way* as she put it.

'I am suggesting that since you failed Phase Two and should be progressing to Phase Three, there might be another *option* for you.'

They both heard a big bang downstairs. Someone had just made an explosive entry, so Kate knew she did not have long.

'Ethan, I'm offering you the chance of joining us, and getting trained up for extractions and wet-work. This is a parasitic organisation and there is plenty of sickness out there to feed off. You would do similar training to the SAS, and I know how much you would like to do something like that.'

Ethan's eyes narrowed with suspicion, 'But why me? Why did you have *me* brought here? There must be plenty of others.'

'Ethan, you are my *son*.'

After a moment to consider this revelation he said 'Well, *Mum*…That would have sounded more *convincing* if you'd said it in a deeper voice with that mug over your mouth.'

29

'Look,' said Kate, crossing to a cupboard, 'I've kept your rucksack here with all your stuff in, from when you were taken on Pen y Fan.' She pulled it out for Ethan to check.

Ethan still did not look convinced. Was she really his mother? Or was she a madwoman? Hadn't she just admitted to being the psychopath of psychopaths? Maybe this was just another of the tricks they played here.

Gunfire could be heard getting closer. It occurred to Kate that unless her girls could overcome the IS attack, at least to ensure a controlled retreat, she may have to set the self-destruct sequence on the whole base. Returning her attention to her son she could see he wasn't taken in by her honesty.

'Let me remove those cuffs,' she came to him and unfastened them.

He rubbed his wrists. Now was his chance to act, but he considered again what if she *was* his mother?

'Oh and there's this I've prepared for us.' Kate returned to the cupboard and brought out a large bag. She opened the zip to show wads of notes, and some false passports for each of them. She thought that Ethan began to look more convinced by what she was saying, unless it was just that he had decided to go with the money option.

At that moment there came a knock on the door. Kate looked round expecting it to be

Eleanor with bad news, but it was worse, much worse. It was Jane with Agent Orange.

'I found her downstairs,' Jane announced.

'Hell Oakley! What are you doing here? Why have you brought Islamic State with you?!'

'I didn't Penelope.'

'Course you have you stupid bitch!!'

'Hey! It's just coincidence!'

'Nothing is coincidence with you Agent Orange. You are *jinxed*.'

Gina didn't know what to say, she was looking at Ethan glad to see he was still alive.

'Who is this?' asked Ethan.

'This is the woman who tried to prevent us extracting you from Pen y Fan. I believe she was asked by the Bests to find you and bring you home.

'As you can see she is not good at letting things lie. Rather tenacious is our Agent Orange, if somewhat failure prone.' Kate turned to Jane who was looking somewhat faint, 'Get back out there and see what support you can provide, Jane.'

'Jane?' Gina chanced. 'Jane Newton?'

'Yes,' she stopped in her tracks sounding surprised.

'Roger has been trying to find you.'

'Well…You can just tell him I won't be coming back.' She turned and left, looking forward to killing some visitors.

There came the sound of another explosion and the lights went out for a few seconds, and then came back on as a back-up generator kicked in. The level of attack was starting to look heavier than Kate thought they could deal with and she grew anxious. Turning back to

Gina, Kate asked 'If you did not come in with IS, how *did* you get here?'

'Via your sewers,' Gina said reaching into her tool-pack and drawing out the dive-bag, tossing it to Kate. 'Which reminds me, how come I found a pair of these breast implants? I thought you had all of them destroyed by ordinance?'

'Oh my God! *Oh my God*!' Kate ran back to her table and flipped her tablet back over but its screen had frozen. The intranet hub was down, and although she could now see the self-destruct had already been triggered, there was no way of aborting it.

'You are such a fucking liability Oakley! When did you trigger the timer?!'

'Ooo about ten fifteen minutes ago. But don't worry I disarmed it, as you can see.'

'That's only one of them, I acquired all of them and they are all here and interlinked. Shit! The whole base is going to go up and now you've gone and jinxed the network I can't save it. Damn it!!'

'We best get out of here then.' Gina announced calmly, reaching for Ethan.

'*You* are not going anywhere.' Kate said lifting a Sig P266 from her desk draw. 'It's time you paid for your damages.'

'Come on Penelope. Let's just get the boy out of here,' Gina tried to reason with her before it was too late to get away.

'Sit down!' Kate ordered Gina into the seat that Ethan had been sitting in.

Gina flung one of her nunchaku at Kate's head but she was not quick enough and Kate dodged, pulling the trigger of her pistol as she moved. The bullet caught Gina in the left arm twisting her and causing her to drop the remaining nunchaku.

Kate came around the desk to stop Gina reaching for the nunchaku on the floor. 'Ethan dear, find something to bind her to that chair, quickly,' she urged as she stepped a little closer.

Ethan did as his mother said, and reached into his rucksack for the only thing he could think to use. He drew out the roll of cling-film he had bought for his *hard routine* and began wrapping it around Gina and the chair back while his mother pressed the muzzle of her weapon against Gina's forehead.

Kate knew that common sense would dictate that she simply pull the trigger and get the hell out of there. It wasn't as if it would disturb the boy. However, another less rational part of her wanted Gina to feel the full punishment for her interferences. She wanted her to count every last second before she burned in the hell she had brought.

Ethan brought Gina's arms together behind her as he tightened the wrap. Blood trickled down Gina's injured arm, and with every drop of blood to hit the floor the three of them were conscious that it might be their last moment.

With the plastic holding Gina firmly in place, Kate pulled Ethan away, not towards the office door and possible enemy fire in the corridors, but to the cupboard. Opening a hidden door at the rear she ushered Ethan through with the bags, then closed the door after them. Then they were gone.

They left via a deadfall escape pod, which decelerated immediately before the bottom.

Though the drop was a short one the G-force was nevertheless a bit stomach churning. Kate opened the pod door and they stepped out into a secret corridor. Two strides further and Kate opened a blast door then closed it after them with a sigh.

Though she would rather they were much further away from The Clinic, preferring to have set off the self-destruct sequence in her own good time, this relative safety would have to do. Nevertheless, she pressed on down the corridor with Ethan at her side, still with a bit of a limp, waiting to hear the explosion above them any second.

'Why did you never keep me?' Now seemed as good a time as any, Ethan thought, to interrogate her.

'What?' she was not prepared for this question, right now.

'Why did you give me up for adoption? Was I not a *nice* baby?' He wondered if even then he had seemed to her too much of a chip off the old block.

'Ethan, you need to understand I *did* love you, and *have* missed you. I have kept an eye on you from afar. The problem was I was convinced that I was not a good mother and that if you had stayed in my care I am sure I would have killed you.'

'But why?'

'It is difficult to control dark needs when you have someone so helpless in your care, when you have a burning need to watch them suffer. Do you see now?'

He thought about it as he followed her deeper into the tunnel. 'I think so.'

Soon they passed through a secondary blast door, but still there was no quake of the expected explosion. Kate began to think through again how the self-destruct system worked. It had been such a long time since The Clinic's construction, when the ring of devices had been placed into the foundations. Besides which, with all the secrecy concerning the whereabouts of The Clinic she never expected she would need to use the system.

She led Ethan up what seemed like hundreds of steps back to the surface, and was quite out of breath by then. Nevertheless, even with his bad ankle and heavy rucksack *he* was not.

'Why hasn't your bomb gone off?' he asked.

They could both hear the battle continue inside The Clinic.

'I think,' Kate said between gasps as they headed across the lawn from the exit hatch, 'the trigger devices…work through the building's intranet….So the central server has to manage the delay…and trigger the devices together.'

'What do you mean?'

'Well…when we had that power-cut earlier…I think it caused an additional delay…as the system rebooted…and then it will have either reset the count or continued from where it left off…Either way, it looks like we may have a chance to make good our escape after all.'

'But what about all of your friends in there?'

'There is not the time to warn anyone else.'

'What if the bomb has been aborted by the power-cut? Won't they need you to command them?'

'I doubt the self-destruct will have aborted. It is there to ensure the destruction of all our intelligence data, so that no one finds out about our satellite bases all around the world. They are the future of my dream. Come on,' she urged, her breath almost back. 'The armoured Range Rover is in a shed just at the back of the piggery.' She jingled the car key's that she held in readiness.

Heavy machinegun fire smashed through a window and let out the screams of men and women dying.

Kate could see that Ethan was still trying to get to grips with everything she had told him. 'Are you forgetting that I am a psychopath too, Ethan? I make my decisions based on logic and need to cause suffering. I cannot help my girls by going back. Either they win out and I can take control again, or they die trying. They are all highly trained.'

They passed close by the pig pens at the rear of the piggery and the pigs became excited expecting a feast.

Suddenly Kate felt a terrible pain in her back as if she had been hit in a kidney by a stray bullet. The pain made her legs buckle and she dropped the keys, turning to grab the rails of the pen to her side.

Looking back to check that her son was okay she saw Ethan was just standing there, watching her, holding a carving knife. It was one of the knives he had taken from the old woman's house in Hereford.

Before Kate could comprehend what she was seeing, her son plunged the knife deep into her chest, drew it back out, and dropped it. Then as she began to tip forward he lunged at her once again. He shoved his shoulder under her breasts, his hands on her hips, and heaved her up over the railings and in with her pigs. The squealing of the pigs peaked as they rushed for his mother to sink their teeth into her legs. She desperately scrabbled to get back out of the pen, pulling herself up the railings, looking with utter astonishment into Ethan's cold eyes.

'This is where my nightmares end,' he announced.

'No Ethan, no!' her face was a picture of confused disbelief, to have misjudged him so.

'Sorry *mother*. You have no idea how long I have wanted to do something like this.'

She screamed as flesh was ripped from bone, till he silenced her by picking the blade back up and slicing it across her throat.

He watched calmly as she coughed up blood with her muted screams before collapsing onto the blood stained straw. At that moment he no longer cared about any bomb blast, he felt invincible, avenged for being made into the monster he knew he was. 'Thank you.'

David could hear all the explosions and gunfire and wondered whether it might be the police coming to arrest these women for their crimes against humanity. The only problem he saw with his fantasy was that police didn't typically use guns, never mind explosives, so possibly it was someone else.

The shooting, in short bursts began to draw nearer. He could hear screams and foreign voices. He slid off his bed and made his way across to the door on his stumps. It could be another of their wicked games, to trick him, but what did he have to lose? He began to call for help.

Soon enough his calls were answered and the door opened, but the man who looked down at him with a sneer of disgust was no policeman. It was not the dark skin that seemed so wrong, nor the stolen security card with a nurse's picture on it, it was the way the man pointed his weapon and pumped David full of rounds.

Jane returned to the corridor where Mel, Rosie, and Tina still lay unconscious and bleeding. She tried to rouse them with the toe of her boot, but only Rosie showed any signs of coming round. With her one working arm she knelt down and gently slapped at Rosie's cheeks. Rosie blinked a few times then her eyes opened wide. She appeared to be staring passed Jane's shoulder. Jane turned and saw two IS troopers had crept up on them unheard, probably because of the sound of Jane's laboured breathing, trying to cope with the pain of her injured arm.

The two men disarmed her and dragged her aside laughing. They hadn't had it so good before. They considered themselves truly blessed to be able to shoot women, especially any who now could not defend themselves.

Unable to escape the grip that pinned her against the wall, or the free hand for that matter which was forcing her head to look in the direction of her colleagues, she was made to watch as with much hilarity the other man shot the girls. He placed his rounds between the legs and then between the eyes, leaving shooting Rosie till last to give her false hope as she tried to lift herself up.

Watching as Rosie fell still, Jane was then flung to the floor with the others, but as she put her good arm out to break her fall her hand went under Tina's torso and she felt the grip of her Glock 9mm. Whipping it out Jane took the smiles of the men's faces as she returned the favour.

Both men fell to their knees hands clutched to groins, as Jane got back up and put a bullet in each man's head, splattering brain matter across the corridor wall.

Discarding the Glock for an AK47, checking how full the magazine was and taking a spare magazine with her, Jane ran on. The Clinic had become strewn with dead bodies in such a short space of time. Some had been colleagues but many more had been IS.

Jane made it to the sick-bay where Clare still lay in a coma. She arrived to the sound of laughter as men took it in turns to defile Clare's body, believing it their God given right.

Jane helped them on their way to hell, dousing them all with rapid fire. Clare's monitor seemed to register the result of Jane's action as it hummed a monotone. Jane turned and left, with a fresh magazine loaded, and made her way to the control centre where she expected the fighting would likely be the heaviest.

However, by the time she got there, it was swarming with unwanted visitors trying to take as many of the storage devices from the computers as they could carry. She opened up on them till her magazine ran empty and she took a round to the throat.

As Jane slipped away she had no regrets. She didn't feel sorry for anything she had done. Thanks to Kate she had got to live out a fantasy which few would understand, and Jane had enjoyed what life she had had.

Will had no idea how so many people could just appear out of nowhere, many of them armed, and all intent on death and destruction it would seem without the police or even the military coming to stop them. Where were they? But then it had all happened so fast, and without sufficient warning, he assumed.

There were not so many people arriving now to join the ranks inside. All of the best IS operatives were already inside fulfilling the demands of Allah's Fist. It had been unreal to watch, like a scene out of some Tolkien tales of a fortress being stormed by greater forces, and Will felt helpless to do anything about it. He had tried phoning the police but there was no response.

Nevertheless, he couldn't just stand there while Gina was clearly in trouble. He knew in that moment that he loved her, and it was up to him to get in there and save her.

His mind now made up, he decided to leave the security of the Astra, and that was when it happened.

There was a very bright light, like an extra sun as The Clinic disintegrated in an instant, with what reminded Will of the clip of the H-bomb test in the Pacific.

Will closed his eyes to save his retinas, bringing a hand up, uselessly. The pressure wave hit next, picking Will up and hurling him over the hedgerow. Then the heat arrived, burning the hedges, burning the forestry all around. Then the Astra was aflame, windows popping just before the petrol tank went up. Will had turned to face down into the field to save his face from the scorching heat.

Next he heard heavy thumps as if the field was under artillery bombardment. Will thought not only do the army turn up late, but they shoot at the wrong thing.

It turned out to be just chunks of The Clinic's masonry coming back to Earth.

He lay there sobbing, thinking how no one could have survived *that*; no one any closer than him. Then he noticed he couldn't hear himself sobbing. He decided his eardrums were probably shot.

He picked himself up and walked down the smouldering field along the burning hedge till he came to the broken and burning remains of a gate and stepped through to the drive. From there he walked to the smoking edge of what looked like a meteor crater.

It was then that he noticed a shadow and looked up to see two black Augusta Westland helicopters coming in to land. He felt rather than heard the sound of their rotor blades as he walked towards them.

Troopers jumped out even before the skids were down and rushed towards him. He expected the body language of rescue, but instead was forced to the ground at gunpoint, where a black hood was pulled over his head and his wrists cuffed behind his back.

30

After landing at some unknown airfield, Will had been led from the helicopter to a car, where he had been placed between two people on a back seat.

With his hearing returning he had asked where they were taking him but there was no reply so he did not ask again.

Later, he sat on a chair in a room, still cuffed and hooded.

The door opened up and someone came in and removed his hood. He blinked in what seemed like very bright LED lighting as the man took a seat in front of him, preparing a new report document on his tablet.

'Name?'

'Where am I?'

'MI5…Name?'

'I want to see Dave.'

'Dave who?' the man frowned.

'Defendor.'

'Oh…*You* wouldn't happen to be Will Norton would you?'

'Yes.'

'Can you prove it? You didn't have any ID on you.'

'Of course I can prove it,' Will sighed at the stupidity. 'Get Dave!'

The man left and after half an hour or so Dave appeared. 'Sorry Will,' he apologised as he undid the cuffs.

'What's going on?'

'I was hoping you could tell *us*. It has been manic. We have captured more IS people than we know what to do with…Where's Gina?'

'I don't know. My phone went up with everything else in the car. The explosion was *so* big. Nothing could have survived that. Could it?'

'Well you did…And two others.'

'Two others?'

'Yes an IS woman breast-feeding her baby. Apparently she ran to the SAS troopers, clearly confused by the explosion, asking if she and her baby were too late to help fight for the cause.'

Will shook his head bitterly. 'The whole world is losing its humanity.'

Dave was going to say something but his phone rang. 'Dave Fendor…Hello…Yes.' He looked across at Will.

Will's heart began to lift, was this Gina?

'Okay,' said Dave handing his mobile across to Will, 'It's Tom Norton.'

That evening Mr and Mrs Best sat on the sofa together, because a spring had gone under Mr Best's chair. Mrs Best was engaged with her knitting while Mr Best was as usual moaning about the rubbish on their 3D HDTV. He flicked through the channels, in loops.

He stopped at one point and flicked back to CBBC in disgust where he thought he had heard a girl yelling 'Cat shit!' but found it was just children playing a ball game. Then flicking onward he arrived at a news channel showing a big crater, and he stopped flicking.

The report showed an image taken by an iPhone from an airliner preparing to land at Heathrow, showing what looked like a nuclear bomb going off some distance away. The red ticker-tape line at the bottom of the screen read Terrorist bombing in the Chilterns.

The next images on the screen showed police and security personnel battling to hold back a tide of people at border control points, and road blocks.

Then there was footage of the air force and navy attacking aircraft and boats.

'It's a bloody invasion Irene!' Mr Best urged his wife to look up from her wool.

'It's been happening for years dear,' said Mrs Best, looking over her glasses at the screen. 'It's just that now they've decided to make a last mad dash I suspect.'

'*Mad*. You're right there. Who'd want to come here when we have bombs like that going off? And what has it achieved?'

'Ruined a bit more countryside I expect.'

'Looks to me like it has been the biggest suicide bombing in history.'

'Well they should have done it in their own country…I just hope Ethan hasn't got caught up in any of that nonsense.'

'That detective you hired said he had gone to Hereford. That's miles away from the Chilterns, so he'll be fine.'

'I just wish he would let us know where he is.'

'Well that *is* the irresponsibility of teenagers.'

The doorbell rang and Mr and Mrs Best looked at one another to see who would get up.

'Well I'm watching the news,' Mr Best excused himself.

As the doorbell rang again, Mrs Best sighed, shook her head at her husband, removed her glasses with her still bandaged hand, put her knitting aside and went to see who it was.

Shuffling down the hallway she opened the door and made out a young soldier, accompanied by a woman with a black eye.

'Ethan!'

She hugged her son, and he tried returning the show of affection, clearly not used to it but now of a mind to try. Following his recent experiences he might even try and change his ways.

'Come in, come in.' Mrs Best said excitedly and turned to call behind her, 'It's Ethan!'

'Sorry, I can't join you,' said Gina, 'I have to get to hospital.'

'Thanks Gina,' said Ethan, meaning it.

'Remember what I said about mentoring.'

'Sure. I'll see you next week then.'

Gina had had a long talk with Ethan on the drive back to Birmingham, after they had found a safe spot to change clothes, tend to injuries, and make some urgent calls.

She could see that Ethan had had something of a life changing experience from what he told her had happened to him. She wanted to keep an eye on him nevertheless, and offered to be his mentor, to keep him on the right track.

Just as she got back to the Range Rover she heard *Enter the Dragon*. It was Tom getting back to her with news.

The hospital visit was too long, but luckily the round to the arm had been more of a bad graze than a major wound.

Bandaged up and warned not to drive she got right back into the Range Rover and drove down to London through frustratingly slow traffic on the M1. After the further delay of security checks at the MI5 building she was allowed to see Will in Dave's office.

'I tried to call you. I thought you had died in that blast.' She wrapped her arms around Will, wincing at the pain she was causing herself.

'I lost my phone with the car. I can't believe my luck that you made it out of there.' He kissed her until Dave grew so uncomfortable watching his ex with her new man, that he verbally prized them apart.

'I need a complete debriefing Gina. You may be a hero amongst the security services now for blowing up a large number of the most dangerous terrorists on record, not to mention enabling us to capture many of the others on our *most wanted* list, but there is one large hole that needs filling in.'

'Hey! That crater was not my fault.'

As Gina had been forced to sit down on the chair in Kate's office she willed her intuition to give her some clue as to how she was meant to get out of this one.

Ethan had come behind her with the cling-film, pulling her arms together, but she felt him place something sharp into the palm of her good hand. She didn't know whether he had expected her to react immediately with what he had given her, but her intuition told her that if she reacted immediately then they would all die, so she sat still.

The muzzle of Kate's Sig pressed hard into Gina's brow while the polythene was wound around and around.

Gina wondered in their final moments together why Kate had not just shot her. She was risking Ethan's life as well as her own with every second's delay. What hold did she think she had over the boy? Gina decided the Penelope she had once known and trusted had gone insane.

She was surprised to see Ethan being pulled into the cupboard. It was going to have to be one hell of a safe-room behind there to survive the imminent blast she thought, until she saw a door close then suddenly drop away to reveal a dark cavity behind the cupboard.

She had already been working on the plastic with the object Ethan had given her and soon had the cling-film removed. She could not reach all the way up but had cut through enough to release her from the chair. Standing up she had shrugged the cling-film off over her head and looked at what she held in her hand. It was one of Ethan's shurikens. Placing it in her tool-pack as she dashed to the cupboard, pulling a torch out in its place, she looked down the shaft.

There was no lift cable. It was a dead-drop system. She could see a hatch in the roof of the pod some four floors below. That was her way out. She flicked the torch beam up to examine the walls. They were too far apart to execute a chimney descent and there was no ladder or anything else to climb down on.

Time was running out, and she knew if she just jumped she would likely break a leg and die down the shaft rather than where she was. She turned her attention back to the office.

Looking around for an immediate solution, Gina's eyes fell upon the sofa. Quickly she grabbed up the four cushions and threw them aside, as too small for the job. Then gritting her teeth against the pain in her arm and elsewhere she lifted off the two sofa-seat cushions. She sped to the shaft chucking them in. She returned for the remaining sofa-back cushions and threw them down the shaft too.

There was nothing else for it that she could think of. She stepped into the void, relaxing her body, a difficult thing to do but known to help the body absorb impact. She hit the cushions below awkwardly, bouncing and banging her head and right knee into the shaft wall. The extra pain was bad, but she could not let that stop her, her whole body was aching from one thing or another. She knew she could be dead any second, but would not quit.

Pulling up the cushions; pushing them above her, she reached for the hatch and opened it. Falling through in her haste, head first she turned over to land heavily on her back, which knocked the wind out of her.

Spilling out of the pod door into the corridor, blinking back stars, she saw a door. Opening the door it was clearly a blast door. She moved through closing it behind her and limped on.

Her whole body was crying out for her to stop, she was exhausted, but she was not giving in. She relied on the Special Forces training which she had received through Five, to maintain her focus.

Another blast door led her to stairs. Upwards and onwards she went. The last part of the stairs was a short ladder up to an open hatch, which brought her to a lawn. She was some distance from The Clinic now and could hear the battle raging inside, but she could also hear screaming, and it sounded like Penelope.

Gina raced, the best she could, across to the piggery and round the back to where the screams had come from. There she found Ethan standing next to a set of car keys watching as pigs devoured what was left of Penelope.

If she wasn't dead already she soon would be. There was no saving her from that pen, and with the self-destruct about to go off, barely time to save the boy.

'Come on Ethan,' Gina urged firmly as she snatched up the keys.

He turned but did not seem surprised to see Gina standing there.

Ethan did not look like he had a care in the world. Something had just happened which seemed to have left him *done in*. Though Penelope was clearly insane, she was not mad enough to climb in with the pigs when escape was on the cards. The only thing Gina could conclude was that Ethan had put her there.

Grabbing the material of Ethan's clinic pyjamas, she pulled him away from the scene of blood and gore, and as he came to his senses and followed, she pressed one of the key fob buttons and heard the twoink-twoink of a car in the shed in front of them. Pressing another button she heard the garage door opening.

Quickly she helped Ethan shove his two bags into the car and was soon accelerating across the lawn even before seat belts were secured. There would be time to sort themselves out *if* they survived.

She spotted a gap in the trees ahead of them and continued to accelerate for the security fence. As they sped nearer, she could see that the fence directly in front of a possible firebreak in the forest, looked like it might be meant to open in some way.

Gina gave it no further thought crashing through them and onto the rough track on the other side. The ride was bumpy but Gina dared not slow, she used all her rally training to get them as far away as she possibly could, but it was difficult to control the 4x4 on the track with her left arm being so weak from the bullet wound.

Both of them bouncing around, Ethan was trying desperately to get his seatbelt clicked in when the intense light came from behind them, and then the fireball gave chase.

Although the Range Rover, being armoured, had slowed their getaway somewhat, it saved them now as the trees around them were devoured by the firestorm that gave them an extra push on their way.

EPILOGUE

Ethan Best, in the weeks that followed his capture and then escape, found a number of things had changed for him, even before the moment he had been returned to his adoptive home. As much as he had been welcomed back, there was a definite smell of death to his room, despite the open window and two plug-in air fresheners.

Having had Mr and Mrs Best try and look after his animals in his absence, they had certainly *taken care of them*. He could hardly have done a better job himself as it turned out.

Not appreciating the finer points of aquarium management neither Mr nor Mrs Best noticed when the filter pump packed in on the piranha tank.

The problem had begun when they had both mistaken the frenzied feeding activity of the fish as a voracious appetite. The last half kilo of minced beef from the reduced shelf at the supermarket had therefore gone down like a muck spreader at a foam party.

The fish, already hidden by their cloudy water, were left to asphyxiate in the protein stew.

Upon their return the next day, that steadily worsening smell, which Mrs Best had already commented on twice, had now become the eye-watering and lung-searing assault of a gas attack.

Opening the windows and then removing the lid from the tank, the fish were found floating, half poached by the strip light. They all faced the pump outlet as if an intentional clue as to their killers.

Only when Mr and Mrs Best were confident that what they were seeing was not a clever trick to bring fingers within reach of their razor sharp teeth Mr Best removed the fish and left Mrs Best to clean the tank out.

However, this care and attention came all too late to save the latest Percy who, on later inspection of his cage and nest, was found to have quite clearly chocked on his own vomit.

Ethan was done with pets. His biological mother had taken away his need for animal cruelty by way of her treatment process. Then her death at his hands in the piggery he had developed a new need.

He had no interest in victimising the small and defenceless any more, he now relished the idea of getting the better of those bigger and more dangerous than him.

There was something else that he had learned whilst captive too, that it was also easier and often much more effective to manipulate people by being nice to them.

He had heard the saying *having to be cruel to be kind*, but he thought there was also some merit to *having to be kind to be cruel*. By showing Kate respect even though he thought she was clearly mad as a March hare, it allowed him to catch her off guard.

It had also occurred to Ethan that the key to success was to tell people what they wanted to hear, or do as they expected you to do, as long as it got you to where you wanted to go.

For now, his goal was SAS selection, and Gina had promised to help him with that through her mentoring.

He wasn't going to open up about what was really going on inside his head, but as long as his past deeds and behaviours could be put behind him then all was well and good. In fact on return to school he had gone to Bertie and to the lad's surprise given him a roll of ten twenty pound notes and an apology for the way he had treated him.

Ethan didn't know what that would gain him, but the money was small change compared to what else was in the holdall from his mother's office.

On Gina's return from London with Will, she had taken Ethan to see DI Dunn where he gave a statement about the coincidental meeting and then filming of the suicide truck driver, and his account of his subsequent running away and kidnapping.

Ethan still didn't like the police, probably never would, but he was getting a better appreciation of how things worked, and how to work the system, whilst potentially reforming his behaviours of course.

Gina received a call from a prospective client one afternoon and agreed to come and talk to him around five o'clock, but it sounded like another fishy one that would turn out to be no case at all.

All the man had said was that he needed help to catch someone who was ruining his business. She was to meet him at the travelling fairground, now visiting Sutton Park. He would be at the Mirror Maze, which she would find to be closed.

She thought she would invite Ethan along to the fair for a mentoring session so as to kill two birds with one stone. He could amuse himself for half an hour while she spoke with the client, then they could reconvene the mentoring before she returned him home again.

She knew as a mentor she was expected to keep her eye on her mentee the whole time, but she considered this a bit of a test to see if he could keep out of trouble.

When she had picked him up however, she noticed he already had a split lip. Mrs Best told her that Ethan had been in trouble at school that day, so as Gina drove over to Sutton Park she quizzed him.

'So Ethan, do you want to tell me about what happened today?'

'A fifth-former threatened to rearrange my face if I didn't give him two hundred pounds.'

'What made him think you *had* two hundred pounds?'

'I think Bertie must have blabbed about me giving *him* two hundred pounds.'

'What? You are losing me. Who is Bertie, and why did you give *him* two hundred pounds?'

'I used to bully Bertie, a first year. I'd mug him for his dinner money and pocket money.'

'Ethan!'

'I know, but I'm over that stuff now. Anyway I apologised to Bertie and gave him back what I took, maybe a bit more, I didn't really keep count of what I was taking.'

Gina sighed. 'So I guess you resisted being mugged and this bigger lad punched you in the mouth.'

'Yes.'

'Then what happened?'

'He tried to punch me again but I took him by the arm and did that thing I saw you do up on Pen y Fan. I rolled him over my hips and smashed his knees into the playground.'

'You saw that?'

'Yes,' he laughed. 'You were pretty awesome up against those troopers. Shame two others got to me before you did.'

'A difficult situation,' she nodded. 'Some of it still doesn't make sense to me. Like why Penelope changed her name to Kate and pretended to run a clinic of all things as a cover for black-ops units. It wasn't even signposted as a clinic, it had no address.'

'Like I said when you rescued me, when Kate told me she was my mother she said she had created a haven for psycho-bitches to deal with their needs, by extracting money and life from criminals and terrorists.'

'But if she was truly psychotic she would have felt no remorse over whoever they brought in, so why go to the trouble of pretending to fight for good? She let some people go, like me, and fed others to the pigs, didn't you say?'

'I guess not all psychopaths are alike.'

After a long pause Gina continued with the previous track of questioning, 'so what has the school had to say about all this?'

'I never told them any of what happened.'

'The boy never said anything either?'

'The boy? Oh I thought you were talking about The Clinic…No, the boy had to be taken to hospital.'

'Ethan. You need to use more *restraint*, and avoid fighting; As Bruce Lee used to call it, *the art of fighting without fighting*.'

When they arrived and parked up, it was quarter to five and Gina walked around the attractions with Ethan until she spotted the Mirror Maze, off to one side.

She told Ethan not to get into any trouble and she would catch up with him shortly. Parting company she walked across to what looked like four prefab units joined in a 2x2 fashion, with no windows just walls covered in mirror chrome style graffiti, spelling out Mirror Maze.

Just as she had been told the attraction carried a closed sign but there was no one around. She looked at her watch. She was a couple of minutes early. Then as she looked up she saw a big man approaching her.

He looked like a stereotypical muscle-man, more appropriate to a circus than a fair. All he lacked was the iconic handlebar moustache. She expected him to speak with a thick accent betraying more brawn than brains but was surprised by his more educated welcome.

'Miss Oakley?'

'Yes.'

'Pleasure to meet you,' he said offering a hand. 'I do hope you can help me with my little problem.'

She shook his hand. 'I will try, but I need to know more before I can comment on what it is possible to do.'

'Do let me show you.' He opened the lock on the door to the Mirror Maze, and ushered her in as the lights came on inside. 'You need to appreciate what I do before I can explain myself properly.'

Gina stepped in ahead of him but as she turned it was clear he was not intending to follow. 'Aren't you giving me a guided tour?'

'Ha no, that would defeat the object.' He closed the door with its mirrored back.

Then she heard the padlock being put back on. 'Hey!'

'Sorry, I don't want anyone else getting in. Some kids can't read *closed* signs. Meet me on the other side.'

She heard him walk away. She shrugged and turned her attention to the maze. The walls were a mix of flat, magnifying or distorting mirrors and as if that was not disorienting enough the lighting began to strobe at irregular rates. She expected loud music to suddenly blare out for the full effect but instead it remained quiet.

'Head towards my voice,' the man called.

Then the lights went out completely leaving Gina to feel her way in and through, trying to build a mental map. She turned a corner and then felt what seemed to be a dead end.

The light came back on and she looked at her confused face and stepped back, then spotted a crawl space below the half mirror. Bending double she shuffled through. It brought back thoughts of the drain, and the explosive and her palms began to sweat, leaving marks on the mirrors as she passed.

Getting up she found herself facing a T-junction. Both led to apparent dead ends, but one had a large mirror and her intuition told her to press one edge, and as she did so the mirror swivelled and changed the maze form, sealing off the passage she had arrived by and opened up a new section. She turned left, just as the strobe lights plunged her into darkness again.

'How are you finding it?' The man asked, sounding nearer.

'Touching it with my fingers,' she responded flippantly intending to indicate that she had had enough now.

Squeezing through a tight gap, the mirror to her right shifted and she moved in to an open area. She had not covered enough distance yet to have reached the other side of the maze; this had to be the middle, yet the man was waiting for her here.

'I must thank you for that.' He stepped closer beaming a smile in the flashing lights.

'I don't see how that has helped,' Gina wanted him to cut to the explanation now, so that she could get back to Ethan.

'You have helped me catch the person who is ruining my business.'

'What?'

'There were others but it seemed you blew them away. You also killed many of my people, but that is of no consequence. They are ten a penny.'

'Who are you?'

'I am Allah's Fist, Agent Orange.'

'Sorry but I have no idea who you are, or what you are talking about.'

'Come now. I am infamous for my support of crime and terrorism.'

'Nope. Never heard of you.'

'You are a dangerous woman Agent Orange, but Allah's Fist is *more* dangerous.'

Gina's mobile began to ring. She took it from her pocket and saw that Ethan was calling her. However, as she lifted it to her ear Allah's Fist launched himself the last two metres and punched her in the face. He blacked her other eye and made her drop the phone.

She grabbed for it, intending to head back into the maze but the mirror she had entered by had sealed behind her. She did manage to touch the phone but that was all, as a heavy kick to the stomach lifted her off the floor, winding her. Then the lights went out. She rolled aside, hearing another kick hit a mirror.

When the lights came back on she was already back on her feet, trying to focus; trying to breathe. Allah's Fist stood the opposite side of the mirrored room.

'I could not trust those remaining in my employ to do what I wished to see done to you, so I have decided to do it myself. I intend to beat you to death with my bare hands.'

Looking at the size of him, protected by so much muscle, he might just achieve his wish if she could not outwit him. And all the while she had the worry of what might be happening to Ethan.

This was like the computer-gamers big-boss level, only if she failed this there would be no coming back to try again.

She stepped forward feinting an attack with her left foot. As he bent slightly to block the kick she whipped it away and round to deliver a reverse round-house kick with her heel to his ear to stun him. But she did not stop there she moved in with a series of rapid blows to the neck. He fell away in a strange stop frame fall with the strobe lighting. Then the lights went out again.

The phone started to ring again. In the dim light of the screen she could see that Allah's Fist was no longer where he had fallen. He had not been sufficiently stunned by her blows. He hooked an arm round her ankles and flipped her to the floor. Only her fast reactions prevented her from hitting her head as her arms met the floor first pushing her aside, avoiding the follow-up attack of the man's massive fists.

Instead of being frustrated by missing, Allah's Fist took it as all part of his game. 'I know quite a bit about you Agent Orange. I know about your combined martial arts skills, stemming from your love of Bruce Lee's Jeet Kune Do. You use that ringtone because it is your favourite film. Why do you think I wanted to end your days in a hall of mirrors my dear? Admittedly there are a number of differences. I did not want to use a claw to attack you like Han…'

Gina thought about smashing the mirrors like Bruce had done, and possibly using a shard as a weapon.

'...And the mirrors are these days made of plexiglass, for health and safety reasons you understand. So we won't be instigating any seven years of bad luck.'

Gina needed to keep him talking by saying anything she could to give her time to plan her next move. 'I don't get why people like *you* are bothering with jihadist extremism.'

'You need to understand it as Monotheism. Once Islam is the only faith left on Earth, with all of the infidels cleansed from the planet, there will be peace on Earth at last.'

'You do realise you are talking rubbish. Diversity is nature's way, your God's way. There will always be people who come to believe something different to the rest. People are not clones, or robots.'

'Then we will find these individuals and kill them, as is Allah's will.'

'Allah has spoken to you personally I suppose. Your need to kill Allah's creations will mean you believe Allah has made a mistake. In your madness you will be constantly killing *your* own people then.'

'Once anyone thinks differently, they are no longer *our* people, but infidels.'

'Shall I tell you something else?'

'Go on then Agent Orange, tell me more. Prolong my amusement before I kill you, with *these*.' He smacked his knuckles against each other across his large chest.

'I think you know this is all bullshit, but you have realised that if you prey on the weak minded you can make money and become powerful. That is your only concern, isn't it?

That is why you have not simply died for *the cause* yourself.'

Gina stepped forwards all relaxed as if the point had been reached where they could just continue to talk this through, and he let his guard down a little.

She dropped to a low crouch, turned her back on him then as her buttocks touched his shins her left hand assisted her right fist as she drove a right elbow strike up into his genitals.

As he toppled forwards, she forced herself upwards, just as the lights went off again. His back crashed down in front of her, but she could not see his neck to follow through with her intended stamp kick to the throat. She knew she had to get the better of him soon or his superior mass would grind her down.

The light came back on to show him reaching for her right ankle. She was not able to move it fast enough this time and both his meaty hands took a firm hold. Standing back up as if her attack had been no more than a slap he had her on her back and began to pull her round. In seconds she was airborne, her head and hands hitting the mirror panels on all sides.

'So there is room to swing a cat!' Allah's Fist cheered, before letting go.

Gina crumpled into a corner, desperately thinking what to try next. His muscles shielded all of her blows to vital organs, and even protected his nerve bundles.

Her only chances were when the lights were out and he could not see her, and then it dawned on her she had to do the unthinkable; attack his eyes.

He lunged for her, a big grin on his face, and the lights went out again and she was gone. He grunted his disappointment. Gina had to move as quietly as possible, but she knew even that was not enough.

She had to distract him to get in close enough, and had to get the timing right so that the distraction occurred just before the strobe lighting came back on again. Reaching into her pocket for something, anything to throw, her fingers grasped her lucky-star, the shuriken Ethan had given her and she had kept close.

With a flick of her wrist it was away, just as the light returned. There was no clatter to distract Allah's Fist though, but Gina was committed to her attack.

As soon as she had him in her sights she was flying across the room. His arms came up but too late, she was inside his defences and he could not prevent the wicked thumb jabs that mashed each eyeball, nor the double palm heel strikes that went on to destroy his nose as he crumpled to the floor. Then she was on top of him intending to strike the soft part of the throat but he seemed to be ahead of her there, protecting it with his hands.

His strangled scream of anguish turned to disbelief as he felt his energy leaving him. 'How is this possible?!'

Gina ceased her attack and pushed herself aside reaching for her phone. She grasped it just as it stopped ringing. Rather than call Ethan right back to see what was wrong she switched it to torch mode just as the lights went out again.

Returning to Allah's Fist she saw his hands fall away from his neck to reveal the shuriken had embedded itself in his jugular. He was bleeding out.

She did nothing to stem the flow but phoned DI Dunn. She informed him where she was and that an ambulance would be needed. Then so as to avoid unwanted questions about illegal weapons she returned the shuriken to her pocket. Allah's Fist bled out all the quicker then.

As it turned out Ethan was just bored on his own. He had thought if he kept interrupting Gina she would finish her meeting all the quicker. However, when he saw the police and ambulance coming he abandoned his bumper car ride and ran to see what was going on.

It did not bode well that they pulled up outside the Mirror Maze. Then he saw DI Dunn and DC Watkins turn up, so moved closer to find out what was going on.

Shortly after Gina found her way out, and saw that Ethan was okay, she led the ambulance crew back inside the Mirror Maze to retrieve the now dead body.

It was some minutes before they all came back out. Ethan watched as the blood-stained blanket-covered body, which clearly hid dreadful neck, nose and eye injuries, was loaded into the back of the ambulance then he turned to look at Gina with her freshly blacked eye.

'What was it you were telling me about *restraint*?'

Stevie Kerrigan had lived with his parents while he attended college and learned bricklaying, plastering, joinery, and became a qualified electrician. Nevertheless, he left home shortly afterwards to, as he saw it, take life by the horns.

He soon found however that he did not work well with others, so he took the first opportunity to set up on his own, which proved a challenge.

That was twenty odd years ago. Nowadays Stevie was still a one man band but now he had things going just the way he wanted them to.

He no longer kept in touch with his parents and didn't bother with mates to go down the pub with. He drank at home in front of the TV and enjoyed watching episodes of Cowboy Builders which he often recorded.

He had come to realise early on in his career training, which he considered had been the equivalent of teacher training for paedophiles, that it had put him right in the thick of his fantasy life.

The violation of having your home burgled was nothing compared to having it destroyed. He loved watching the faces of family members; angry and tearful, especially distressed mothers of disabled children when their life savings had been taken and their home destroyed.

Stevie would even pause the recording and drink in the distressed expression. It wasn't that he found it funny in any shape of form, it aroused him, and he became a monster led by his lust for misery.

Stevie considered that while many other cowboy builders probably gained the same pleasure from causing such intense misery for the helpless, he was a sharper operator than those who had been caught on TV camera.

Not only did he know how to do the jobs right, which maybe *they* didn't; he knew how to use this knowledge to most effectively lead people on with hope of a quality job on the cheap.

Once he had his victims hooked, and got underway, he knew when best to leave work unfinished and how best to ruin their home's services and structural integrity.

This was vandalism on a monumental scale; working in plain sight of the victims. He loved it. He used a false name and address, so he could only be contacted by mobile. His victims had to pay cash or suffer intimidation, *and* he regularly moved to a new area to keep ahead of reputation, printing new business fliers each time.

Inspired by the Cowboy Builders programme he purchased a Gopro video camera with his ill-gotten gains, and began to covertly capture the distress he was causing as he tore these people's hearts out.

Over the last few years he had been building his personal collection of video clips, which he did not intend to share with anyone. He didn't even use the Internet for anything. No one was going to track *him* down.

One night he was just settling down to a string of his favourite clips, imagining the misery and hardship those victims must still be suffering, unable to rectify the mess he had left them in, when he heard a splintering sound out in his back yard.

He raced to have a look and could not believe his eyes when he saw some idiot had reversed a black van into and over his back gate. What did they think they were doing? He raced into the kitchen and flung open the back door, expecting to have to chase after the driver.

However, he was confronted with the sight of the rear doors opening and armed black clad figures charging out. One carried what looked like a syringe, and another carried a body-bag. Behind them, their unmarked vehicle gave no clue as to who these people were.

When the heart of a dark family is removed, resilience can lead that which remains on to something darker.

Other titles by
Kevin H. Hilton

Northern Darks

Breakfast's in Bed

Imogen Powers Trilogy:

Possession

Afterlife

Singularity

Printed in Great Britain
by Amazon

81910244R10212